THE AFTERMATH | BOOK TWO

IN THE
UNBREAKING

BRIGITTE CROMEY

YARROW LEAF PRESS

Cover design by EAH Creative

Copyedited by Deborah O'Carroll

Formatting by M.H. Woodscourt

Published by Yarrow Leaf Press

ISBN: 979-8-9850208-3-0

www.wordsinmyblood.com

CONTENTS

IN THE
UNBREAKING

THE AFTERMATH | BOOK TWO

The Earth Defense Force banished the xenos back into the depths of the galaxy, before turning on their founder who risked everything to save humanity. Then, they abandoned regions they deemed not worth protecting. Regions like this one—the beautiful desert where I was born, where the very air tries to kill you and the sky is endless. People who live here are born resilient, and only survive because they love each other and their homes more than they love their own comfort and safety.

Earth's heroes abandoned this desert to chaos. They'll learn that we won't fall so easily.

STAGE ONE

Thunderbird Heights
Santa Cruz Valley
February 26

I COULD BARELY REMEMBER a time Before.

This place had once been filled with natural light, quiet voices, bright colors, and the smell of thousands of books—a combination that never failed to bring peace. Mama and I would collect stories from the children's section, sitting hip-to-hip on a couch covered in geometric patterns and diving into tales of heroes, villains, and Wild Things.

Now, it was desolate. Broken. Filled with the sound of violence, as gunfire echoed where voices had once been hushed. A handful of reddish humanoid figures moved in my periphery, their presences pinging in my mind like the sound of ghetto Spanish spoken three rooms away.

"Two in the kids' section, and one more in the computer lab." It'd been months since I spoke out loud when communicating mentally, but sometimes the old habit sneaked in. I crouched behind what had once been the reception desk, the recoil of my rifle a familiar sensation as I took another shot at the gang members firing on us. "And two more outside. I think they're watching the exits."

A crack of blue light answered my words, and a woman's voice resounded through my head. *Got one.* Intense focus and a sense of crackling energy marked Tara's presence on the other side of the open space from me, her husband Caleb beside her. *We'll hold their attention.*

We've got it, Gabriel, Caleb said. *Don't worry about us.* His voice sounded the same in my mind as it did through my ears—level and calm, with courage running through every fiber of his being. *Do you have eyes on the objective?*

I cleared my throat, forcing myself out of the past and into the present. We'd deviated from our usual patrol route to retrieve something from this place, the encounter with the Blood Angels an unfortunate byproduct. *Yeah,* I reassured him. *I know where I'm going. Just hold them off for another minute.*

More gunshots cracked as I broke cover, bullets splatting against the dome of light that formed around me. Grit and broken glass crunched under my boots with each hurried step toward the opposite side of the building, where my power painted a row of bookshelves in cyan light.

A yell from one of the gang members shook my concentration before a shotgun blast took him down. Sudden pain went through my stomach as the Blood Angel fell, and my footsteps stuttered.

Gabe, you okay? Tara asked. Clearly, she'd noticed my stumble.

I shook my head, banishing the shock of nearby death to the recesses of my mind. *I'm fine.* I threw my weight against the nearest bookshelf before ducking a bullet as it pinged off the wall to my right. *Almost there.*

The ones outside, what are they doing? Caleb asked, his mental voice clear despite the gunshots muffling all other natural sounds. *They're not moving in, and I don't like it.*

I ducked behind the bookshelf I'd been trying to move and slapped a hand to the ground. A moment later, I had the answer I'd been hoping for. *They're running. Running, and...* Bringing my power to focus on emotions rather than physical form was like narrowing the aperture on a camera, and I closed my sixth sense in on the single remaining Blood Angel in the building. *The last one inside is panicking. If you leave him an opening, I think he'll also run.*

Copy.

Another sharp crack came from Tara's vicinity, and I caught the moment when the gang member decided he no longer had the stomach to fight. His fear and frustration traced an almost visible path in the air as he fled, leaving the three of us alone in the library.

Well that was a waste of time for everyone, Tara said. *You'd think they'd learn not to tangle with a patrol with two Shattereds.*

Don't hold your breath, I told her. *They've never been the smartest, and I think they're getting desperate.*

Tara and Caleb came around the corner, Tara's hand glowing with barely-contained power as I released my rifle to hang on its strap over my shoulder.

"I didn't realize it would be so messed up in here." The blue light extinguished once Tara stood beside me, her height barely topping my shoulder. "You lived here how long?"

"About six months. It didn't used to be like this; I think it got trashed after I left." I braced my shoulder against the tarp-covered bookshelf I'd been trying to move earlier. Caleb added his weight to mine, and the shelf finally rolled aside to reveal a narrow doorway. Nothing moved other than a handful of crickets under the couch, and I closed my eyes at the sudden wave of memories brought on by the sight of the little room.

Rain on the roof.

The book in my hands; old even before everything fell apart.

A breaking sound—glass.

Heavy footfalls outside the door.

Fear flooding my veins.

Caleb and Tara felt it too, as the fear rebounded from me to them. In a single pace, Caleb was beside me, gripping my shoulder and projecting my name through all three of our minds. *Gabriel. Breathe.*

I took a deep breath, counting to four on the inhale and the exhale. After two more measured breaths, the memories subsided.

Sorry, I finally said. *I'm fine now.*

Caleb released my shoulder. He'd lifted the visor on his helmet to reveal silvery-grey eyes surrounded by fine scars and filled with concern. "You sure?"

I nodded. "It's fine—let's just get what we came for and get out of here before they come back." I walked into the room, passing empty shelves that had once held my belongings before crouching to peer under the couch. "I hope it's still—ah." Stretching my arm to its fullest extent, I closed my fingers on the woven strap of a book bag and hauled it into the open. A row of spiral-bound notebooks lay within, their spines reflecting the light with a dull gleam.

Your oldest stories? Tara didn't bother saying the words out loud.

Yeah. I lifted them out of the bag, brushing fingertips over the spines. Nowadays, I color-coded all my notebooks—blue for work, red for stories—but two years ago, I'd written in anything I could find. *It's my memories from Before.*

Understanding passed immediately between her and Caleb, who nodded and closed his visor. "Did you have anything else you wanted to get while we were here?"

"There isn't time." A sour note pinged at the edge of my awareness. The Blood Angels were regrouping, no doubt realizing they'd left two of their number behind. I slid the backpack straps from my shoulder, tucking the notebooks away and zipping the bag shut before taking a last look around the library. "And I don't have anything else. This was home once, but now it's just old memories."

WE TURNED our steps for home, hurrying to put distance between us and the Blood Angels as the February sun lowered into the west. Once a mile had passed with no signs of pursuit, we stopped to catch our breath and I turned my eyes to the mountains. The fading sunlight caught the edges of the Catalinas, washing them in gold and red before fading to dusky pink. The sight settled my heart in a way that almost nothing else could, even on the heels of yet another fight. I'd watched the sun set over these mountains hundreds of times, but every single day brought something unique and beautiful.

We rounded the corner of a neighborhood street to see the floodlights of home illuminating the growing dusk.

Before we got any closer to the base, I flipped a cover on my forearm armor and punched a button. Caleb's and Tara's emotions faded to background noise, and I sighed with relief as the pressure against my mind decreased.

Tara chuckled. "One of these days, we'll have to modify your software so you don't have to worry about surprising all of us when you walk too close to the base."

I flipped the cover closed. "Yeah. It'd definitely make it easier for me to avoid accidentally syncing everyone." I shook my head in frustration. "I hate having other people unexpectedly in my own head, so I *really* hate it when I do it to all of you."

"We know you don't mean it," Caleb reassured me. "At least it's only happened a few times." With the link between our minds turned off and my power operating without technological assistance, his emotions had retreated behind the most impressive mental walls I'd ever known anyone to possess. "There's got to be some option for picking who you sync with... I remember there was in the old days."

"There was." I eased my shoulders under my backpack and rifle straps with a tired nod of agreement. "Deadeye's been working on it, but she's having to reverse-engineer software that she didn't create in the first place."

Our footsteps crunched on gravel as we walked into the pool of light cast by the floodlights. The edges of a rooftop solar array stood sharply against the sky, a quiet hum emanating from the transformer boxes. The base—decorated with a stylized number thirty-six and affectionately termed "Station Somewhere"—had been a fire station before the xeno presence eliminated most regional and federal governments. With less of a population to serve, it had lain unoccupied for years after the Earth Defense

Force succeeded in kicking the xenos out of the solar system.

Now, it was home.

Caleb input a code into a lockbox mounted to the wall, and the bay doors began rattling open. "Good patrol, everyone. Who's writing the report this time?"

Tara ducked into the vehicle bay as soon as the doors cleared her diminutive height. "Not me." Her helmet came away to reveal dark brown hair in messy French braids and cyan eyes that almost glowed in her suntanned face. "I did the last one. Or maybe it was the one before that; I forget. Besides, why write reports anyway?"

Even after knowing her for over half a year, Tara's eyes never failed to unnerve me. For that matter, my own still caught me off guard every time I looked in the mirror. I pulled off my helmet, the heads-up display inside going dark as I reminded Tara, "You know how Bandit is." My free hand made quotation marks in the air as I said, "Even if we're not 'official EDF' anymore, he still wants things done to their standards."

"All right, then." Tara tugged open the Velcro closure at the neck of her armor padding. "*You* write the report." The door to the living quarters opened on a waft of delicious smells as she added, "You're the best writer out of the three of us, anyway."

"That's not fair!" I called after her. The door swung closed as I looked at Caleb with irritation. He was laughing, a chuckle that I could feel deep behind his mental walls as well as hearing it naturally. "Well, it's not." I thumped my rifle into its slot in the rack along the wall. "Her memory is terrible; I don't think she's written up a report for *weeks*. And I really wanted the chance to look through these"—I gestured at the backpack weighing against my shoulders—"before dinner tonight."

"Don't worry; I'll talk her into it," Caleb said, the laughter still evident in the crinkles around his silvery-grey eyes. He put his own weapon—a lethal-looking shotgun—in the locker alongside mine. "It can wait until after dinner, anyway. You go take some time."

With our armor and weapons stowed, we hit the showers before going our separate ways. Returning to my room with damp hair and clean clothes, I unzipped my backpack and laid the three notebooks we'd recovered from the library on the bed. Opening my closet, I withdrew a box in which over a dozen red and blue notebooks stood in chronological order. The edges of the pages were worn and dirty—not even my best attempts at keeping them clean had succeeded against the pervasive dust.

So many memories lay in that box.

I settled on the bed and paged through the most recent of the three notebooks. The date at the front told me I'd begun it the year before I'd joined the Defense Force, the smears of blood at the end informed me that it covered my run-ins with gang members. The other two—though older—told a similar story of living in fear while someday hoping to become brave. Finally, I closed the last notebook and set all three in their proper place at the back of the box.

As I withdrew my hand, something snagged my finger. A moment of fishing between spiral-bound spines yielded a plastic ID badge on a metal clip. I pulled it free and sat on the bed, looking solemnly at the image of my younger self.

Not so much younger, I reminded myself. *It's only been a year.*

The photograph had been taken the day after I'd graduated training. Rubbing my thumb over the edge of the badge, it struck me again how *different* the Gabriel of a year ago had looked. The dark hair was the same, even if the curls made it messier than regulations liked. My facial structure hadn't changed either—not much could change the angles of a face passed down from parent to child. Then again, my eyes had once been deep brown, not unearthly cyan. And the expression, so cautiously optimistic...

I sighed and tucked the ID badge into the box once more. A year ago, Surveillance Specialist Gabriel Mendoza hadn't had any idea of what was about to happen to him.

Back then, I'd considered Shattering a rare event. Those whom it happened to were legendary, heroes to be respected and feared. They'd turned the tide of humanity's resistance against the xenos, and their power on the battlefield was awe-inspiring. Shattering itself was rare and unpredictable—leaving the survivor with inexplicable abilities—and I'd never in a million years expected or hoped it would happen to me.

I returned the box to the closet before letting my sixth sense expand to survey the station. My power presented itself to my mind like adjusting the filters on my old surveillance system, and the others' presences lit up in my mind's eye as humanoid shapes outlined in bright blue. Perhaps it was a nervous habit, checking on my newfound family during quiet moments, but the EDF *had* trained me to keep an eye on everything around me.

Our German technical specialist Reneé—Deadeye, as she preferred to be called—was gone on a mission of her own, and the office where she normally worked was quiet save for the hum of computers. Tara and Caleb were in their room, Caleb reading and Tara sulkily scratching away with a pen on a paper form. *I guess he talked her into writing the report.*

I jumped as Tara slapped the page down in front of Caleb. He jumped as well—I caught unguarded fear swirling before his mental walls went up—and I wondered what he'd been thinking about. Without our comms program turned on, I couldn't tell what memory she'd triggered, but I made a mental note to check on him later.

A flurry of irritation sounded somewhere in the kitchen, and I stifled a snicker at the image my sixth sense presented before getting to my feet and heading for the living area. As I came out of the hallway, the sounds of angry Spanish fell on my ears.

"Josephine?"

I peered into the kitchen to see a petite Latina standing on a stepstool below a high cupboard, dancer-graceful hands straining for an object just beyond her reach.

I was about to help her when footsteps sounded behind me and someone brushed my shoulder. "I've got it, *mijo.*"

Bandit, our squad commander and Josephine's boyfriend, was tall enough that lifting Josephine was as easy as lifting a child. She squeaked in surprise as Bandit set her on the floor before retrieving the item she'd been reaching for and handing it to her with a kiss to her cheek.

"Carlos! I had it! You didn't have to—" Her dark eyes flicked to me, lurking at the edge of the kitchen, and I realized too late that I'd been laughing out loud. "Gabriel! *Ay,* you're just as bad as him."

"I'm not *that* bad," I complained, going past her to collect bowls from the drying rack. "What else do you need help with?"

JOSEPHINE WAS a good cook and tonight's dinner was no exception—though chicken and rice for the third time in a week had the others grumbling. I didn't mind the repetition *or* the simplicity. Eating the same food day after day had always been normal to me, and it was fun to sit quietly and listen as the others tried to complain without making it obvious. Tonight, though, the conversation took a different tack.

"I heard Regional's getting quite the staffing shake-down," Deadeye said, her "I've-heard-something-interesting" tone piercing my after-mission exhaustion. "We might be getting some new blood around here."

I looked up from shaking hot sauce into my food. "Oh?"

"Where'd you hear that?" Bandit asked from across the table. He'd kept wearing his EDF uniform shirts long after the rest of us had jettisoned them, and his captain's bars gleamed silver against his shoulders.

"Benny, at St. Augustine's today." Deadeye's chair screeched against the floor as she pulled it closer to the table. A grey-blue eye narrowed under the strap of her eyepatch, worn over pink-streaked dark hair. "I swear, that guy's network of 'insider contacts' only increased after Command disowned all of us. Saltori's got him in charge of St. Augustine's logistics depart-ment now. Josephine, do you remember a 'Dr. Kartchner'?"

A bright spark of recognition flitted past the edges of my mind from Josephine, and she hummed meditatively. "Yeah! He was an odd one, but had some groundbreaking ideas. He wrote a couple of papers on the correlation between Shat-tered power and the xenos' dampening fields that were really insightful."

"I knew him too," Caleb said. Unlike Josephine, his

recognition carried distrust. I'd been only half listening to the conversation, but his reaction made me set my fork down and pay attention. "He was part of the med team when I was rescued, but I think he switched over to Research and Development. They demoted him?"

"Not demoted, exactly. From what I heard, it was more like shut down. Or reassigned, or dismissed, or *something*—both his specific lab and the entire R&D cell at Regional Command." Deadeye reached across the table to take a jar of salsa from Tara. "Benny made it sound like they were taking the opportunity to clear some dead wood."

"Yeah, but you mentioned new blood?" I said. At least, I *thought* she'd said something along those lines. "They're coming down here?"

"Not all of them," Deadeye clarified. "Not the *eier*—uh—eggheads. A couple of techies—maintenance guys mostly—took their discharges and found their way to St. Augustine's, which is how Benny knows about this at all. With Regional dumping them, they had no reason to stay." She gave a sharp-edged grin, the thought of new forces a bright spot of hope in her mind. "Command might regret their decision once their equipment breaks down with fewer people to repair it, but hey, it's their loss."

"Yeah, pretty much..." I muttered into my food, my interest squashed at the mention of those who'd once commanded us. "To hell with them."

The others continued discussing Deadeye's new information as I returned my attention to eating. Last year, our superiors had sworn to bring all of us to court-martial for remaining in the region when they'd given the order to abandon it, but nothing had come of the threat. Bandit's theory that they'd been reluctant to expend more resources on a lost cause had made me respect them even less, and the chaos overtaking the city had forced the worry into the subconscious parts of my mind. Now that we'd reached a deadly stalemate with the enemies that'd originally forced the authorities out of the region, I couldn't bring myself to take the EDF's promises seriously.

And it is *a stalemate,* I agreed with myself. *No one's winning, and we're both losing.* I'd been hopeful, three months ago, that we could restore peace in the city where I'd grown up, but now—

"Gabriel?"

Josephine's gentle voice broke into my introspection, and I looked up in surprise. Most of the other seats at the table were vacant now, Deadeye having returned to her computers, Tara to her report, and Bandit and Caleb to the kitchen to clean up.

"Sorry." I shoveled the last few bites of rice into my mouth. "Sorry, I just—"

Josephine picked up my empty bowl, switching to Spanish as she said, "You were miles away, *mijo.*"

I answered in the same language, some of my tension ebbing at the familiar cadence. "Just thinking."

"Thinking, or worrying?"

"Both." I leaned my elbows on the table with a heavy sigh. "Last year, there was only us, the Blood Angels, and the desert. Now, I feel like there isn't a safe place to take a breath." I looked around the kitchen. Bandit and Caleb were washing dishes, and I doubted they could hear me over the sound of running water and clinking silverware. I propped my forehead against my clasped hands and addressed Josephine without looking at her. "I'm so tired of fighting, tired of looking over my shoulder, tired of the Blood Angels, and tired of half the barrio avoiding me while the others look at me like I'm a freak." The calluses on my palms felt rough against my skin as I buried my face in my hands. "Actually, I'm just *tired*. I don't know how long I can do this."

Josephine was silent for a long moment. As I looked up, something stirred behind her eyes that I couldn't place. Like worry, but deeper. I was about to ask what was wrong when she blinked and the strange emotion vanished. "That's understandable. I don't think any of us anticipated Regional's departure to have so many far-reaching consequences." She gestured toward the door to the vehicle bay. "Maybe take some time by yourself? Don't worry about dinner; we'll clean up."

THE BAY WAS DARK, bordering on cold now that the sun was down. I flipped open the tailgate of the truck and clambered up to sit cross-legged on the textured floor of the passenger compartment. Deeper in the compartment, the lights on my surveillance station blinked in a steady on-off rhythm. I sat watching for a long moment, a loss-tinged ache filling my chest at the thought of how much had changed in the year since I'd first learned to use the system.

With a sigh, I pulled a digital voice recorder from my pocket. Its red light pulsed as I turned it on, a different cadence than the surveillance system's readiness. Keeping track of everyday occurrences had been a habit even before joining the Defense Force, hence the notebooks we'd recovered from the library that morning. After I'd Shattered, the practice had taken on new purpose—getting churning emotions out of my head before I inflicted them on the others through the mind bridge. Tonight, my thoughts settled on the events of the previous October, and the mess we'd been in ever since.

I took a deep breath. It was always like this when I opened a new file or turned a page in my notebook, the strange silence a certain sign of far too many words demanding to be turned loose.

"I'm not sure what I expected after the cloning facility went down." I laughed halfheartedly—this was *not* where I had expected to start. "When the roof collapsed, I expected to die. When I didn't, I thought it would just be over, somehow. Like in the books, where the heroes finish their mission and everyone goes home and has coffee. Instead, we got disowned by our superiors and handed a city on fire. And riots. And looting, and murders. There—there were a lot of deaths the first month."

My voice went thin as I admitted it—here, in the darkness of the stationary truck, I could acknowledge the pain that each death cost me. I'd gotten lucky three months ago, in that first month of nonstop violence. My power's radius had been smaller, and I hadn't felt deaths as acutely as I did now.

"We were able to knock the Blood Angels into a stalemate after that, but without Regional backing us up, there's nowhere to send our opponents other than hell." My stomach twisted at the thought. "Once they realized we couldn't let them retreat and didn't have anywhere to put them if they surrendered, they backed off. Well"—a bullet graze across my tricep, earned in a fight a few days ago, burned as I shifted positions—"most of the time."

I tugged the edge of my T-shirt away from the healing wound and lifted the recorder closer to my face. "I guess there's less violence now, not that it does anyone any good. Now it's just wearing each other down and trying to survive.

Corporations stopped sending shipments in once they realized the EDF was gone—I mean, why *wouldn't* they? There's no guarantee their merchandise would make it to the intended recipients, or that they'd get paid for what *did* arrive."

I uncrossed my legs and let my feet swing free over the edge of the tailgate. "And power production is starting to suffer now that no one's maintaining the solar fields. There's nowhere to get parts, and no guarantee that the city stays calm while we fix what breaks. I guess the grids are okay for now, but next winter could be different."

The bay doors were closed against the cold, but I still shivered. We'd lost power a few times when I was a kid, once in the dead of January, and the idea of an entire winter without heat was literally chilling.

"And after all of it, there are the ordinary people." I heaved a sigh. "I've heard enough stories. Everyone here is living the same way I was—they're desperate for an escape or a reason to get up and fight. And the ones that gave me both escape *and* purpose abandoned us to chaos." My voice choked at the thought. "This region won't survive much longer if things continue like this. The people here need stability, safety, a chance to raise their families and do more than survive...they don't deserve this."

"Who doesn't deserve this?"

I looked up as Tara came around the corner of the truck, motion-sensing lights clicking on as she approached. I'd been so deep in thought that I hadn't noticed her coming, and the realization brought a flash of accusation into my voice. "Did Josephine send you?"

"Yes," she said, not a hint of embarrassment in her voice. "She's a little concerned about you." The truck bounced as

Tara climbed up to sit beside me. "Were you bringing your log up to speed on the state of the region?"

I clicked the voice recorder off with a frustrated huff. "I didn't realize how much it'd been bothering me until I started letting it all out."

Tara pulled a knee up to balance on the edge of the tailgate and let out a sigh. "It *is* frustrating, I'll give you that. The Angels and Regional and all that... It's like this place got dropped down a hole and forgotten about."

"Exactly," I muttered. "And that's my biggest fear." At her raised eyebrow, I explained, "Region 520 *was*. That's what I'm afraid the reports will say in another five years. Not 'is.' Was. Like it'll be gone from the map with nobody to remember beyond what it *used* to be." I squinted to keep tears at bay as Tara put her arm around my shoulders. "That's why I bother keeping a record of things that already happened. I do it because maybe, someday, someone will listen. And even if this place is gone, its story won't be."

Tara didn't say anything in response, but I knew she understood. Images—memories—swelled past the edges of my mind, sharpening as I reached up to rest my fingers against the back of her hand.

Misty green forests stretching to the sky, tumbledown buildings squatting beside muddy roads, derelict cars rusting amid tangled undergrowth, ferns uncurling against logs crusted with mushrooms, the sound of a fiddle playing in the distance.

I'd seen the place enough times through the mind bridge to recognize it as Appalachia, where she and Caleb had grown up. Both of their voices had been purged of any accent long before their arrival to Base 36, but I'd overheard them using words with each other that were as unfamiliar to me as my first uses of Sonoran dialect had been to them. From everything I'd heard, the mountains of their childhood —old as the skies, with the legends to match—were viewed in a similar way as the desert of mine.

For Tara, it'd been home. And she'd had to leave.

The memories broke apart as Tara took a deep breath. "Some places stick with your soul, even after everyone else is ready to leave them to time and chaos. I know, Gabe. But cheer up." Her arm tightened around my shoulders. "We're with you. And we'll fight alongside you for this place, one story at a time."

STAGE TWO

Station Somewhere
Santa Cruz Valley
February 27

THE NEXT MORNING, I was in the middle of a workout with Caleb when the dispatch lights flared in the bay. He'd just flipped me on my back and knocked the wind out of my lungs, and for a moment I didn't notice the change in atmosphere. Then, urgency flooded my system as each person in the station dropped what they were doing.

Not even a full day. I groaned and let my head drop to the mat. *I knew hoping for a breather was stupid.*

Caleb pulled me to my feet as my vision cleared. "Weren't you saying something the other day about how it'd been too quiet?" he asked with a grin.

I rolled the kinks out of my shoulders. Caleb was stronger than he looked, and sparring with him always left me feeling like my limbs were about to get popped loose.

"Look, I know better than to say 'quiet.' That's just begging for a beating."

We pushed through a swinging door into the living area. Bandit was already there, switching on the wall monitor and bringing up an outdated satellite map of the city.

"What happened?" Tara demanded as she and Josephine emerged from the hallway leading to our makeshift medical area.

"You remember that gas station where we broke up the fight last week?" Bandit asked as he entered coordinates into the map.

I nodded and rubbed the bullet graze on my arm as Tara said, "Yeah, weren't the Blood Angels trying to strong-arm the owner into putting a lock on the pumps?"

"Something like that." Deadeye had come in on Tara and Josephine's heels. She leaned against the hallway doorframe, a pair of wire snips dangling from her fingertips. "It's a big source of income, and they couldn't stand not getting a cut." Her brow furrowed. "And I think they need the gas for their trucks; they don't use power cells like we do. He said no, didn't he?"

"Yeah, hence the fight," Bandit said. "And they weren't going to let him get away with it. He reached out to Dispatch a little while ago; says his son didn't come home from school yesterday. He asked around, and a couple other families said the same thing." His face darkened, lines deepening around his eyes. "Then he got a ransom demand this morning."

I groaned at that, not that the news was a surprise. The Blood Angels had decided a long time ago that adhering to common nicety wasn't for them.

Tara swore under her breath. "Kids? They're targeting kids now?"

"Don't act so surprised," Josephine said. Her face pinched with sadness that went deeper than just her expression. "They're getting desperate."

As frustrated as it made me, I had to agree that the statement was accurate. Most of the original Blood Angels had been killed or fled by the end of last year, and the ones that remained were abandoning even the shreds of fair play that their predecessors had abided by.

"Well, this latest thing is right in line with their new MO." Bandit zoomed to focus on a tiny house surrounded by barren land. "This is where he was told to come."

Deadeye leaned over the back of the couch, her good eye narrowed as she examined the map. "There's no cover except the wash. We'd have no way to get close without them seeing us."

"They know *someone* will be coming. The trick is getting close enough to shield the kids before the Blood Angels hurt them." Caleb looked at me. "How's your power?"

I turned my gaze toward the floor and concentrated for a moment. I'd slept uninterrupted the last few nights, and my power thrummed full force through my veins. "I'm good. I can draw fire if Tara's able to sneak through the wash." I pointed to the top of the map, where a line of trees and rundown buildings lined a dry riverbed. "She can get behind them and shield the kids while the attention's on the rest of us."

Bandit's free hand had drifted to rest near his handgun grip—the weapon as much a part of him as wise guidance was. "Whatever you two do, make sure you don't endanger the kids." He checked his watch. "Let's get moving, everyone. I'll send the map to your helmets. *Mijo?*"

I stopped on my way out the door. "Sir?"

He tapped his temple. "Let's use the mind bridge. I'm not sure what we're walking into, and it's better if our comms stay silent."

Caleb followed me out to the bay as the others dispersed behind us. Throwing open our lockers, we swapped our workout clothes for cargo pants and tan-olive T-shirts before squirming into the reinforced underlayer of our armor—the right sleeve of mine shortened to allow my monitor access to my skin. After throwing my armored vest over my head and buckling it tight, I booted my monitor cuff and called to Caleb, "Chirp the PA system; I'm about to sync everyone."

He reached over to the mic system hanging alongside the door, clicking the microphone twice before calling, "Mind bridge booting."

I pushed the button to bring our comms program online as the echoes of the PA announcement died out. In a split second, the world stretched like a rubber band and snapped together as technology melded with Shattered power to blend my consciousness with that of the others. Memories, emotion, thoughts, and dreams combined in a swirl of sight and sound, and I gritted my teeth as *I gasped awake from a nightmare, the darkness of the room and Tara's measured breathing reassuring me that yes, it was just a dream this time.*

It's always something like this, Caleb muttered inside my head. His mind and mine always linked first each time we turned on the comms program, probably *because* of all the times I'd pulled him out of nightmares like the one that'd just flashed through the bridge. *I do have good memories; why can't this tech ever hit on them?*

I tried to reassure him, but Bandit's presence sent both of us spiraling into another memory.

"He's all yours."

The nurse placed a bundle in my arms, guiding me to sit in the chair at Maria's bedside. I pulled away the edge of the blanket and marveled at the chubby cheeks and dark eyes of my newborn son. "Hi, Cruz," I whispered. "Welcome to the world."

The image flickered, stabilizing briefly before shredding into *a dark hallway, illuminated by strips of emergency lighting. I strode after the others as they cleared room after room, the energy in my blood pounding in my veins and demanding to be released.*

"Tara, stop!" Michael's voice ricocheted through my head as I rounded the corner, too late to avoid seeing what lay beyond. "They found him, but you're not going to like what you see."

Every muscle tensed, and I fought the urge to cry out in response to the wash of anxiety that flooded from Tara's presence. *It's just a memory, Tara! Let it go!*

From inside the swirl of everyone's emotions, I felt her take a deep breath, then another. *Sorry.* A final shiver went through her, my own limbs tremoring in response before she said, *I'm okay now. Are we all here?*

I'm here, Deadeye said, her deadpan mental voice making me jump with surprise. *I think my interface kicking in got drowned out by yours.* If I'd been able to see her face, I was certain it would've been touched with a sarcastic smile.

"Sorry," Caleb said aloud, the sentiment sparking through the mental link as well. "It's not like we're able to pick which moment it latches on to."

We know, Bandit reassured him. *It's okay.* Even through comms, his mental voice was determined and kind. *Are we all good,* mijo?

I think so. I flipped my monitor cover closed, smacking it to make sure it stayed latched. It, like most of our other gear, had seen more action than its makers had ever predicted. My rifle was a reassuring weight as I retrieved it from the rack, the others coming to grab their own weapons as Caleb opened the bay doors. Winter sunlight spilled in as the door rattled upward, the outside air refreshingly crisp.

It was Deadeye's turn to drive. The road rumbled under our tires as we left our pocket of civilization and sped toward the mission site, Bandit and Caleb strategizing as we went. I leaned against the compartment wall and tried to get my nerves to settle. This bumpy, adrenaline-inducing drive was my least favorite part of any mission, when we were too far from conflict for my power to warn me of what lay ahead. Luckily, I didn't have long to fret about what might be coming. Less than ten minutes passed before we slowed to a stop and Deadeye shut off the engine.

I squinted through my helmet visor toward the tiny house as we clambered out of the vehicle, Tara raising a precautionary shield over all five of us. There was no immediate hostile response, but a black truck similar to ours stood outside the building.

"What do you think, *mijo?*" Bandit asked.

I had to bite back the first thing that came to mind. *No one should be allowed to paint their truck that color in the desert, and that many antennae just look stupid sticking out of the top.*

Deadeye laughed aloud as the thought reached her, and I caught Tara and Caleb trying not to smile either as I said aloud, "It's the Angels' patrol unit, sir. Even numbers with us."

"That we know of," he responded. "And the kids?"

I stepped behind the bulk of the truck. "I'll look now."

"Thanks." Bandit nodded at the tangle of undergrowth and trees on the other side of the open expanse. "Deadeye, Banshee, circle around and start moving into the wash. Phantom, watch Gabriel's back."

"Yep." Caleb came to stand beside me. This close to him, I could sense the fear that he kept carefully caged in stern discipline. It leaked through the cracks in his mind like dark ink spiraling through water, a reminder that he'd endured more darkness than anyone should have to experience.

I knelt to place a hand flat on the chilly ground, grateful that my gloves allowed my fingertips to meet the dirt. Tara always laughed at me for doing it, but I found the physical gesture helpful in focusing my powers. With my eyes closed, I imagined flipping to a new filter in my surveillance system. The squad's emotions faded into the background as the physical world around me came into sharper "focus."

Taking a slow, measured breath, I counted to four on inhale and exhale. My senses expanded outward—past the truck, over Deadeye's and Tara's cyan-illuminated heads, through the dusty ground riddled with snake and rodent burrows, into the house, around the terror-laced forms of the kidnapped children—until they ran into something that sparked like battle fury and ozone.

I withdrew my hand from the ground with a sharp inhale. *They pulled out the big guns. Their Shattered's here.*

The Blood Angels had once had two Shattereds fighting for them, until Tara and I dropped a mountainside on one of them last October. After that, there'd only been this one—a teenager wielding a fearsome amount of Shattered power with ferocity that bordered on recklessness. Memories of crackling electricity streaked across the words as I clarified, *It's the lightning wielder—the girl.*

I couldn't hear exactly what Bandit said, but it felt like a swear word. Deadeye's voice came through the bridge loud and clear. *Are they crazy? They'd send their best for a conflict over a gas pump?*

Crazy or not, they need that station owner's cooperation, I said as I straightened. *The Blood Angels haven't updated their trucks to power cores like we have. Makes sense they'd go to bat over a gas pump.*

He's right, Caleb said calmly. *Banshee, how's your power? Running hot?*

I'm fine. For a moment, Tara's power flickered through our bond, and my own answered in a wash of cyan across my vision. *Gabe and I can handle her.*

A shout of alarm echoed from the house. Bandit ducked behind the truck and drew his handgun as a gunshot rang out. *They're not interested in talking.* His words cut through my distraction as he ordered, *Banshee, get the kids.* Mijo, *hold that Shattered's attention! Try to keep her from engaging anyone else!*

"Yes, sir!"

I moved several yards away from the truck, bringing up a shield around myself as Caleb joined Bandit in opening fire against the Blood Angels pouring out of the house. With a deep breath, I opened my hands and gave the energy swirling in my soul an escape route. Pure cyan light poured out of my palms and streaked toward the sky as I coaxed it into a beam. If previous experiences with this Shattered were any indication, she wouldn't be able to resist a counter-attack—and hopefully, it would keep her from turning the full force of her power loose on anyone else.

Her response was almost instantaneous. The hairs on my arms stood on end as a lightning bolt slammed down with a heart-shaking crack less than twenty feet away. Even though I'd been expecting something like this, I jumped.

Good, Gabe! Bandit shouted over gunfire. *She sees you. Let it go and engage!*

I gritted my teeth and forced all of the energy—shield included—to boil down into my bloodstream. It pounded at the back of my head and scorched through my veins as I ran to Caleb's side and released a fraction of the pent-up power into the advancing Blood Angels. Gouts of dirt and blood flew up as several fell, their deaths sending invisible punches through my stomach before adrenaline eased the pain.

As I caught my breath, searing battle rage mixed with cold calculation in the mind bridge—Tara and Deadeye as they pounded through the close-grown trees near the wash. The edge of the house shuddered as Tara's destructive subtype reached it, and for a disorienting moment, I was several places at once—huddled in the kitchen, crashing through underbrush, and standing tall with power coursing through my veins.

I shook my head with annoyance, my helmet display flickering at the sudden movement. This had been happening more and more; my awareness splitting when I needed to be most focused. Tara said it was my power growing, and more practice would help. For the moment—

Gabe, shield! Caleb yelled.

I obeyed on instinct, a glowing blue bubble winking into place around us as another lightning bolt streaked across the dusty sky. It slammed into the shield, and a shiver of electricity passed through my limbs as the charge dissipated.

With a yell, I launched a sphere of energy at the other Shattered, who'd finally emerged from the house encased in a shield of her own. The girl's fury turned to surprise, then panic, as a corner of the building shivered and broke apart under Tara's power. In the kitchen, the hostages' fear spiked through the roof, making my own heart rate rise as another shield appeared over them.

Tara's urgent shout echoed through both my mind and in-ear comms. "Get out! Run!"

Relief washed over me as the kids realized what was going on. They scrambled out the jagged hole in the wall, a Blood Angel swearing and starting after them before a streak of light from Tara obliterated him.

They're all out? I asked, uncertain if the relief I'd felt had been my own or the kids'.

Deadeye's mental voice wasn't out of breath, but the adrenaline coursing through her system was plain as she said, *They're out. We're getting them away from here.*

Bandit acknowledged from behind the truck, firing his handgun another two times before saying, *Good work, you two.* His attention broadened to include me and Caleb. *Let's see if we can convince the others their best bet is to run. Back up, everyone.*

Caleb and I did as he said, taking measured steps backward as the weapons' fire abated near the house. I tapped Caleb's armor to get his attention before saying, *I'm going to try to command them. My shield might drop, so watch out.*

The others' acknowledgments sifted past the edges of my mind as I stepped behind the truck. Casting my consciousness across the bullet-riddled expanse, I focused every bit of my attention on the Blood Angels. They appeared in my mind's eye as red humanoid figures, the emotions drifting from them clouding the air with hostility and fear.

I collected my will and envisioned a new layer of light

falling across the battlefield. Once I had the command in my mind, I unleashed it with all the adamance I could manage.

Run while you can.

Most of the Blood Angels obeyed instantly, save one. A defiant spark flickered across the field as the Shattered's allies retreated. The mingled emotions and voices of the squad faded to a subsonic hum in the back of my mind as I bent my will toward the girl's cyan-and-red presence. As I did, my power slid against something resistant, like glass covered in oil.

Just like Judge. The images of my former squad mate's bleached hair and cyan eyes flickered through my head, aching in their familiarity and tinged with grief. *Someone taught her to guard her mind.*

The command snapped across the field again.

Run.

The resistance gave slightly, and I slammed all my awareness into the weakening barrier.

Run.

My power rammed through, and the world dissolved into a confusing whirlpool of scattered memories; myriad fragments of a life I'd never lived.

Laughter in another language.

The feel of a skateboard deck beneath my feet.

Sunlight reflected off turquoise water and rushing waves.

Horrible helplessness driven out by a sudden burst of cyan energy.

I froze. That helplessness...I'd felt that before. Right when I Shattered.

A single word cracked through my mind with the force of a lightning bolt.

OUT.

I reeled back a pace. **NO.** Someone—probably Caleb—caught me before I fell. I regained my balance to push more power through the cracks in the girl's mental wall. ***This won't end well for you. Leave. Now.***

For a moment, I thought she was going to resist again, and a stab of panic skittered through my mind at the thought of continuing this battle of wills. Then, her resolve crumbled, the connection between our minds failed, and the sense of ozone faded into the wash as she retreated. On the other side of the open space, the black-painted truck's engine started with a rumble, a cloud of dust rising as the remaining Blood Angels fled.

I sagged with a sigh of relief, hands going to my knees and limbs trembling as I fought to catch my breath. It took me a long moment to realize that the mind bridge was still up, until a question from Tara pulled me back into reality.

They running?

Yeah. Caleb gave an impressed whistle. The sound warbled through my in-ear comms as he commented, *I know you weren't directing it at us, Gabe, but even I was tempted to run.*

Yeah... I frowned. "Which command did you hear?"

"Just the one. 'Run while you can'?" He walked past me to reach into the truck for a water bottle. "Worked great, even if it took a moment for all of them to listen."

I joined him at the tailgate, popping the top off my own water and taking a swig. "Most of them listened, but the Shattered was able to guard against it."

"Is that what happened?" Caleb asked.

"Yeah." I winced as a headache made its presence known. "You didn't hear me command her specifically?"

"Nope, not a word. Your shield did drop, though. I figured something was up; that's why I grabbed you."

"Thanks." I took a deep breath. "It did work the second time; I was able to override her resistance, and the others were already running." I let my senses expand to follow the Blood Angels' retreat. From the feel of things, they'd stopped to pick up their comrades who'd fled on foot. "They're still in retreat. Oh—" I returned my focus to the immediate area, and my awareness to the mind bridge. *Tara, you can bring the kids back. Are they okay?*

They're okay, Tara said. *Kind of shaken up, though.* A brief image flashed through our connected minds of tears streaking dirty faces. *Do you think you can help with that?*

I can try, I said, eyes following Bandit as he walked into the no-man's-land between us and the crumbling house. *Sir? Are you all right?*

Bandit was kneeling over a Blood Angel. It was a long moment before he answered, a hand scuffing over the corpse's piecemeal armor before going to his helmet in something close to a salute. *This one's just a kid.*

Their Shattered's young too, I said. An ache had hollowed out my chest, the sensation coldly informing me that more than one person had died today. Now that the immediate conflict was over, all I could feel was deep exhaustion. *I think she's close to my age.*

Bandit's sigh came through the mind bridge with the weight of years fighting behind it. *They didn't deserve to go this way; none of them did.*

Kids or not, Shattered or not, they're still our enemies. Tara's voice and mind held little remorse as she and Deadeye ushered the rescued hostages in our direction. *Keep your thoughts on that, El Bandito.*

The sorrow in Bandit's mind shrank at Tara's stern-edged usage of his old call sign, as if being compacted into a ball and stuffed in the dark recesses of a closet. He holstered his handgun with a definitive shove before saying aloud, "I think we're done here. Let's get going before they realize they've left their dead."

UPON FURTHER INSPECTION, two of the kids had sustained injuries that neither Tara nor Bandit felt comfortable treating in the field. As the sun crested the sky, we made for St. Augustine's Hospital. Josephine had remained at the station, but several of her Medical Corps colleagues were happy to get the kids patched up before releasing them to us.

I stayed by the truck to help Caleb restock our medical compartments, a little nervous around the hustle of the Emergency Department. Most of the hospital staff were former Defense Force or current Medical Corps, and they all knew exactly who I was and what my power entailed. It wasn't overt or malicious by any means, but the stares and whispers made my skin prickle each time I walked the halls.

"Are we out of 4x4 gauze pads?" I asked from behind our clipboard. "I feel like we had to use a bunch last week."

Caleb flipped open a compartment and fished through it. "Yeah. Good thing we're here." He jumped down to stand next to me. "I'll go swipe some."

Caleb had disappeared inside and I was sorting IV fluids when a guy in civilian clothes sauntered over to engage Deadeye—who'd stayed in the driver's seat—in conversation. Most of my attention was wrapped up in counting, so I didn't catch what was said, but after a moment she hopped out and followed him into the hospital.

"Do you know who that was?" I asked as Caleb returned with a cardboard box of supplies.

"Who?"

I leaned down from the truck and brushed my fingertips against his shoulder, envisioning the newcomer's face and projecting the image into Caleb's mind. "This guy Deadeye was just talking to; I've never seen him. Recognize him?"

His forehead creased with a frown. "Yes, but I can't remember from where. Could be he's a technician who came here from Regional." He passed me a package of gauze pads. "Just ask her when she gets back."

A few minutes later, Deadeye returned with a plastic bag full of printouts slung over her shoulder. "A little light reading," she explained when I shot her a questioning look. "Remember how I was telling you about the lab that got shut down? That was one of the guys from there."

"I wondered." I nodded at the bag. "And that's..."

"Encrypted data," she answered, pulling out a stack of paper and riffling through it. "Recovered from a destroyed xeno site—did either of you guys know there was a whole wing of labs in the upper levels of the facility we trashed last year?"

My breath caught in my chest.

...They're built like labyrinths, those places, Bandit had once said. The memory of that night in the Ridges jumped into sharp relief, like a recording played back on my screens.

"Found it." I pressed my hand into the ground, fingers digging at the gravel like it would help me see better. "It's really big; it just keeps going."

"No." I drew back in shock. "How?"

"We were only there to destroy the cloning operation," Caleb reminded me. "So the Blood Angels wouldn't have more Brutes to keep throwing at us. We didn't stop to wonder if there could be anything else there."

I groaned, more frustrated at myself than anything else. "I should've known to look."

Deadeye snorted. "*You* had only just figured out how to keep track of more than one mind at a time. I'm surprised you were able to fight at all, much less scan for stuff we weren't even interested in. But yeah, Regional sent a team in to clean out everything after you and Tara wasted it, and this was part of what they found."

"The lab that Regional closed was continuing that research?" Caleb slammed a compartment door shut and came to peer at the stack of paper. His eyes narrowed, and a flicker of suspicion sounded behind his mental wall. "What *was* it?"

I tilted my head to better see the abstract page of the massive report. "Wavelengths and frequencies? Energy field analytics?" I looked up at Deadeye with confusion breaking through my frustration. "Isn't this outside your sphere of knowledge?"

She plucked the paper from my hands and slid it back into the bag. "Never underestimate my ability to fixate on a pet project." Her good eye shone under her eyepatch strap. "I've been thinking about something for a while, and this might be a godsend. If I can make the pieces fit together, it might actually go a long way to helping people."

Caleb and I exchanged looks; mine uncertain and his suspicious. I thought he was on the verge of asking more questions, but at that moment Bandit and Tara reemerged from the Emergency Room doors with the kids in tow.

"Hey, pack it up!" Bandit called in Spanish, oblivious to

the tension that had spread around the three of us. "Let's get these guys back to their families."

WE RETURNED the kids to the relative safety of their barrio compound. Bandit warned the families to be on their guard, and we left before anyone could thank us or accuse us of not doing more. As we pulled away from the gas station where all the trouble had originated, I caught sight of the farthest pump handle. It was covered by a bright yellow plastic shell, and a combination lock glinted in the noonday sun.

"Did anyone else see that?" I asked, a hollow growing in my stomach. *That entire fight might've been for nothing.* "They've got controls on the pumps now."

"I saw," Deadeye said from the driver's seat. "Must've settled with the Blood Angels. That's nice of them, to cave without letting us know."

"They wanted their kids back and they didn't trust the Blood Angels' guarantees," Tara said. "We don't have to like it, but I understand." She slid a hand under her own monitor cuff and rubbed her wrist with a grimace. "At least the fight went in our favor."

"This time," I said with an edge to my voice that hadn't been present before seeing the power dynamic shifting for the neighborhood. "But now it's going to get worse in this barrio. Things might not go this well the next time we have to respond here."

"True." Caleb put his arm around Tara as she leaned into him as much as their seat belts allowed. "But at least for today we're still safe and telling the tale."

I nodded and fell silent, too discouraged to speak. *Some tales I still barely believe. If you'd told Gabriel at graduation that he'd Shatter in less than a year's time, he'd have called you crazy.* I rubbed my face, the ache from earlier pulsing behind my right eye. *And if you'd told him he'd end up fighting for the same region he'd tried to escape from, he'd have called you cruel.*

And now?

Now, I wasn't even certain there was a way to win this fight, or if the pain would be worth it when we did. The gaping sorrow that Bandit had let slip welled into my recollection, twisting my stomach into knots. It wasn't often that our stoic commander showed that much emotion, but he had a well-known soft spot when it came to kids—and not just the ones on the civilian side of our run-ins with the Blood Angels.

Every encounter ends in death, and it's not always of the ones who deserve it. I shifted in my seat and renewed my attention on the city as it flew past us. *I know they're our enemies, but I don't know how long I can keep doing this.*

STAGE THREE

Thunderbird Heights
Santa Cruz Valley
March 5

A WEEK LATER, the knots in my stomach hadn't subsided. I stood—once more—under a shield, rifle juddering in my hands as shot after shot cracked through the air.

Mijo, what's going on down there? Bandit asked through the bridge. I couldn't see him, but I could feel his presence on a balcony above us. The rest of us had taken cover at the edge of a business plaza's parking lot, where we'd come in response to a report of shots fired at a community clinic. The source had been credible, so we'd loaded up and responded. We were greeted with gunfire from all directions, a firmly barricaded enemy, and no victims—all clear and demoralizing signs that we'd been duped into an ambush.

Three in the barber shop, I answered from where I crouched behind the truck, both hands on the ground with power streaming out in all directions. Frustration and exhaustion pulsed through my mind—this was the third time we'd been called somewhere, only to walk into an ambush. *Four between the thrift store and the clinic. One of them...*

I dug my fingers into the ground, concentrating my power on the person firing on us from the derelict barber shop. Blood Angels appeared to my Shattered abilities as reddish outlines, sounded like Spanish spoken several rooms away, and—these days—carried a sense of anger and desperation. This individual, however, felt off. Bluish and scared, like...

The ground stirred in the center of the parking lot. Dust spiraled up, the air grew heavy, and a faint rumble began under my feet.

Guys, they've got a new Shattered with them! I yelled. *It's a vortex; a big one!* The uncertainty churning in my stomach grew to terror as the dust rising from the ground became tinged with cyan—a color that deepened and intensified as the infant vortex grew, and grew, and grew, and—

Retreat! Bandit shouted. I caught the sense of him scrambling away from the edge of the balcony. *Get out!*

A flurry of movement marked the others obeying; Tara sprinting to join me behind the truck, Deadeye breaking cover and dodging behind the taller building. As they did, the vortex continued to grow—and now, I could sense the panic coming from its wielder.

I yanked my hands from the ground and shot to my feet.

Tara, he's brand new. Certainty built in my heart as the hum of the vortex overwhelmed even my helmet controls. A shuddering vibration built in the air, energy coalescing under the influence of Shattered power running haywire. *He can't control it!*

The information flew between all five of us faster than I could track.

—*run?*

Shield?

No time—

Bandit's voice pierced the chaos. *SHIELD NOW!*

Tara's hand shot out to grasp mine, our gloved fingers interlocking. Light spread to envelop both of us, then shot outward to protect the truck. My power stuttered in response to the fear that even this wouldn't be enough, that we were about to get blown to pieces by the raw power churning into the sky. We'd done this once before, melding our power to create a shield that could handle an uncontrolled vortex, but that was months ago, and I didn't know if—

Hold on, guys. Caleb skidded to a halt behind us, his gun hitting the dirt as his hands went to each of our shoulders. New strength filled me, and the shield surrounding us stabilized not a moment too soon.

In the blink of an eye, the cyclone of Shattered power collapsed into itself, becoming a tiny, spinning ball before exploding into violent curtains of pure destructive force. From inside the shield, all I could see was blue and white, twinned with a concussive blast and earth-shaking impact against the ground and surrounding buildings. Tara's and my hands tightened on each other, our power pulsing and flaring against the onslaught before the chaos subsided.

Sound off, Tara gasped. *Everyone okay?*

I'm fine, Bandit said. I caught the sense of him cautiously circling the building as it groaned and shuddered.

I...think I'm fine. Nausea spiked from Deadeye, and I let

my shield go to focus on her more clearly. *Got slammed against the dumpsters.*

You are not *fine.* From deep inside her head, I could tell that her vision was unfocused and everything felt swimmy. *Can you get over to us?*

Caleb released my shoulder. *I'll help her.* He stepped from behind the truck, surprise jolting from him as he did. *Guys—*

Tara braced herself and peered around the truck. A deep sort of sadness stirred. *He lost control,* she softly said. *Didn't have enough juice to shield, or maybe he never learned how. They didn't have a chance.*

I didn't have to guess at what she meant, but I was still unprepared for the destruction that greeted me. It looked like a bomb had gone off in front of the buildings where the Blood Angels had been barricaded. Only the farthest walls had survived, the destruction centered around what had once been a barber shop. I swallowed hard, the knots in my stomach becoming more pronounced as I let my power wash over the ruined buildings.

There were no Blood Angel survivors.

Seven of our enemies, gone just like that.

I raised a hand to my forehead, the gesture instinctive despite wearing a helmet. Pain throbbed behind my eyes. This ambush was no different from the others, I told myself. There'd been no avoiding it, no way of stopping the destruction once it had started. And if we'd refused to respond, we'd have been no better than the authorities that'd first abandoned this region.

They didn't have a chance, I agreed with Tara. Exhaustion running through my limbs, I sank into a crouch on the newly cracked ground. *But neither did we.*

COMPUTERS and small rooms were never intended to mix. A few days later, Deadeye and I were in the cluttered workspace that had once been a fire chief's office, pitting our collective three brain cells against our chimera of a computer. During the winter, it had been chilly in this room, tacked like an afterthought on the side of Station Somewhere. As nature stirred outdoors, the computers were making the room stuffy and warm. I'd ditched my hoodie about halfway through the task of updating my comms program, and now it draped over a stack of totes in the corner as I sat at the end of the desk.

"That ought to do it." Deadeye's German accent came out stronger whenever she was dealing with technology. She sat hunched over the keyboard despite the lingering headache from her concussion, editing the code we'd jimmied together from old patch logs and half-deduced recollections. My monitor cuff lay on the junk-covered desk, its indicator lights flickering in test patterns of green and red. "As long as it doesn't..."

She trailed off into German muttering as I yawned and propped my chin on my hand. The ambush hadn't been the only action we'd seen a few days ago. I'd been up late each night, quelling disturbances as the Blood Angels reacted to the disaster. Despite the setback to the Blood Angels' goal of gaining control over the sparsely populated city, the last few days were doing their part in convincing me that this was a battle neither of us could hope to win.

"Gabriel, pass me the—the—" Deadeye snapped her fingers several times before pointing to where her helmet sat atop a messy pile of folders and printouts. "The—"

I raised an eyebrow and went to dig through the mess. A

pile slid free to spill over the floor—the report she'd been given by the fugitive researcher at St. Augustine's. I set it aside and asked, "The...folder, maybe?"

"Ah! Yes! The grey one, *por favor*."

"Stick to the languages you know, okay?" I plucked the folder from the pile and handed it to her. A grin tugged at my mouth as I added, "Your accent is hard enough to understand in English."

"Don't tell me what to do." Deadeye flipped the folder open and retrieved a printout scribbled with notes. "I'm—what is it now, nineteen years older than you?" A new dialogue box came up on the computer screen, and she began typing. "I'm twice your age. You should respect your elders."

I rolled my eyes as the lights on my monitor cuff began blinking in a new pattern. "Fine, *elder*. What are you doing now?"

She nodded at the computer screen. "I wrote a new script for the startup sequence while I was at the university yesterday using their computers. It'll make it easier for the software to boot, and about ten times faster." Her shoulder hitched in a shrug. "I figured we might as well update everything while we're messing with this thing's brains."

"You mean my brains." I touched the back of my head, where my bio interface made a now-familiar ridge beneath my fingers. "Or does thinking about that not help your focus?"

"Shut up, Gabriel," Deadeye said with a grin, fingers flying faster over the keyboard than my eye could track. With a final, dramatic keystroke, she sent the code into the depths of the computer and turned to face me. "That should do it. It has to back up and restart, and when it does, we'll know if it worked."

I frowned and rubbed my forearm. I'd been wearing my monitor so consistently these days that it felt strange to not have anything riding against my skin. "And I'll be able to connect with individuals, instead of just throwing the bridge open to everyone?"

"Mm-hmm. Here, see?" Deadeye reached over to adjust a setting on the monitor cuff's flexible screen. "We can set it now. I'll tell it to restrict to just the two of us." She rubbed her good eye with a grimace. "It'll be obvious if it worked. Either it'll just be us, or we'll be yanking *everyone* into the bridge with no warning."

"I'll let you make the apologies if it fails." I resumed my seat at the end of the desk, balancing my chin between my hands. "It'll be nice if this works."

"Not to mention easier on you." Deadeye leaned back in her chair and put her feet on her desk, shoving aside folders of paperwork and tangled cables to make space. "Michael always felt the strain when there were a lot of us to keep track of."

I wriggled my voice recorder from its hidden pocket on the outside of my thigh and turned it on as Deadeye nodded her agreement. The deceased founder of the EDF—a Shattered whose abilities closely resembled my own—was a distant figure to most, obscured by urban legend and propaganda. To the others in Squad 36, though, Michael had been more than a commander—he'd been a friend. It'd taken me forever to get comfortable referring to him by his first name, but the others bore no such hesitation.

"Was he able to instinctively choose who he bridged with?" I asked. "Or was it software?"

Deadeye frowned around her eyepatch strap. Based on the expression crossing her face, the strain on her eyes was developing into a migraine. "It was both. If he focused on someone, he could narrow things to only him and them, but most of the time he used software to make it easier. The command team would select from a list, and suddenly you'd have Michael's voice in your head telling you to report upstairs."

I winced. "Sounds uncomfortable."

"Oh, it was." Deadeye lowered her feet to the floor, chair creaking as she sat forward. "But very different from how things are with you. When you bridge with us, it's a two-way exchange of information, like a real conversation." Her pink-streaked hair swished as she shook her head. "It wasn't like that with him."

"Right...I guess there are some differences between an empath and a telepath. He never let any of you see inside his head?"

Deadeye scoffed, a cynical sound with a touch of phlegm. "Never. That would have implied weakness, and the resistance years were so life and death that he couldn't afford any weakness." Her voice dropped, and she turned away with a hand going to rub her eye once more. "Not even from himself."

I was about to call her out on the evasion riding behind her words when the computer beeped. A startled yell escaped me as the mind bridge surged open, dropping me smack into the middle of the memory Deadeye had been dwelling on.

I wasn't supposed to be in the command module, but I'd heard the alarms from the security room. Michael was slumped on the ground with his back against the wall, the lines etching his face making him appear much older than thirty-three. He had his command helmet off to reveal blond hair and pale skin, cyan eyes mere slits as spasmodic tremors shook his limbs.

My heart rate surged with concern as I dropped to a crouch beside him, reaching out to grasp his shoulder. "Michel? Was ist los?"

His brow furrowed as a scrawling spiderweb of cyan light flashed across the wall he was leaning against. A robotic voice warned of overload, red emergency lights blinking from the command console. My pulse surged into my ears and I grabbed his wrist, muscle memory and long practice guiding me to the tiny buttons on his monitor. "Michel!"

He didn't seem to hear me, but his eyes had opened all the way. I caught a hint of recognition before they sagged shut and his head dropped backward.

"What...happened to him?" I asked aloud.

Deadeye's breath caught and the keyboard rattled as she smacked a command key. The memory vanished as she snapped, "Nothing."

"Reneé—"

"I said, nothing!" She spun in her chair to point at the door, her jaw tight and good eye bright with unshed tears. "Get out of here, Gabriel."

I snatched my recorder off the desk, clutching it to my chest as she hustled me out of the office. The door slammed behind me and I caught a flash of tears, like the breaking of a dam under a flood, before I was left alone and confused in the hallway.

She's never acted like that before when we've talked about him. I rubbed my arm again. My monitor was still plugged into the office computer, but the surging grief and loss behind the door made me fear for my life, should I reappear before Deadeye was ready to talk. *What's gotten into her?*

I NEVER DID MANAGE to corner Deadeye about what happened that afternoon. My monitor cuff was lying on my bed when I returned from working out, and Deadeye had reemerged from the office and was acting like herself. We tested the software that night with the rest of the squad, and if she seemed a little more closed off than usual, nobody cared to comment.

We had another several run-ins with the Blood Angels over the next four days. Grief for the lives lost in the failed ambush—or maybe desperation—was driving them to take stupid risks, and all of us were feeling the strain of battling an unrelenting enemy. Finally, we had an evening without chaos interjecting. I was on kitchen duty while Deadeye doodled at the table, a fact that didn't go unnoticed by my cleanup partner.

"It wasn't until Michael went to pull the whiteboard over that she remembered what she'd drawn," Tara said, elbow-deep in dishwater as I dried plates with a worn-out towel. "By that point it was too late to stop him, so we were all left staring at this profanity-spewing horse-octopus-*thing* drawn in purple dry-erase. Michael was just like—" She closed her eyes with an exasperated sigh, the image of the EDF founder appearing in my mind's eye as my elbow brushed her shoulder. "He just stayed like that for a second, then took the eraser and started *scrubbing* the whole thing."

I snorted a laugh. "Was there any fallout?"

Deadeye grinned. She'd annexed my notebook for her artistic pursuits, and a whole page was already covered in roughly sketched figures. "I had my whiteboard privileges revoked after that. Never had to do another briefing for the rest of the war. But Alexi definitely heard from me about it later."

"Oh? Why, was he there that day?"

"What, you think I drew a monster on purpose?" Deadeye said. "NO! I drew a horse! And it was one of my better horses, I'll have you know."

Tara gave the forks a last swish through the dishwater before passing them to me for rinsing and drying. "Alexi now...he added the tentacles, the extra eyes—"

"—and the mohawk. Michael knew *exactly* who was responsible." Deadeye tugged on her eyepatch strap. "But that was before they realized how much of a pest he was, so they let him get away with it."

I rolled my eyes. I'd only ever known Alexi by his call sign "Judge," but his death had left me with a much deeper understanding of the cocky Shattered than anyone else realized. Judge hadn't allowed anyone into his mind until his last moments, when he'd thrown open his mental barricade and dumped twenty-seven years' worth of memories and secrets into me. "It always surprises me how much he matured over the years."

Tara pulled the plug from the sink and spoke over the water gurgling into our greywater tank. "That's right... I sometimes forget you have all his memories. You ever do anything with them?"

I ducked beneath the sink to detach the drain tubing from the tank. "When I have a bit of time, I sit down and get them written out. I'll probably see if I can find the moment you were talking about, once we finish here." I raised my voice loud enough for Deadeye to hear me. "I will need my notebook back, though."

"Ugh. FINE." Deadeye flipped the notebook closed and skimmed it across the table as I lugged the greywater tank toward the back door. "You work on your project, and I'll work on mine."

"Data decryption?" Tara gave her a thumbs-up from the other side of the counter. "Sounds great. I love turning my brains into tapioca for fun."

"Now see here..."

I snickered as the door closed on Deadeye's indignant words. It was chilly outside now that the sun had set, but there was a lighter feel to the air that told me spring was on its way. The greywater tank sloshed as I hauled it to the edge of the yard, where we'd constructed a pair of raised garden beds that were now filled with spring vegetables and infant tomato plants. A snow pea vine had opened its first cluster of white flowers, and I stopped for a moment to run my fingertip over their velvety edges.

I should get inside. There's no telling how long it's going to stay quiet.

Even with the reminder, I still took my time watering the plants. The dusky light had completely faded and the flood-lights clicked on by the time I'd finished.

Chores done, I retreated to my room with my notebook. The station pulsed with quiet around me as the others went about their own business—Deadeye puttering in her office, Bandit sorting paperwork, Caleb reading, Tara watching a movie with Josephine. By the time I'd finished transcribing

Judge's perspective of the whiteboard incident, everyone else had long since turned in.

I was nine pages in and getting sleepy when a scream ripped through my head. I jerked upright as my mind's eye filled with ruby light and glistening chrome. Even from across the hallway and through two closed doors, the fear set my teeth on edge.

Caleb.

I supposed it had only been a matter of time. He never really reacted to any of the things we saw in combat, but I knew the stress took its toll where no one else could see. He never made noise during these episodes—not aloud, anyway—but I could sense the terror leaking from him like ink spiraling through water.

Caleb. I pushed his name into the night, envisioning a beam of sunlight piercing the darkness surrounding him. **It's a dream.**

Sometimes, the mental reminder was all it took to banish the nightmare and free his formidable will to act on his benefit, but not tonight. Pain crawled across my skin, and my muscles spasmed as another silent scream ripped into my mind.

The cracked tiles were cold under my bare feet as I slid out of my bed and crossed the hall. The room was dark, but I didn't need light to find Caleb huddled at the edge of the mattress. His breath shook as he curled into a tighter ball, fists closed on handfuls of the bedsheets.

I dropped to sit at the foot of the bed. Past experiences had taught me that it was foolish to touch him when he was like this, so I reached out with my power instead. The barriers that encircled his mind had grown flimsy, fragile, and it was the work of a heart-stopping moment to step through them and into a world of *chrome, glittering crimson light, the high-pitched whine of machines, aches that ran deeper than my bones, and a pervasive feeling of cold, cold, cold.*

A stark metal ceiling loomed above me, angled at the corners and laced with pipes and glowing conduit. Something held my limbs fast, a burning sensation running through skin that had been sliced and restitched in too many places to count. I craned my neck to look around, and a dull crimson gleam caught my eyes amid the blinding metal. Fresh blood glimmered at the edges of a wound, leaving a metallic lattice of alien circuitry exposed on the inside of my left arm.

A spasm seized my muscles, and the circuits shimmered in response as I screamed again. This time, the voice was familiar, and I arrested the noise with the realization of where—and in whose memories—I was.

I swore as I clawed my way back into my own consciousness. Power bloomed in the corners of my vision, cyan in stark contrast to the crimson and metal as I plunged back into his memories. ***Caleb, this isn't real. This isn't real. This isn't real.***

Xeno voices chattered back and forth, and a blinding flash of ruby light illuminated the underside of the ceiling.

Caleb! I had a grasp on the boundaries of the memory now—dark and fogged where his mind had tangled past with present—and more importantly, I could tell where he began and I ended. ***Hey, it's a dream. Wake up!***

Tendrils of power wrapped around both of us, the familiar fearful darkness closing over the edges of my cyan light. Aloud, I yelled, "Caleb, wake up!" and, like cutting off the mind bridge connection, hurled us both out of the memory.

The light around us vanished as my awareness broke into reality, and my eyes refocused on the stillness of his and Tara's room. Caleb shot upright with a gasp, a flailing arm catching me on the shoulder.

I bolted to my feet, ready to dodge if he tried to hit me again. "Hey," I gasped, light breaking from my upturned hand to illuminate my face. "It's okay; it's me. You had a bad one, is all."

He looked bewilderedly around the room—the ceiling, floor, myself. Finally, his gaze fell on the upturned palm of his left hand. The circuits embedded below the skin of his arm glinted dull silver in the sparse light. He examined them for a long moment before whispering, "It was a dream this time?"

I sighed. "Just a dream, yeah. You're safe." I closed my hand over the light I'd summoned and cautiously resumed my seat at the foot of the bed. "Sorry I had to wake you; you were pretty deep and it pulled me in too."

A long breath hissed between Caleb's clenched teeth. "Geez. I'm sorry, Gabe." He'd pulled his elbows tight to his torso, shoulders quivering with barely noticeable tremors. "Were you already asleep? Did I wake you up again?"

I shook my head. "I was still awake."

He gave an exhausted snort. "What was it this time?"

"It was quiet, and I was writing."

"Your power won't regen if you don't rest," Caleb warned. He reached over to tap his fist against my arm. "Go to bed, and actually sleep this time."

"I will in a minute. If—" It was then that I realized the other side of their bed was empty. "Wait, where's Tara?"

"Fell asleep on the couch." Affection filled his voice. "She looked so comfortable that I didn't want to move her."

"Oh." I looked toward the living room, projecting my power through the walls to scan for Tara. Sure enough, her sleeping form pulsed in muted cyan somewhere near the far end of the common area. *Maybe it's for the best. She hates seeing him like this.* "I'm sorry I wasn't faster. It's been a while, hasn't it?"

Caleb took a deep breath and let it out slowly. "Yeah, but I'll be fine. You got me out again, just like the other times."

"Sure, but still, it—"

"Could be much worse," he interrupted. "There's always a cost when you fight day in and day out like this, but it's worth it if it means we protected someone who couldn't fight for themselves. At least all I'm losing is sleep." Caleb tipped a no-nonsense look in my direction, steely grey eyes catching the light from the hallway. "And speaking of, *please* go to bed."

I wanted to argue. I could feel the fear continuing to prowl the corners of his mind, but breaking the nightmare's hold had left me exhausted. "If you're sure you'll be okay."

"I'll be fine."

I was about to return to my room when the overhead lights clicked on. Both of us jumped, Caleb's eyes flicking to the ceiling and my hands tightening into surprised fists. The electronic voice of our station-wide alert system echoed through the cinderblock hall, words long garbled past the point of coherency.

I swore quietly. "Something's going down again."

"Sounds like it." Caleb stood with a groan. "Let's go."

"Will—will you be all right?"

He settled his shoulders and gave me a smile. "Don't worry about me. Really. I'm fine."

It was a lie, but I didn't have time to call him out on it. By the time we'd gotten to the bay and armored up, the devastation from Caleb's memories had disappeared behind a will stronger than steel. We peeled off into the night, Bandit's briefing through comms half-heard as I tried to calm my nerves and shake off the terror that lingered after these nightmare encounters. *It's still worth it,* I told myself as we hit a pothole that cracked my helmet against the compartment wall. *Saving the people I care about will always be worth it. But* this?

I glared at the map as it populated into my helmet display. As far as I could tell, the multi-family compound we were racing toward would've stayed secure had it not been for someone allowing interlopers inside. *This can't go well for anyone involved, and how do they expect us to deal with it?*

My cynical musing turned out to be accurate. The gates of the compound stood open and splattered with blood, the screams of children sounding in crescendo behind gunfire as their parents battled the handful of Blood Angels that had snuck in. Once the dust settled, anguished cries pierced my stomach as inspection revealed several of the compound youths—freshly recruited and in the middle of initiation—among the dead Blood Angels.

"Couldn't you tell the difference!" a bereaved mother shouted in Bandit's face. Her grief and anger practically colored the air red as she cried, "They're just kids!"

My stomach churned at the raw emotion building in the air. *Don't they realize we had no choice? Just like the ambush the other day, we can't sit back and do nothing.*

Tara's shoulders drooped under her armor. She'd done her best to save the newly recruited barrio kids, but not even her considerable healing abilities could replace lost blood.

They keep pushing like this, and we're all going to end up dead.

We saved their lives, Deadeye said sourly. *Some would call that victory.*

I don't know if this type of victory is worth it. I turned and climbed into the truck. *I'm shutting down comms. Come get me when it's time to clean up.*

The others didn't follow me, though I felt their concern even without our bio interfaces connected. By the time Bandit had talked down the parents and the dead had been sent to the St. Augustine's morgue, it was past two in the morning and I was reeling with exhaustion.

I stumbled into my room as soon as we got home, muscles aching as the adrenaline of the last two hours worked its way out of my system. The base went quiet around me, everyone trying to recoup as many precious hours of sleep as they could.

As I slid into bed, a new pang went through my left arm —sharply different from the soreness left by combat. I shuddered, cradling my arm to my chest and flexing my fingers against the residual pain from Caleb's nightmare.

"He might think the cost is worth it, but I don't know," I whispered into the darkness. "It's *not* just sleep, it's having those memories and carrying that pain with you wherever you go. And the people you risk it all in order to save might not care what you gave up in order to protect them." I let go of my arm. Lying back against the pillow, I closed my eyes and did my best not to think about the swirls of emotion that now accompanied every mission.

Kids fighting for our enemies. Shattereds losing control and taking out their allies. Families grieving, even when we restore peace to their homes. Even our enemies sound so much like us. For that matter, I could've been like those kids if things had been different. I rolled to my side, the silence insufficient to calm the emotions painting the insides of my eyelids with cyan light. *No matter what we do, it's not enough and it always costs us. And it's never quiet—not even inside my own head.*

I shuddered. *What I wouldn't give for a moment of quiet.*

STAGE FOUR

SPRING in the desert was its own special kind of magic. None of us liked summer, and winter was unpredictable enough to leave my heat-loving heart suspicious. Spring came heralded by poppies, opening bold faces to the sun and carpeting gravel patches with golden petals and feathery leaves. In the wilder places, the dead-looking sticks of ocotillo cactus sprouted leaves and tassels of flaming orange flowers, and the creosote bushes burst into clouds of yellow flowers and tiny leaves.

Some of the exhaustion we'd all been feeling lifted with the advent of warmer temperatures, even as the conflict with the Blood Angels kept making life miserable. The next week and a half after Caleb's nightmare saw us fighting for our lives and civilians' lives over too many encounters to keep track of. We won back the area where the secured compound stood, then lost it again, then helped the grieving families relocate to the far north side of the city. My power was kept in constant demand—Tara's too—and I was getting used to the constant nausea that came with riding close to burnout.

I was on patrol that afternoon, Deadeye my partner as we made our rounds south of the station. It was a little close to the barrio where the Blood Angels had made their newest foothold, but Bandit had insisted we not adjust our patrols. I hadn't argued—there was a *tortillería* nearby, and with how worn down I was, the idea of simple food was a godsend.

"Any trouble today?" I asked the shop owner as she passed me two dozen tortillas wrapped in a crumpled sheet of foil.

She shrugged, but her eyes darted over my shoulder as she said, "Not today. It's getting harder to find gas for the generator, though—Loren said that his supplies aren't available to the public anymore."

"Those jerks," I muttered. "Are the Angels here a lot, then?"

"Now and then." Her eyes went to the window again, or maybe the street beyond. "They come in here sometimes, but they don't bother us too much."

"Right..." I could sense the evasion in her voice even without digging, and the thought of trying soured my stomach. *I don't want to bother her. It looks like she's already having a tough time.* I held up the foil packet. "Thanks for these. Reneé." I turned to Deadeye, switching from Spanish to English mid-sentence. "I don't think you've ever tried *paletas* before, right?"

We hadn't turned on the mind bridge today—I'd run my power down the previous day, and a patrol with one person wasn't worth burning my reserve—but Deadeye still caught my nudge to change the subject. "No, I don't think I have." She went to peer into a small, glass-topped freezer. "I don't think Josephine will mind if we get a snack."

We paid for our things, talked a little more with the shop owner, and left. Between replaying the conversation and trying to ignore a headache, I wasn't paying nearly as much attention to my sixth sense as I should have been. By the time I felt Blood Angels nearby, it was already too late. Both Deadeye and I jumped as a bolt of cyan lightning streaked into the pavement near us, exploding the asphalt and sending a shower of debris into our faces.

"Dammit, this again?" Deadeye stepped closer to me and I raised a shield over us, the road distorting in a swirl of blue light before the shield stabilized.

"The shopkeeper did make it seem like they're moving into this barrio. You'd better radio the others. I can only feel three of them, but they might call for reinforcements."

Deadeye groaned and craned her neck to talk into the radio clipped to the shoulder of her backpack. I tugged up my shirt sleeve—I hadn't worn my armor underlayer, and was already regretting my decision—to throw the mind bridge wide open. The last bits of Deadeye's report to base echoed through my head in duplicate; first through my mind, then my ears.

It'd only taken me a second to shield and turn on the mind bridge, but the enemy Shattered was already moving. She and two other gang members crossed the parking lot opposite us and ducked behind concrete barricades at the edge, a cyan shield just like mine popping into existence above them. I flinched as another bolt of lightning broke against my shield, residual energy making the hairs on the back of my neck stand up.

Beside me, Deadeye drew her handgun and fired, hissing in annoyance as a shot missed the Blood Angel's shield entirely. *What is it with her? This is what, the fourth time this month?*

The fifth, I answered grimly. *You'd think she'd learn that using lightning all the time isn't the best use of her power.* This lightning wielder and I had matched wits enough times that we could've been on a first-name basis—even *without* considering the unsettling moment a few weeks ago when I'd accidentally broken into her mind.

Didn't you say she's young? Deadeye answered. *Wasn't that other one a few weeks ago young as well?*

Yeah. I sent a pair of energy blasts toward the Blood Angels, flinching as another lightning bolt came in response. *She might not have learned how to conserve her energy. And she fights like she expects every strike to be her last.*

As the thought crossed my mind, the dirt began stirring, spiraling into the air near our feet. The energy in my veins thrummed in response, and panic shot through my chest.

Vortex! Run!

I sprinted toward the road, Deadeye at my heels as a churning funnel of power opened in the spot where we'd been standing. Stopping behind another line of concrete barriers, I yelled, "Close your eyes!" before facing the vortex. Drawing up as much power as I could, I pushed everything I had into a secondary shield around the spinning tower of light.

I was almost too late.

The vortex collapsed downwards and inwards into a pulsating ball of destruction. Brilliant light exploded outward a millisecond later, slamming into the shield I'd cast around it.

A shockwave went through my bones, and I staggered under the impact.

Deadeye steadied me. *What is she thinking?! Forget killing us; that could have flattened the whole barrio!*

You were right; she doesn't know how to moderate her power. I didn't stop to wonder where the certainty had come from as I added, *I don't think she was ever taught.* Warmth flowed down my arm as I pulled another energy ball into my hand, sparing a glance at the display of my monitor cuff as I did so. The tiny lights were blinking red with a warning that my power was dipping low. My shield pulsed, and a stab of pain went through my right eye. *I might be able to outlast her, but I can't keep this up for much longer. Are the others on their way?*

I caught the silent confirmation from Deadeye, but there was hardly a need. As if in response to the thought, Tara's voice sounded in my head.

What's going on?

I could feel them now, half a mile away and closing fast. Deadeye answered as I deflected another lightning bolt with a well-placed secondary shield. *It's that girl again! The lightning wielder!*

Again? Caleb sounded annoyed and exhausted. As the truck drew closer, I understood why. Dark clouds swirled through his mind, the fear and pain closer to the surface than it had been in weeks. Without even asking, I could tell he'd been awake most of the night after another nightmare.

Keep your guard up, Bandit said. *We're almost there.*

I took a deep breath, counting to four as I let it out. I didn't have enough power to send another fireball at the Shattered, but there was still something I *knew* she hated— maybe enough to stop attacking us.

Don't like me in your head, huh? Try countering this.

Confusion and uncertainty flashed from the rest of the squad as my concentration diverted to breaking through the enemy Shattered's mental wall. She pushed back with equal fury. Blood roared in my ears, matched by the pulse of power. For a moment, we were balanced—will versus will—before the barrier between our minds fractured. The world spun around me as I caught sight of what lay behind the Blood Angel's helmet.

A sunset glimmering off an ocean, and the sound of gulls fighting raucously over scraps of food. Laughter and happy conversations in broken Spanish. A whoosh of water filling my ears, and a triumphant yell as I breached the surface in a spray of crystal-clear droplets.

Desperation filled the tenuous connection as the Shattered attempted to wrest control away from me. A girl's scream echoed through my mind, and the memory suddenly shifted, solidified, *entrapped.*

Terrible weight pressed against my limbs, helplessness locking my jaw shut. A sense of horror, betrayal, panic coursed through me, then power erupted in a surge of cyan and the helplessness faded.

In an instant, I knew.

Someone, somewhere, had terrified her enough that power had burst out of her in self-defense. She hadn't had a choice in the situation that had led to her Shattering.

Not like I had.

No wonder she never holds back. She's still scared.

The brief glimpse cut off as sharply as a trap closing, and a thunderbolt slammed out of the blue sky into my shield. The impact was a death knell for my power, and my shield evaporated. The voices of the others vanished, the world collapsing to just myself and my own thoughts.

"Deadeye, I'm out," I gasped, doubling over as the pain from my head spread into my limbs. "No shield."

Deadeye fired her handgun again as her radio crackled, no doubt the others panicking at the sudden loss of the mind bridge. "Get down. I'll cover you."

I took a deep breath and abandoned our now-demolished barrier for the one beside it. My handgun felt more familiar in my hand than it had when I began training, its weight grounding me into reality. I couldn't tell for certain without my power to guide my vision, but I thought I saw one of our enemies lying on the ground. The shield they'd been hiding beneath was gone. *She's burned out too.*

All at once, the gang member stood upright, their arm arcing as something flew through the air.

"Duck!" I screamed, tackling Deadeye at the knees. Time stretched as the grenade went off immediately behind us. A brilliant flash scorched my eyes behind my visor. The blast thumped hollowly in my chest. Something zipped past me like an angry hornet, and a burning pain tore across the outside of my neck where my helmet left a gap above my vest. I was conscious of other, smaller pains elsewhere as I rolled to my back, instinctively grabbing the wound.

My fingers came away coated in blood as Deadeye leaned over me.

"Gabe? Aw, no. Gabriel!" Her hands covered mine, returning it to the wound and pressing down. "Press it here, buddy. Hold on!" She released my hands and moved to fire over the barrier, gunshots echoing funny through my helmet.

This can't be good.

I knew I should be getting up, but the panicky note in

Deadeye's voice made me stay down, my hand growing slippery as I pressed it into my neck. I rolled to my side and curled into a ball as more gunshots sounded overhead, the reports louder and faster than Deadeye's handgun had been. Blue light flashed into the corners of my blurring vision, matched by growing darkness as something warm seeped past the edge of my helmet and into my ear.

Someone's feet scuffed the gravel beside me. As they turned me over, the light of a blue-glowing shield filled my vision.

"Tara," I gasped.

"Breathe," she commanded, her voice distorted inside her helmet. "Just breathe and let me help." She peeled my fingers away from the wound, swapping her hands for mine. Blue light streamed down her arm and into my body, the pressure almost enough to cut off my breathing.

Something crawled beneath my skin and I gasped, twisting in Tara's grasp and shivering uncontrollably. The feeling of her power running through my veins was familiar but foreign, like I was hearing my own voice played on a distorted recording. Another tremor sped through my core, and I thrashed again before a second set of gloved hands grabbed me.

"Hold still," Caleb's voice warned. I swam through foggy blackness to stare up at him, aware now that he was leaning into my shoulder with enough of his weight to hold me to the ground. "She's almost done."

After another minute, Tara removed her hands from my throat. Caleb helped me pop the releases on my helmet, and I sat up to realize that the fight—what remained of it—was over. Bandit and Deadeye were on the far side of the parking lot, arguing about something, and Caleb had moved a hand to Tara's knee. A blue glow was fading from his helmet; a sure sign that he'd had to boost her power.

Still disoriented, I stammered, "*Angeles—¿adonde?*"

"*Huyeron.*" Caleb jerked a thumb toward the main road, then switched to English. "Skedaddled when they saw the truck. I think their Shattered burned out; at least, she should've after that lightning bolt."

"It's good we were that close." Tara scrubbed blood—my blood—from her hands. A shiver went down my spine as she warned, "Another minute, and you would've been pretty far down the rabbit hole."

I took a deep breath, counting to four and letting it out as my hand went to my neck. Stickiness met my touch, more in keeping with a scrape than a life-threatening injury. Some rational part of my mind coldly informed me that I should be relieved, but in the moment all I felt was shaky and sick. "Thanks. And thanks for scaring them off."

"What happened?" Caleb asked, popping the release on his own helmet and sliding it off. "Reneé said you burned out, and we all felt the mind bridge drop."

"But you were distracted even before then," Tara said. "Like, you were there but not there. What was going on?"

"I..." I pulled my knees up and leaned my forehead against them, limbs tremoring and my voice shaky. "I think I ticked off the Shattered." The things I'd seen in the lightning wielder's mind flooded back, and I raised my head with urgency. "I managed to break past her walls."

Caleb looked at me with wide eyes. "I wondered what that was. Right before you burned out?"

"Yeah. It's not the first time, either. You remember when we were rescuing those kids?" Both of them nodded. "I did it then too. She resisted the command to run, so I had to push harder." I looked at my hands, suddenly realizing how much blood there was coating them. "She didn't like it."

Tara gave a rueful laugh as she pulled off her own helmet. "I can only imagine. Didn't Judge knock you backward onto concrete the only time you made it into his head?"

"More or less." I gave a halfhearted laugh and sat straighter. If Tara could crack jokes in the face of what had almost happened, I could follow suit. "Anyway, the same thing happened today. I needed her to leave us alone, and I knew I'd be able to break through." I closed a bloodstained fist against the ground, uncertain how much to say.

Don't be ridiculous, there's nothing to protect here, the cynical side of my heart snapped. *She almost killed you.*

My uncertainty left in a huff, and I blurted, "Something happened to her when she Shattered. It wasn't a choice to be in that situation—and it's still dictating how she fights."

Caleb and Tara exchanged a cautious look before Tara asked, "You're sure?"

I thought back to the glimpses I'd see in the enemy Shattered's mind. The helplessness, the fear, the sudden rush of power—all reminded me so much of how I'd felt when I first Shattered. *Except I was in that spot because I was trying to protect someone else, not myself.*

I looked up at Tara and Caleb, unexpected emotion welling up in my voice. "Yeah, I'm sure. She might be fighting for the Angels now, but it might not have been her first choice. And she's just as scared as I was."

AS LUCK—OR Murphy's Law—would have it, Josephine was gone. She and a handful of other doctors with the Medical Corps had set up a clinic downtown, and she'd been spending more than half her days there. Bandit wanted to take me to her anyway, but I insisted otherwise. "I'm not sure why we had this run-in today—might've just been wrong place and wrong time, or patrols bumping where we shouldn't have—but I don't want the Angels to attack the clinic to try to finish me off." I gestured at the living room, the farthest I'd made it without my knees shaking. "If I'm here, at least the rest of you can—"

I closed my mouth tight on the words "warn them off."

I hate being the one who needs protecting.

Tara understood what I wasn't saying. She'd washed her hands, but the cuffs of her long sleeves were still stained with my blood. She sat on the couch beside me, blue light wreathing her fingers as she splayed them against my chest. I fought the urge to squirm away as her power wound through my body. She looked up at Bandit as the light faded. "He lost a lot of blood, but nothing I can do will fix that. I think he just needs time."

"But Josephine—"

"I'm sure Josephine would say the same thing." Tara cast a suspicious look at the wall monitor where we normally received word of trouble. "Let's just pray that things stay quiet for a little while."

Bandit's jaw muscles stood out against his cheek, tension running through the lines of his shoulders. "Your power's gone, right?" he asked.

I nodded. The nausea and pain from the initial burnout had subsided, but the world still felt empty and silent. "For a while, at least."

"Josephine can't do anything about that," he admitted. His fist tapped restlessly against his holster. "You're certain sleep is all you need?"

"Time," Tara corrected. "Not sleep. Though, sleep would be best." Her cyan eyes pierced mine. "You need to go to bed and stay there. No writing, no reading."

"No lying awake, obsessing over the weight of the world's troubles," Caleb added. He raised a sarcastic eyebrow at my offended expression. "There's no way my nightmares are waking you from a dead sleep every single time, and don't think I can't guess why."

I opened my mouth, ready to argue, when Tara raised a hand. Blue flame flickered between her fingers. "Stop. Don't fight us on this, or I'll *put* you to sleep."

"And if she doesn't have enough juice, I'll do it myself," Deadeye added from the kitchen. She brandished a cast-iron skillet in my direction. "Shut up and listen."

Equally frustrated and grateful, I raised my hands in surrender. "All right, all right! I'll sleep, for crying out loud."

My knees only wobbled a little as I got up from the couch, but Bandit still caught my arm in a strong grip. "Here, *mijo*. Hold on to me."

With his help, I managed to get down the hall and into my room. There was no question of my being able to stand long enough to shower, so Bandit sat me on the edge of my bed. "Wait here. I'm going to get stuff to clean up the rest of those cuts."

His footsteps retreated down the hall. Alone in my room, I raised shaking hands to my throat. Tara's power hadn't sealed the wound all the way—I assumed because she'd been running dry—and it stung as my fingers touched it. A shiver built in the pit of my stomach, and a racking gasp tore out of my throat. I doubled over, shaking and feeling like I might throw up as tremors spread across my limbs.

"Whoa, hold on there," Bandit exclaimed as he returned.

He put the bin he'd been carrying on the floor and sat beside me. "Hang on, *mijo*. Breathe."

His hand moved in gentle circles across my shoulder blades while I counted breaths in and out. Only after my shoulders had relaxed did he ask, "What's wrong?"

"Nothing." I scuffed my sleeve across my eyes once, twice, before letting my arm drop with a sigh. "Nothing happened." I mastered the shake in my voice and insisted, "*Nothing happened.* Tara was there in time. I'm still alive to fight another day."

"But..." Bandit let the word hang there, his hand not moving from my back.

I wrapped my arms around my torso to try to control the shivers. "We got lucky. I'm alive, we sent them packing, some people would even say we won. So—why do I still feel like we lost?"

"You almost died. That isn't 'nothing.'" Bandit shifted to put his arm around my shoulders. I'd only hugged him a few times, even after all these months, but I leaned into him nonetheless with a lump building in my throat. "And even if that hadn't happened, it's still okay for you to feel like this. The stuff; it all builds up. Nobody ever told you what happened to me after our victory?"

I shook my head. With my power gone, I couldn't reach past into his mind to see the memory, and I didn't care to at this moment.

Bandit didn't wait for me to answer. "We knew that clearing the xeno command facility would take everything we had. If we failed, it wouldn't matter how well we'd distributed our forces, so *we* held nothing in reserve." His free hand drifted to the spot behind his ear where his bio interface sat. "Those of us with interfaces were linked through Michael, so he could feed us up-to-date information on the weakest parts of the facility. At the time, there were over twenty-five of us."

I shivered despite myself at the thought of keeping track of that many minds.

Bandit noticed and nodded. "You know what that must've been like. Even with the strain, I could feel his determination. Things were taking their toll, but he desperately wanted to ensure peace before letting go."

I tipped my head to look at him, forgetting the stinging in my throat. "He let his own emotion reach you? I thought—Deadeye said—"

"Normally, he didn't. Inside the mind bridge, he was all professionalism. That day, though, he let us catch a glimpse of the man inside the helmet." Bandit looked up at the ceiling. "I think he was getting too tired to keep his own wall up. When the last xeno ship left Earth's atmosphere, all of us felt the change. We'd been living free of the dampening fields for months, but it was *still* like a weight had lifted off all our chests."

He sighed and readjusted his arm around my shoulders. "I'd lost a lot of blood a few days previous, but they insisted on sending me on this last mission. I'd spent so much time with Michael, been exposed to so much of his power, that I was easy for him to interface with. It made me an ideal squad commander."

I couldn't help the smile ticking up the corner of my mouth. "You're a good commander even without that."

Bandit shoved my shoulder. "Shut up, *mijo*. Quit trying to flatter me."

The smile had spread to genuine fullness now. "Yessir."

"Anyway." Bandit sat back and crossed his arms. "I was

exhausted by the time the fields dropped. I remember I passed out in the Thunderbird on the way back to base. I thought it was over."

I frowned as I examined his face. Even without my power, there was something else riding at the back of what my mentor was saying. *Loss. Regret.* They shadowed his face the same way nightmares shadowed Caleb's.

My arms slid from around my torso as I connected the dots. There'd been a reason why Bandit and Josephine had taken so long to admit they loved each other, and it was tied into the grief surrounding that day of victory. "It wasn't over, was it?"

"No." Bandit took a sharp breath. "No, it wasn't. We weren't aware of the riots, though *someone* should've predicted that something would happen once humanity got their free will and emotion back." His hand went to the chain around his neck where—like all of us—his ID tags rattled in a constant reminder that death stalked our steps. "Region 520 didn't even have a particularly violent population, but..." He stopped and turned a helpless gesture to me. "Well, you know."

I uncomfortably nodded. I'd been ten on the day the xenos' emotional dampening fields dropped worldwide, and had huddled under my bed in terrified silence while my grandmother was gunned down by looters. "Yeah."

"By the time I found out what had happened to Maria and Cruz, all I could do was pray for their souls."

Deadeye's voice echoed softly through my memory, a statement she'd once said with no idea of what it meant to me. *Bandit's son would have been a bit younger than you, if he'd survived.*

I took a deep breath. "Victory felt like a loss to you as well."

"Yeah." Bandit shot me a stricken look. "You can ask Josephine how I reacted. I'd say compared to that, your response to today's 'victory' is perfectly normal." He bent to pick up the bin of medical supplies he'd brought. "Let's get you cleaned up so you can sleep. I promise, you'll feel better once you do."

For someone who'd made a career of killing, Bandit's hands were gentle as he swabbed the wound with disinfectant and taped a gauze pad over it. My shock symptoms were being taken over by profound exhaustion, and I barely objected as he helped me out of my shirt and surveyed the smaller wounds that Tara hadn't taken the time to seal. "These just need Band-Aids," he muttered. "We *really* got lucky. Wear your underlay next time you go on patrol, okay?"

"Yeah," I whispered as he passed me a clean shirt. "Thanks, Bandit."

He pulled me into a tight hug. "Don't scare me like that again, okay?"

"Okay."

I SLEPT through the rest of that day and into the next—almost twenty hours. Near noon, I staggered to the kitchen and retrieved a piece of toast. Even with the extra sleep, I still felt as heavy and slow as if dumbbells had been tied to each limb. My power was back—at least, the world no longer felt heavy and silent—but I shuddered at the thought of having to use it so soon after burning out.

No sooner had I retreated to my room than Josephine

came to check on me. I didn't have to imagine her concern when the others told her what happened—it was projecting so far from her that I could practically feel the adrenaline building in my own veins. She bustled around, checking my monitor's readouts, taking my temperature, cleaning and dressing the wound on my throat, and radiating worry until I snapped at her, "I'm fine! I just needed to sleep."

Josephine gave me a measured look. For a moment, I feared she would hear *my* thoughts if she listened hard enough. "If you think that's what will get you recovered fastest..."

"It will," I insisted. Blue light bloomed in my palm as I raised it to show her. The rest of my body and mind only felt exhausted in the usual bone-deep manner that followed weeks of strain—or blood loss, which felt almost worse than burnout. "I'm sure I'll be fine by tomorrow."

"Okay, *mijo*." She picked up her tablet and slid it into her bag. The light clicked off as she left the room. "Try to rest, then."

I curled up in the darkness and tried to go to sleep, but my attention was immediately taken as Bandit's voice came from the hallway. "How is he?"

"Sleeping again," Josephine said. "His power's coming back, but it's slow going. Normally, he regenerates fully with a full night of sleep, but now..."

I knew I shouldn't be eavesdropping, but their voices— bare murmurs in Spanish outside my bedroom—sounded so concerned that I slid out of bed and padded closer to the door.

"It's been a tough few weeks, Josie," Bandit answered. "Cut the kid some slack; he's been running himself dry trying to keep all of us safe."

"I know." Josephine sighed. "It's just—Carlos, he's so tired. Tara says she had to wake him when you had that skirmish the other night, when normally he's first out the door because he sleeps so lightly. Yesterday, he burned out in *minutes*. Any of those things could be just from the season, but all together—" A memory loomed large at the edge of her mind, but it vanished as Bandit shushed her.

"Shh. You want him to hear you?"

Josephine's muffled apology faded as their footsteps receded from the door. I returned to bed and sat in the quiet for a long moment.

First Deadeye, and now Josephine and Bandit. I put my elbows on my knees and leaned my chin against my forearms. *What's scaring them so bad?*

I STILL COULDN'T GET the things that I'd learned about the lightning wielder out of my head, and it was forcing me to see our interactions with the Blood Angels in a new light. The time immediately following my injury was spent mostly sleeping, but my unease about the situation continued to grow even after I'd recovered. I didn't have the chance to talk it through with anyone until a few days later, when St. Augustine's requested our help with a community clinic.

A brief rainstorm had washed the dust from the sky, and the air held a pleasant humidity and chill while we stood guard at the entrance to the open tent. I didn't *think* the Blood Angels would stoop to attacking doctors, but I couldn't deny that their leaders lacked the restraint you'd expect from another human being. The Medical Corps had things well under control, and Josephine was in her element among the people she loved so much. While I kept myself busy scanning the area for threats, I could tell that Bandit was more than a little distracted.

I glanced at the tent where Josephine, dressed in scrubs, knelt holding the withered hands of an ancient *abuela*. I couldn't hear what was being said, but I got the feeling that Josephine was being treated to this woman's entire life story. The compassion swirling through every fiber of her being as she listened sent a smile to my lips.

The same smile touched Bandit's face as he watched. Speaking Spanish, I commented, "I see why you fell for her."

The first time I'd confronted Bandit about his feelings for Josephine, he'd yelled at me. Now, his smile only deepened. "She cares so much about the people here, enough that she'd rather stay in a war zone than leave for somewhere safer." He shook his head, his broad-brimmed hat casting a shadow across his face. "If the Blood Angels only had a few people like her on their side, we'd make so much progress toward peace."

I closed my hands tighter around my rifle. I'd been wondering for days how to broach the topic, and he'd just handed me the perfect opportunity. "What makes you think there aren't?"

Bandit frowned. "Say again?"

I tried it again, a different way. "The other day—when that Shattered and I were fighting—I broke into her memories again. That's why she reacted with the lightning bolt that broke my shield and dropped the mind bridge."

"...'Again.' You've done this before?" He gave an exasperated sigh. "*Mijo...*"

"The first time was an accident, sir." I avoided his stern gaze as unspoken admonition drifted from him. "But Bandit,

I don't think she had a choice on whether or not to join them. Which isn't that surprising." I shifted my grip as my hands began getting sweaty. "I mean, if things had been different, I might've gone the same way. Before the EDF deserted the region, there was at least an option for something different. Now, there's no guarantee of safety unless it's with the gang."

"You're not wrong," he agreed, surprising me. "People without stability will run to anything that promises it, even if it's not the best thing for them." He turned his gaze toward the east, amber eyes searching the rain-washed sky over the Rincon Mountains. "I wouldn't even argue, if it were like the old days. The earlier generation of leaders had some pretty messed up priorities, but at least they ran things with care for the people around them."

"Sounds like you got along with them." I squinted against the sun before turning to keep my face in the shade. "But didn't they kidnap you and hold you for ransom?"

Bandit chuckled, and I caught flashes of memories behind his eyes. A dusty, cracked strip of highway, the feeling of a tightly wrapped dust scarf, and the hum of a generator all whirled past and were gone before he said, "Sure. Like I said, messed up priorities. But after a while, we came to an understanding. The guy that ordered me to be kidnapped—Santana—he was decent. And he liked Josie."

I raised an eyebrow. "Liked her how?"

He snorted. "Not like that. She was like everyone's little sister." Bandit grinned over his shoulder at Josephine, who was now reading the riot act to a teenager who looked like he'd traded his last crumb of food for something more reality-numbing. "If anyone else had come to negotiate for me, Santana would've spat in their faces. But not her. And *because* of her, he decided we were worth leaving alone. For a little while, there was peace." He tucked his free hand into the shoulder strap of his armor, the other never straying far from his holster. "Then the xenos stepped out of the shadows, and everything *really* went to hell."

"Is Santana still alive?" I asked. My cynical side rumbled deep inside with the knowledge that this was grasping at straws, but I stuffed the emotion down and persisted, "Would he be willing to help us take out the current leaders if it meant he could bring things back to the way they used to be?"

Bandit stayed quiet for a long moment, but interest filled the empty space. I could almost hear his thoughts churning as he looked between Josephine, the mountains, and the sky before he answered, "Last I heard, he'd escaped the city. The Angels didn't do so well under the xenos, and a lot of them split when people started dying. If I had to guess, that's how the current leadership got into power in the first place." Bandit gestured at the northern mountains, where a ridge stood in relief against the greater bulk of the sky island. "There was a rumor a long time ago that he was up in the Catalinas. Somewhere above the canyon."

Hope stirred in the part of my mind worn out from battle after battle. "You think we could find him? If he *is* up there?"

Bandit shrugged. "I couldn't. He's always been good at keeping a low profile. But with your abilities, you could. He might shoot us, or he might be curious—if he's up there at all. Why don't you ask Benny at St. Augustine's to do some digging?"

I never knew what to make of Benny. Engineer by trade, informant by nature, and I didn't think *anyone* knew where he got his information. Deadeye had once said that she suspected he listened to the roaches. "If anyone would have an idea of who to talk to, it's him," I agreed. "We have that meeting at the hospital later this week...think he'd turn up anything before then?"

"Might be too soon, but I've been wrong before," Bandit said, turning as the sound of an argument came from near the medical tent. "Even if he can't get answers that quickly, you can at least pick his brain and see what he knows." He began walking toward the tent, loosing his hand from his armor and calling back, "I trust you to take point on this one, *mijo*. Once we get back to base, send him a message. Sooner or later, he'll get the truth for us, and we can go check it out."

LIKE I'D EXPECTED, Benny didn't blink at the request. "I got you, man," he told me that night. "I have some ideas of where to start looking... Gimme a few days and I'll see what I can come up with."

It was a promising start, and the idea of being able to temper the conflict between us and the Blood Angels was enough that some of the persistent ache in my stomach eased. Anxious as I was to talk with him directly, it was several days before we had an opportunity to visit St. Augustine's in person. In the wake of the EDF's departure, the hospital had become the center of communication for the emergency services slowly coming to life across the city. Today, all of us were piled into the truck for a meeting with the different department leads. Deadeye was driving, a fact quickly remarked on by Tara as we took a corner at high speed.

"This isn't the *autobahn*, Reneé. Take it easy!"

"Next time, you can drive," Deadeye answered. "Until then, don't comment."

Tart words aside, she slowed to a moderate speed as we approached the university. It had barely functioned in the last five years, but a handful of faculty and students still toughed it out in pursuit of knowledge. Deadeye and Tara kept talking as we passed the campus, and I did my best to ignore their bickering while examining a satellite map of the place. The landscaping had once been beautiful, but now the fountain beds lay cracked and dry and the palm trees bore massive skirts of dead fronds.

Thinking of enrolling? Caleb asked through the mind bridge. Evidently, he'd caught some of my contemplation of higher education. *Become a doctor like Josephine?*

No. I shrugged my seat belt to a better spot against my armor, both underlayer and vest worn after the almost-disaster of last week. *Maybe if things had been different...*

"What *would* you have chosen, if you had the chance?" Tara asked aloud.

I couldn't fault her for eavesdropping, not with our bio interfaces making it hard to tell whose thoughts were whose. "I don't know. I like words and things, but I don't think that's something I would've wanted to *study*. I guess —" I stopped, unsure if I should continue before realizing it was pointless to try to hide. "I guess it would be cool to understand how people think." Amusement flicked over from Bandit, and my face warmed. "I mean, I know *what* people are feeling, but not always *why*. Is there a name for that?"

"Psychology," Deadeye supplied from the front seat. "I could see it. You can have it, and I'll keep my computers and code; which reminds me—hey, Bandit?"

"I already told you," Bandit said, "the lab time is fine. Tell me when you want to go, and we'll cover you."

"Wonderful." I could practically hear the wheels humming behind Deadeye's thoughts, images of wavelengths and a whiteboard covered in complex mathematics flickering through the mind bridge as she anticipated more time to work on her pet project. "I got some ideas from that report they gave me the last time we were at Augustine's, and I think I'm close to dialing in the right frequency. Soon I'll be able to test it and..."

Trying to piece together what Deadeye was working on was only going to give me a headache, so I turned my attention back to the conversation at hand. "What about you, Tara? What would you have studied?"

The thought came through Tara's mind first. *Nothing.* Then, the explanation. "With where we came from—our backgrounds—nobody expected us to do much with our lives." She looked at Caleb, affection swelling through the mind bridge. "He showed them all, though; was going to school for nursing when everything ended."

Really? I looked up at Caleb, who'd decided to stand rather than take a seat for this trip.

Yeah, he said, adjusting his grip on a handle in the ceiling. "I got pretty good grades in high school. Not like *someone.*"

Tara made a face at him. "I didn't need to worry about college. Everyone assumed I'd marry you right out of high school and spend the rest of my life making sourdough bread and babies." An unexpected pang of sorrow went through both her and Caleb's minds, the rebound reaching mine before fading away.

"It didn't matter anyway," Caleb said aloud. "The blackouts started at the end of my first year." His jaw tightened on the statement, and I caught grim determination behind the rest of his words. "After that, the only thing that mattered was staying alive."

ST. Augustine's hadn't changed in appearance from when it'd been an EDF base. The top floors of the old hospital gleamed in the sunlight as we approached, their original color faded over the years to a whisper of pink. The only thing different was the Maltese cross, emblazoned where the Defense Force logo had once overlooked the cracked parking lot, and the air of dedicated busyness hanging over the area as we parked beneath a concrete overhang alongside several other vehicles. They were as run-down as the building—like the EDF before it, the Medical Corps didn't have nearly enough funding or manpower to maintain equipment properly.

The meeting we'd come to attend was boring, but necessary. With police and fire departments coming into their own, we needed some way to make sure our communication between agencies was seamless. I did my best to pay attention, but most of my thoughts were preoccupied with wondering what information Benny might have found regarding Santana. Halfway through, Bandit noticed me fidgeting and motioned discreetly that I could leave. A pat on the elbow was all it took to get Deadeye's attention, and within another minute we were rattling down the stairs toward the basement.

"Thank God you got me out of there," Deadeye said from three steps below me, her voice echoing through the column of concrete and metal that was the stairwell. "I was on the verge of throwing a smoke bomb and disappearing in the confusion."

I chuckled. "Bandit is too, but he's hiding it better than you were. Where can we find Benny?"

"Logistics." Deadeye leaned against the crash bar of a door whose paint bore more scratches than a used lottery ticket. It swung open to reveal the hospital underbelly—a twisting set of darkened concrete hallways with pipe-lined ceilings.

Logistics was hidden behind a dented metal door, which opened onto a large room filled with crammed wire shelving. A desk crowded with boxes and a computer to rival Deadeye's setup hunkered in the corner by the door, the monitor's display flickering through pictures of different anime characters.

"Benny!" Deadeye called from the entrance. "Are you back there?"

I felt the presence of our informant friend long before he rounded the corner—a tallish, lanky guy with rich brown skin and a giant bush of dark curly hair. He'd already been eccentric when employed by the EDF as a techie, and I was used to seeing him in scruffy civilian clothes. Now, he seemed to have traded up for a set of pale blue scrubs. He dropped an armful of junk into a plastic tote on the desk and greeted us enthusiastically. "I hoped you'd venture into my kingdom! And boy, have I got some news for you."

"Great!" I returned his fist bump with relief. Maybe Bandit was wrong, and Benny's network of contacts had pulled off the impossible.

"I need some stuff first," Deadeye said, producing a handwritten list with a flourish. "Then you can talk as much as you want."

"Let's take a look." Benny's eyes narrowed as he examined the list Deadeye handed him. "Parallel processor, voltage meter, memory card, solenoids—what're you fixing, a washing machine or a computer?"

"That's for me to know, and you to guess," she answered. "You have them, or what?"

Benny waved at the shelves. "Somewhere. Go look in sections 2-16 and 7-31—they're labeled at the tops of the racks." He stabbed a finger at a pile of cardboard boxes. "Oh, also, Corps sent us like five boxes of liquid dish soap, but it's all packaged in refill bags for dispensers we haven't used since before the invasion. Take at least a box, 'kay? I don't have time to figure out what to do with it all."

I shook my head as Deadeye disappeared into the rows of shelving. "Can't say I have any ideas either, but okay. You said you have news?"

"Yeah, man." Benny pulled his chair out from beneath the desk with his foot and crashed into it. The smile had disappeared from his face as he said, "I was actually going to come find you, if you hadn't come to me first."

"Did you find Santana?"

"Still working on it," Benny said. "I have some leads I'm following, but while I've been digging I learned something else. You'd better have a seat." The computer screen came to life as he bumped the mouse, revealing a command screen and Medical Corps logo. "Does the name 'Kartchner' ring any bells to you?"

"Yes," I answered immediately. Uncertainty and more than a little nervousness made my muscles tense. "But I'm not sure why. Caleb doesn't like him; I can tell you that much."

Benny snorted a laugh. "Knowing how protective Caleb

is of his wife, it makes sense. Kartchner was curious to the point of obsession about Shattered powers. He was the lead at the lab that just got closed at Regional, and... You remember that facility you guys shut down last October?"

I dropped my gaze to the desk, unbidden memories of towering tanks, a stench of decay and chemicals, and shuddering ceilings immediately springing to mind. "It's not like I'm going to forget that."

"Right." Benny gave a half smile by way of apology before pressing on. "Command sent some folks in to check it out after the fact, right? Like, after you guys destroyed it. And whatever they found, they were looking into more at that lab." He planted skinny elbows on the arms of his chair and leaned forward to look me in the eye with the air of someone who'd found a bomb while looking for sparklers. "I think the stuff they learned was pretty spooky—enough that Kartchner and a couple of his *compadres* fled with the findings instead of making them public."

I sat up straight against the edge of the desk. The recording device's plastic housing creaked as I tightened my grip on it. "They...ran?"

"They ran," Benny confirmed. "Official word is that the lab got dismantled, but I hear they split and took their findings with them. After that, there was no need for the place, which is why the maintenance guys ended up here."

My thoughts whirled to Deadeye's current project. "I think Deadeye might be trying to reverse-engineer the project from the data they brought with them. Do we know what it was, other than related to Shattered power?"

Benny shook his head. "Whatever got left behind is so encrypted I don't think anyone *except* Reneé can make heads or tails of it. And this isn't even about what we know—

it's about what we *don't* know. And more importantly, who does."

"No kidding," I muttered. "Is Regional doing anything to catch him?"

Benny's eyes narrowed. "When has that ever been their MO?" He snorted. "They've let him go the same way they've let your squad go. Sweep all the embarrassment under the rug, y'know?"

"Right..."

"Look, just take it as a warning, from one black sheep to another. If there's a mad scientist on the run with an obsessive interest in powers like yours, you could become an object of interest." He straightened in his chair as Deadeye emerged from the shelves with a box under an arm. "You get what you needed?"

"All set!" She tucked her list into a pocket. "Gabe, you ready?"

I got up from my seat. "Yeah... Yeah, I think so. Thanks, Benny," I said over my shoulder. "You'll tell me if anything else comes up?"

"Yeah, I got you. And I'll keep working on finding Santana."

He and Deadeye exchanged a few more pleasantries before the door closed and left us in the dank concrete corridor once more. My thoughts tumbled over each other, feet moving on instinct while my brain tried to catch up. This news—whatever it meant—felt weighty, like watching a storm roll in with the knowledge that there was nothing you could do to stop its arrival.

"Have a nice talk?" Deadeye asked as we retraced our steps upward.

"Yeah..." I paused on the word while the stairwell door

clanged shut behind us. Foreboding aside, I needed to see if she already knew about this. "When you got that analytics report from those new techies, did they say anything about their leaders disappearing with most of the data?"

"No." Deadeye stopped on the stair above me. "But it's obvious from the report that I'm only working from part of the whole. I guess it doesn't surprise me." Her eyes narrowed. "Why? What'd you hear?"

Between the stairs and the twisting halls, I shared everything Benny had told me—including his warning of a possible threat. When I was done, Deadeye gave a low whistle. "That's an ugly piece of news. No wonder these new guys have been so evasive when I've talked with them. We're going to need to tell the others—" She frowned as the overhead PA system clicked on to page Dr. So-and-So to a certain line. "Somewhere where there aren't a thousand ways for anyone to eavesdrop."

"You're right." I shivered and glanced over my shoulder to make sure no one else was in the corridor. "I'm going to go find the others and tell them we're good to leave."

"'Kay, I'll be by the truck." She set off down the hall, and I went the opposite direction. It wasn't until I was standing in the atrium of the hospital that I realized I didn't know if Bandit and the others were still in the conference room where I'd last seen them.

No sooner had the realization struck than a voice broke through my confusion. "Lose someone?"

I turned at the sound, and a smile broke across my face at the sight of our friend Logan. Originally assigned to Base 36 as a Thunderbird pilot, he'd transferred to the Medical Corps after our desertion from the EDF. "Hey! How's it going?" I asked, returning the offered handshake. "They keeping you busy?"

"Busy enough," he laughed. "I didn't realize I'd signed up to become a medevac pilot, but it's not so bad. At least no one's shooting at me. You're looking for Bandit and the others?"

"Yeah." I turned in a circle, trying to let my sixth sense pick up on their presences. "I could boot up the mind bridge, but it's been so hairy out there that I don't want to use it unless I have to."

"That's what I heard." Logan's voice always carried a hint of a drawl, left over from growing up in the south. "Your power's been in demand a lot these days. How're you handling it?"

My stomach immediately clenched. Anyone else would've gotten an immediate "fine" and rapid change of subject, well-intentioned or not. Logan, though...he'd been at Base 36 for the first few weeks after I Shattered. Of anyone, he deserved the truth.

I sighed and began walking the direction in which I could now, finally, feel the others. "It's...a lot. Things haven't really slowed down since last year. And I didn't realize how awful being close to burnout all the time would feel."

"I'd heard it wasn't comfortable, running dry." Concern popped through his words as he asked, "Your power recovered fine after that injury? Nothing else feels off since?"

I had to stifle the desire to roll my eyes. "Yep. It came back fine—why does everyone keep asking me that, anyway? What's going on?"

Logan's footsteps stuttered for a split second, and a shockingly familiar sense of evasion pulsed in the space between. "I—we're just worried about you, is all. Your power and everything...how often you're having to use it...it adds up."

That's more of an answer than I've gotten from anyone in a long time. "That's interesting..." I hedged, though inside my irritation was building faster than monsoon clouds over the Catalinas. "What about my power has everyone concerned? What exactly would 'it' add up to?"

Logan's eyes darted to the side. "I don't think I'm the best person to ask; I don't understand enough to answer your questions."

"Questions about *what?*"

For someone ordinarily so confident, Logan was downright stammering. "I—Gabe, if you don't know, I *can't* be the person to tell you. Just—just talk to Tara."

The double doors ahead held squares of sunlight, and the others' presences ranged beyond in the vehicle bay. I set my jaw and walked faster. "Fine. I will."

First Deadeye, then Josephine, and now Logan. What is it they're all so worried about? And why aren't they telling me?

St. Augustine's Hospital
Santa Cruz Valley
March 30

I SEETHED OVER THE QUESTION, saying nothing to anyone as we packed up the truck. By the time we left, I'd managed to whittle the frustration down to something a little more patient, and hopefully more understanding. We fell into our usual seats, with Deadeye and Bandit up front and Caleb, Tara, and I in the passenger compartment. With the tires spinning toward home and the sky fading to twilight, I turned my attention to Caleb and Tara. He'd put his arm around her shoulders, and she was leaning against him with her eyes closed. *Out of everyone, they're the ones who'll tell me the truth.*

"Tara? Can we talk?"

She opened her eyes and cast a curious glance at me. "Sure, Gabe. What's up?"

"Everyone's been acting super weird around me this last month."

As soon as I said it, her jaw tightened, and she looked abruptly at the wall separating us from the cab. Even seeing that distress, I kept talking. "Last week, I overheard Bandit and Josephine talking about how they were worried that my power—or maybe my body—was taking too long recovering from burn-out." I ran a finger across the screen of my monitor cuff. "And when Deadeye was helping me update the software on this, I accidentally dropped into a memory of Michael. I think it was something to do with his death." Caleb's arm had stiffened around Tara's shoulders, and the set of his jaw told me he knew exactly what I was getting at. "Logan was even on the verge of saying something while I was trying to find you guys, and we've barely seen him since he started flying for the Medical Corps. Guys, *what* is going on?!"

Tara was quiet for a long moment, sorrow welling from her like blood from a wound. I could tell she'd decided to stay silent when Caleb spoke up.

"He needs to know."

Her cyan eyes darted to his. "I *know*. Don't rush me."

Silence reigned again as we waited, until finally Tara sighed. "You're right, it's about Michael. Or, well, what happened to him. I'm sorry, Gabe; we should have told you months ago, but none of us have wanted to." She snorted, more out of frustration than contempt. "Or, really, we haven't known what to say."

I opened my mouth to ask more questions, but she held up a hand. "Chill. I'll explain, but let me do it in my own way." Tara shook free of Caleb's arm and sat straight. "You know about Michael's power—similar to yours, but all mental with no emotion. He had a huge power reserve, and he *used* it. Keeping tabs on everything, controlling data through the positioning software, maintaining communication through all of us—it exhausted him on a regular basis."

Her shoulders drooped as I quietly pulled my recorder out, but she nodded consent and kept talking, "There was a while when things got bad, and he ran himself dry every single mission. The demands on his power didn't let up, day after day. He barely had time to regenerate before something new would happen to burn him out again."

I squirmed uncomfortably, a deep sense of foreboding sending shivers through my core. That sounded like how many of our days had gone recently—both for Tara *and* myself. "Then what happened?"

Tara closed her eyes against the memory. I glanced down at the recorder, which had started blinking with a "low power" warning. If this were any other conversation, I'd pause her to change the battery. This time, however—

"I noticed it early on, but soon everyone could tell." Tara's voice had gone soft, stretched thin by the unspoken loss. "He slept more, was losing weight, and seemed like he was in pain. When we talked mind to mind, he sounded like himself, but soon even that felt—tired. After a while, he stopped trying to hide it. I'm just glad we won when we did." Her voice dropped to a mutter. "I'm not sure he would've lasted much longer."

I shook my head. Michael's death two months after defeating the xenos was common knowledge, but evidently it hadn't come as a surprise to those close to him. When my voice returned, it came out charged with frustration and helplessness. "Everyone thinks it was sudden. If people knew he was dying, why didn't anyone *do* something?"

"We tried, Gabe." Caleb looked as tired as he sounded. "We didn't know *why* it was happening. The docs ran every diagnostic in the books, the other Shattereds tried using their power, everyone was doing everything they could think of to figure out what was wrong and stop it. All anyone said was there was nothing they could do." He sighed. "After he died, we did some digging. Turns out, his wasn't the only case."

"Only case—only case of what?" I swallowed hard. "This happened to more than him?"

Tara's eyes had gone glassy. "Michael was first, and no one understood it at the time, but by now it's a known phenomenon." Her next words hit me like a punch to the gut —like a death. "Shattered power sometimes kills its users."

I took a deep breath. Four counts in, four counts out. "How?"

"We still don't know," Caleb said. "Best we can figure is it drains them. Almost like a cancer."

"And there's no rhyme or reason to how fast," Tara added. "Or how soon it happens. Not to mention that some don't survive long enough for it to take effect." Tara raised her head and held out her hand with a grimace. "Here. I'll just show you—if you're sure you want to know."

My seat belt clicked open, then hesitation froze my limbs. *Do I?*

"It's okay if you decide not to see," Caleb reassured me. "We won't blame you."

I counted another breath in and out. "No..." I crossed the compartment and knelt beside Tara. "I think I need to."

My hand closed over Tara's.

Her fingers tightened and a torrent of faces surged through my mind, each with a name, a face...a story.

Sophia; a carbon copy of her younger sister Tara, dead at age twenty-two from a vortex out of her control.

Damien; his cyan eyes shocking against dark brown skin, abandoned by his family and succumbing to exposure-related pneumonia after Shattering as a child.

Nick; his spectral figure wearing old-style EDF armor, killed in a training accident.

Clementine; a teenager with a row of piercings along her ear, wasting away and dying after only a year of Shattered power.

Alexi; his Russian accent, false bravado, and everlasting loyalty disappearing in the vortex he'd summoned while on a rescue mission.

Stories, cut short.

Over it all came the cold knowledge—every death had occurred as a direct result of the victim's Shattered power.

"Why doesn't *everyone* know about this?" My voice trembled as I said it. "If I'd known, I wouldn't have—"

Tara chuckled, a hollow sound. "Wouldn't have what? Shattered? It wasn't in our control, Gabe." Sadness filtered through her voice. "This power is a blessing in many ways. We're forces of nature. To admit that we're vulnerable—" She shook her head.

"Brand new Shattereds are so uncertain, so afraid, so volatile." Caleb gave me an apologetic glance. "Nobody wants to shock them with the news that their power will eventually take their lives."

My mind jumped to the image of Josephine holding the withered hands of the *abuela* at the clinic a few days previous. Another hollow knell reverberated in my chest. "No growing old in peace."

"And no children, either." Tara released my fingers and

wrapped her arms around her torso, a hand resting flat on her abdomen. "They didn't tell me that part until I'd been using my powers for years—I'm not even sure *they* knew for certain."

"That's what you were talking about," I said, tucking my elbows tightly to my ribs and staring at the floor. "You said something about Shattered power taking your future from you, the first time we activated the bio interfaces."

"Yes," Tara whispered. I didn't need to look up to know she was crying. "I keep telling myself that it doesn't matter—shouldn't matter—but—"

"It's a part of your life you'll never get back. And you didn't get the chance to give it up; it was taken." I reached across to turn off my recorder, but saw the light had already died. *It's for the best. I don't want a record of this.*

When I looked up, Tara's eyes held the same dull sheen as the recorder's indicator light. Caleb had pulled her close once more, helplessness and hopelessness warring behind his mental walls.

I didn't want to ask, but I had to know. "Do *any* of us survive to old age?"

"No one knows," Tara said. "Not enough time has passed. Michael barely had his power for five years. Alexi Shattered when he was fourteen, and he was twenty-seven when he died. That's thirteen years without him ever mentioning a difference." She tapped her own chest. "I Shattered almost twelve years ago. So far, nothing's changed."

"It seems to be affected by how often you burn yourself out," Caleb said as he squeezed Tara's shoulder. "Michael ran himself to the limit almost every day."

"So did Judge..." I said, though I wasn't sure it was true.

"When he was young and stupid, yeah." Tara scrubbed

her eyes. "After we saw what happened to Michael, he got a *lot* more careful about not running himself down."

I sighed. "Is everyone aware of this, then?"

They glanced at each other before nodding, Tara with defeat and Caleb with resignation. "We knew we needed to say something," he said. "But none of us knew how to tell you. Especially after losing Alexi, we didn't want to burden you with—"

"With the knowledge that I could lose Tara too?" I cut in. "Or that it was going to happen to me?" A spark of anger cut the hollow ache in my chest, and I couldn't stop myself from saying, "I thought we were past secrets."

Tara's eyes were glimmering with tears. "I'm sorry, Gabe."

I stood up too quickly, pulling away as fast as I could from the genuine apology in her voice. The truck was slowing, and the familiarity of Station Somewhere surrounded us. "Well, thanks for *finally* telling me the truth." I threw the hatch open as we halted. "I'll let you know if I have any other questions."

I jumped down before either of them could say anything else, shut out their concern, and slammed my gear into my locker with too much force and too little precision. Deadeye tried calling to me as I went inside, but I ignored her and went first to my room, then the showers, as fast as I could.

The hot water thawed out the freezing anger, leaving disorientation in its place. Tara must've explained the last ten minutes to everyone who was still out in the bay, and the combined force of sympathy and guilt hit me like a ton of bricks. A knee buckled under the unexpected weight, and I swore as I regained my balance.

I put my hands over my ears, fingers digging into my

scalp. My thumb landed in the space behind my ear where my bio interface sat, and for an impulsive moment, I considered ripping the device out of my skull.

Too much. It's too much.

I'd hated my power when I first Shattered. The legacies carried by others were so heavy that nothing I could do would ever be enough to match them. It'd taken Bandit's trust, Tara's patient training, and Judge's sacrificial death for me to decide my powers were worth embracing.

I'm still scared, just now I have a gun in my hand.

I'd said that to Caleb, the day I'd first pulled the trigger on another person. After coming to terms with my powers, I'd thought the fear was behind me. *And after all that, there really* is *a reason to be scared.*

The water drumming against the backs of my hands finally returned me to reality, and I shut off the shower and got dressed. Casting my awareness through the station, I immediately felt Caleb nearby. It wasn't a surprise to find him leaning against the wall as I came out of the bathroom.

"I don't want to talk about it," I snapped, walking past him toward my room.

"That's why you need to." He arrested my flight with a strong grip on my upper arm. "Hey. Don't act like I haven't had this conversation before."

A yell was forming in my chest before reality sank in. Caleb was quite a bit older than me, and had spent *years* in close proximity to Shattereds. No, it wouldn't have been the first time.

"All right, fine." I shook loose from his hand. "Just let me put my stuff away."

I REJOINED Caleb in the vehicle bay, having dodged cautious greetings from the others as I went through the kitchen. He was in the corner, where our workout stuff occupied a quarter of the open space. The punching bag was still swinging slightly as I walked over.

"Sorry for snapping at you."

"I understood." Velcro rasped as Caleb tightened his sparring gloves. He'd changed out of the long-sleeved shirt he'd worn to St. Augustine's, and the circuitry in his left arm glistened with a dull metallic sheen. The sight—like always—left me more inclined to listen to whatever he had to say. "Did your shower help?"

"No. Just made it worse." I ran my fingers over my bio interface, wishing again that I could rip it out. "Every time I think I've stopped getting surprised by how bad things are, something always pops up to remind me that no, life really *can* get worse."

Caleb snorted. "That's almost exactly what Tara said when we found out. *After* she freaked out and put a crater in the helipad." He tossed me another set of gloves. "Here. Let's see what you've got."

I reluctantly put them on and faced Caleb, the two of us circling cautiously. My frustration from earlier resurged as I demanded, "Why didn't you tell me earlier? It's been over six months since I Shattered; you can't expect me to believe there wasn't a conversation about this."

"There was." Caleb jabbed at my ribs, forcing me to step back to avoid tripping. "Sometime after what happened to Alexi. We weren't sure how you'd react to—"

"To hearing that I'm going to die?!"

"We had no idea what would happen when we attacked

the cloning facility," Caleb insisted. His fist clipped my shoulder and sent me off-balance. I hopped back another pace as he said, "We agreed that we couldn't afford to let you get distracted, in case it threw your concentration."

"That's it?" I squared my stance, blocking and returning the next set of punches. "You didn't want to tell me in case I became useless? Really?" I ducked under another of his jabs to slam my shoulder into his stomach. The momentum carried us both to the floor, before Caleb continued the roll to flip me over his head.

"Listen to me, Gabe," he said as I hit the mat with a groan. "If you'd been distracted at the Ridges, we *all* would've died. We were going to tell you afterward, but there was never a good time." I rolled to my feet as he said, "It's a lot to take in, and *none* of us wanted to be the ones to tell you. Besides, there's still reason to hope that they'll find—"

"What, a *cure*? A cure for having Shattered?" I eyed him past my raised fists, disbelief and anger churning through my blood. "That's ridiculous. Even if such a thing existed, no one's going to let us take advantage of it."

"You know that's not true."

"Don't lie to me!" I yelled, striking with all my strength at the inside of his augmented left arm. Caleb staggered a pace, clutching his forearm as I spat, "The moment the EDF found out that I'd Shattered, they demanded I be turned over so they could figure out how *useful* I was." His shoulders caved around my next strike—a shove to his chest, with my full weight behind it. "And *you* didn't tell me the truth because you needed my power at full strength! What's that supposed to make me believe?" Blue clouded my vision as I yelled, "These powers are the only reason anyone's ever wanted me! Even if there *was* a cure, no one would let us have it. Without our power, we're WORTHLESS!"

Caleb let go of his arm, grey eyes blazing. The force of his unfiltered anger blasted into me, hotter than any fire and colder than any nightmare.

"Don't. Say. That."

Faster than I could react, he grabbed my shirt and yanked me forward. I was braced for him to hit me, but instead his words took all the fight out of my blood.

"You are *not* worthless, Gabriel! You weren't before you Shattered, and you aren't now! You mean the world to us—all of us." He pulled me into a tight hug. Affection surged past the anger, as fierce as the fury had been. "I don't EVER want to hear you say something like that about yourself ever again."

With all that in my head, there was no way I could stay angry.

"Caleb, I—" I crumpled against his shoulder, closing my eyes on tears that refused to be contained. Finally, I choked out, "I'm sorry. I'm sorry I yelled at you, and I'm sorry I hurt you."

Caleb released me, reaching up to brush tears from his own face. "Well, you *could've* blasted me out of the bay and you didn't. And I'm not hurt bad—well, not that bad." He turned his arm over and ran a finger down the circuitry. A bruise was already forming where I'd hit him. "Gosh, you pack a wallop when you're mad."

"Sorry." I scrubbed my hands over my face. "I wasn't even *trying* to pull my punches."

He gave a half chuckle. "Do you feel any better now?"

With my hands still against my face, I took stock. "Yeah. Yeah, I actually do." I plonked to the mat, my limbs feeling like damp, wrung-out washcloths. "You guys have really known about this the whole time?"

"Uh-huh." Caleb pulled off his gloves and threw them at the punching bag. "And I was telling the truth about why none of us said anything. Before the Ridges, we were worried you'd lose it. Afterward, we were afraid we'd lose *you*." He came to sit on the bench of our weightlifting setup. "I'm sorry. I really am. We should've told you sooner. Will you forgive us?"

"Yeah." The answer came automatically, but then I stopped and considered. After a moment, I said, "You should've told me sooner. But you're also right; I *would've* freaked out if I'd found out right after Judge died." A shudder ran up my spine as I considered anew what I had learned. "Is there actually a chance of a cure?"

"Maybe." He slid from the bench to sit with his back against it instead. "I remember they were working on it before Tara and I took off. Tests and energy fields and things like that." His face clouded over, and he tucked his left arm tight against his torso. "I didn't want Tara to be anywhere close to an experiment like that. The guy who was leading it —Dr. Kartchner—he oversaw that research group that went dark."

"That guy again." I sighed, reminded that I needed to update the others on what Benny had told me that afternoon. "He keeps coming up, and nothing I've heard sounds like something I'd want to be a part of. Did he have *any* good ideas before going off the deep end?"

Caleb shook his head. "The only things that had any effect on Shattered powers were the xenos' dampening fields, and they only made Tara's power harder to control. Reneé told us she's developing a way to adjust smaller fields so they'd offset some aspects of Shattered abilities, but I don't have much confidence that it'll get beyond the theoretical." He shrugged tiredly. "So far, nobody's come up with an actual solution to the problem."

"That's what Deadeye's project is? Retrofitting xeno dampeners to block out Shattered power?" I shook my head. "No wonder she's been so cagey about what she's been working on. She'd have had to tell me why, and nobody wanted to." The thought of Tara willingly sitting under a dampening field came to mind, and I couldn't help but chuckle. "Tara would hate being stuck in one place, even if it did extend her life."

"Yeah. She'd go crazy after a week." Caleb smiled, but the amusement came tempered by sadness. "We still aren't sure how many years she has left. From what we saw with Michael, how fast your power drains you is deeply connected with how often you use it to its limit." Frustration flickered past the edges of his mental wall. "If we'd decided to stay out of all this, she wouldn't be using her power as often, and maybe would live longer. But she said a life in hiding was almost as bad as sitting around waiting to die."

"Right..." I looked at my feet. *Things are always better in the desert. But waiting for death sounds just as bad as not knowing when or where it'll get you.* "It's still a big risk."

"Sure." He got to his feet, eyes flicking over at the kitchen door. "But nothing makes you realize what's most important to you like staring down the likelihood of your own death. For us—for her—that's living life instead of waiting for it to end." He offered me a hand up. "C'mon. I know you'll be thinking about this in circles for a long time, but you don't have to do all your thinking tonight. Let's go see what's for dinner."

STAGE SEVEN

I BARELY SLEPT THAT NIGHT.

THE NEXT TWO days passed in something like a blur. Despite my conversation with Caleb, I was crabby and short with the others—especially Tara, who deserved it least of all. By the third day, she got tired of my surliness.

"I know it's a shock to you, Gabriel. It's a shock to everyone when they first hear about it. But there's nothing we can do about it, other than try to moderate our power and live with it the best that we can." With a tug of her hand, she sent the ground bucking under my feet. I lost my balance and hit the ground with a thud, glaring up as she added, "If you can't stand doing nothing, *you* can help Deadeye test her stupid field generation idea. I'm not touching it."

"Maybe I will!" I snapped back. "At least then I'll be doing *something!*"

Practice didn't go very well after that, and I left in a huff to give the scanning system atop the base a going-over. It took a while, but eventually my emotions settled enough that the work shifted from distraction to comfort. Somehow, I wasn't surprised when Deadeye came clambering up the ladder to join me.

"Tara send you?" I asked over my shoulder.

"Not at all." Deadeye swung a toolbox up to the roof before taking a seat beside it. "I just had a burning desire to come up here and get yelled at by someone half my age."

"You're going to be disappointed, then," I informed her. "Yelling doesn't seem to get me anywhere around here." I finished connecting the last control and plugged my monitor into a cable. "You clearly have something to say, so just say it. I won't be able to go anywhere for the next few minutes, anyway."

"That's more like it." Deadeye kicked a foot out in front of her and leaned back on her braced arms. "I assume you've heard enough from the others about what my project is?"

"Field generation," I answered, stabbing a button on my monitor to send a test program running. "Which explains the wavelength calculations on the report I saw. What the hell are you trying to make, anyway?" I half-turned to her and gestured at my eyes. "Something to counteract this thing that's killing us?"

"In a general sense, yes," Deadeye said, not at all put out by my sarcastic tone. "The stuff found at the cloning facility included some kind of xeno field generator designed to keep prisoners contained. It was like a smaller, more precise version of the bigger generators they used to control population centers. My thought is it could be adapted to suppress the parts of Shattered power that drain the wielder."

"A cure, in a sense." I rolled my eyes but turned to face her, keeping my arm at an angle so as not to break the connection between my monitor and the scanning system. "At least, it would be as long as someone stayed under that field."

"If your power can't affect you, it can't kill you," she said. "I connected with some researchers at the university who helped me make some modifications to the device itself. It's almost ready to test. And now that I can talk to you about it..."

I sighed. "Both Tara and Caleb suggested that I help. I take it neither of them wanted anywhere near it."

"Tara's not a good candidate," Deadeye answered immediately. "Her power doesn't respond well to fields of any kind, and I don't want to risk myself *or* my equipment. You'd be perfect, if you're up to it."

I didn't answer for a moment, angling to look across the city instead. From the roof, I was able to see the entire barrio, with the Catalinas rising behind it like a sleeping guardian. The mountainsides were coated in a haze of green—a sign of a happy desert after good winter rains. After a minute of contemplation, I admitted, "It'd be nice to do something instead of sitting and waiting for it to get me. If you think I can help, I'd like to try."

Deadeye grinned and gave me a thumbs-up as my monitor beeped to inform me that it was finished scanning. As I unplugged it and fastened the control box closed, alertness sparked below my feet. A moment later, an electronic voice came through the station intercom.

Deadeye groaned. "Here we go again."

"Guess so. Glad I was able to finish." The ladder creaked as I scrambled down, Deadeye close behind me. "What's—ahh!" I ducked the sweatshirt Tara threw my direction and hurried to my locker while switching uniforms. "What's going on?"

"Don't know," she responded briefly. "Bandit's on the radio with Augustine's now."

We got dressed and armored, and I was waking my screens in the truck when Bandit emerged. "Comms," he ordered. I obeyed, and the sound of the back hatch slamming shut was lost in the whoosh of the mind bridge opening.

I tugged my helmet on and synced it with our systems as soon as I could see through the mind bridge. The map snapped into view and zoomed, fast enough that I could tell Bandit had input coordinates from his console. Thanks to the mind bridge, the others recognized the building he was targeting at the same moment that I did.

"Hang on, isn't that the—"

"The police headquarters, yeah."

Trepidation and irritation filled the bridge before Tara said what we were all thinking. "Are they insane?"

WE'D DEPLOYED so many times into urban settings that my usual trepidation had been worn down to grim anticipation. By the time I was standing behind the truck with my armor weighing my shoulders, we'd established radio contact with the police officers and civilian workers who'd been at the downtown station when things went south. I should've been relieved to hear their account of a handful of teenage Blood Angels breaking several windows and throwing Molotov cocktails before retreating. Instead, a twist of unease went through my stomach.

This doesn't feel right, Deadeye said silently.

You feel it too? I asked, narrowing my attention to just her.

Yeah. The Blood Angels don't typically go for mischief. This isn't their style.

I frowned. She was right. Ignoring the radio chatter in my ears, I craned my neck to scan the barrio. Everything felt heavy with anticipation, like the air tensing beneath the onrush of a monsoon storm.

I cleared my throat. "Guys, something's off. I don't—"

Before I had time to finish my sentence, an unmistakable feral roar split the air. All of us jumped, and more than one person swore.

Brute. A big one.

"Spread out!" Bandit shouted, ejecting the magazine from his rifle and switching it for one marked in lurid green. "*Mijo,* find that thing before it kills everyone!"

How'd they keep it alive this long? Tara asked in wonder as I slung my rifle over my shoulder and dropped to a knee. *It's been almost six months; not even the xenos managed that!*

I don't know. With both hands planted on the ground, I sent power streaming through the dirt, the air, the cinderblocks of the building, until it ran into something massive and hulking that would've smelled like chemicals and decaying meat if we'd been face-to-face.

"Front courtyard!" I yelled through the radio and mind bridge alike. "Just one, but it's big!"

Caleb and Tara acknowledged with a wave and took off,

a few of the braver police officers running in their wake. I got to my feet but left my rifle where it was across my back. We only had enough calibrated-to-Brutes rounds for Bandit's and Caleb's guns, and Shattered power was a more effective weapon regardless.

"What do you think?" Deadeye asked out loud. I could see the reflection of her heads-up display behind her visor, and her voice carried the professional edge that suggested she wasn't talking to me. "Can we finish this with the resources we have?"

The police captain's answer blurred in my ears as Tara's consciousness splintered through my own. A Brute loomed in the shadow cast by a patio overhang, its hulking form more than eight feet tall and resembling a troll from some old story. Screams echoed from the building, and glass shattered as it withdrew a clawed hand from a window. It roared as Tara and Caleb opened fire, energy bolts and shotgun rounds impacting its hide with bloody splatters. Their gunshots were echoed by several others, and it took me a moment to realize I was hearing them from *outside* the courtyard.

As fast as a camera zooming out, my power informed me that several more hostile presences had stepped into the fray. Reddish figures converged on the police building, seething fear and fury marking the newcomers as Blood Angels—and young ones, at that.

"Phantom, Banshee, get out of there!" I dumped the images of the onrushing gang members into Caleb and Tara's minds, before running to where I could see our opponents with my physical eyes. A swarm of figures in mismatched armor pieces and red bandanas were charging the building, firing indiscriminately at police and civilian workers in their rush.

The Brute was a distraction, I warned the others as my shield blinked into place. *The initial attack probably was too. But I don't understand—why are they here? Why are they doing this in the first place? They've got to realize this can't succeed!* The part of my mind trained to assess numbers and defenses rapidly tallied the odds—over a dozen trained adults versus double that number of untrained, brand-new, *young* Blood Angels. *This is going to be a massacre.*

We don't have time to negotiate, Deadeye said. *They brought a Brute, and they're targeting civilians.* Behind me, her rifle cracked, and one of the running figures went down.

I swayed and stifled a groan as the sensation of death reverberated through my stomach. The yells from our enemies screeched through my ears, high and thin and tinged with more fear than fury. *Kids. They're just kids. Why'd they send kids?*

Bandit's voice sounded in my ear. "*Mijo.* This is a bad time to freeze."

An unbidden memory from training rocketed through our combined minds—*noise surrounding me, my hands trembling around a handgun grip, Bandit's calm but firm voice reminding me to keep a clear head*—and with a shock, I realized I'd been standing like a statue while bullets flew into a building full of civilians.

What am I doing?

I flung a hand out, power coalescing into a bolt of light that struck a Blood Angel's helmet. The movement carried into a wall of force, and the gang members tumbled backward to the ground.

"Brute down," Caleb announced through my in-ear comms, out of breath and relieved as he ran to join Tara at the end of the patio. The officers who'd accompanied them were in cover nearby, returning fire against the few Blood Angels still on their feet. More invisible blows went through my stomach with each figure that jerked into stillness, and my shield flickered several times before stabilizing.

They're too young for this. Tara's words from earlier splintered through my mind—*Shattereds almost always die young*—and I caught my breath in a pained gasp.

Mijo? Bandit couldn't see my face from his position behind the truck, but he must've caught my distress through the bridge. *You all right?*

I would've answered him—and in the negative—but my attention was taken by the awareness of another several gang members, emerging from the parking structure on the opposite side of the police station.

"Contact!" I yelled into my mic as I began running, my voice breaking high on the words. "Five new hostiles from the Delta side!" My stomach tightened, and my heartbeat surged into my ears as screams sounded from that direction. I came within sight of the conflict, just in time for a gunshot to send a splatter of red across the cinderblocks. A new death sent a shock through my chest—and this time it wasn't that of a combatant. *Civilians. There were civilians taking cover on that side of the building.*

Memory broke through the bridge; my own, again.

Splintering glass.

My grandmother's voice, raised in terror.

A spray of red on the white wall of my room.

Blue light instantaneously overwhelmed the memory, and I raised my hand with a furious yell. Energy streamed from each fingertip and slammed into multiple hostile targets at once. The enemy presences diminished in my Shattered senses, leaving a hollow sensation in the pit of my stomach.

I opened my eyes, aware only now that I'd been targeting with them closed. Bodies lay scattered between the parking structure and where I stood beneath my shield. One of the Blood Angels was facing my direction, and the smoking holes in an outdated helmet left no uncertainty as to his fate. *He didn't have a choice.*

Sudden, horrible clarity slammed through my stomach, and a stab of pain went through my right eye. *I didn't have a choice either.*

The barrier between myself and my power melted away under the death-knell truth. Fear and adrenaline and help-lessness crashed over me—the emotions of the squad, the police, our opponents—everything in the whole damn barrio. My legs buckled under the strain, and I toppled to catch myself with a hand against the pavement.

"I can't do this," I gasped through comms—a warning, maybe, to the others. "It's too much." Threads of light gath-ered around the arm supporting my weight, shooting from my fingers as I clutched the ground. *I can't take this anymore!*

Gabriel? Tara shouted. *GABRIEL!*

Her voice melted into the noise as chaos unfurled in a storm of blue light. Civilians and police alike fled, the shouts of alarm drowned out in the hum of an opening vortex.

Get them out of there! Bandit ordered. *Clear the area!*

Do something! Can't you do something?! Deadeye, her voice growing panicked.

I can't. Anguish from Tara. *I don't think he can hear us!*

The squad's mental voices blurred with their physical ones, the alarm building in their thoughts sending me further and further into the emotion storm.

We can't let them kill innocent people. But I can't keep fighting like this.

In the turmoil, I felt Caleb stop. His fear melted into steel. "Gabriel!"

I squinted through the growing blue swirl to see him running toward me. He ducked his head and—with a cry of pain that sent an answering throb through my skull—pushed through the vortex surrounding me.

I'd expected him to hit me. Instead, he dropped to a knee, a hand going to the panel on the inside of my right forearm. Frustration flared as he slammed his palm against the row of tiny buttons, and the connection between our bio interfaces cut off.

"Hey." Caleb's hands found my shoulders. "Breathe. Let it pass."

Breathe. I could do that much.

I closed my eyes, blue flickering behind my eyelids, and took as steady a breath as I could manage—too fast, but the first thing I'd been in control of for several minutes.

Somewhere, I could hear Caleb counting down from four. His hands squeezed my shoulders as he said, "Again. Breathe."

I stayed in that spot for what felt like years, every sense focused on Caleb as he coached me through the storm, breath by breath. When I finally opened my eyes, the vortex had dissipated, leaving us kneeling in a circle of asphalt cracked beyond repair.

"Thanks." I sagged against Caleb, limbs tremoring. Now that I could breathe again, I realized that the vortex had drained my power to almost nothing. The world was silent as I said, "The Angels—"

"Gone." By the twist in his voice, he didn't mean "ran

away." "You were right; it *was* a massacre." His helmet shifted against mine with a rasp of plastic. "They're all teenagers; I can't imagine what their leaders' purpose was in sending them here."

I dragged myself upright as my eyelids dipped closed. "Make a statement without losing anyone important," I said, the words coming slow and messy. "Discredit the police. Make a biiig mess..."

"...Yeah." Caleb got my arm over his shoulders with a sigh. "You need to rest. Let's let the police clean up."

I LAPSED in and out of wakefulness as we drove home. Once inside, it took every ounce of focus and willpower I possessed to put one foot in front of the other as I put away my gear and dragged myself to the shower. It took long minutes of careful thought before I was able to stand under the warm water, letting the steam ease the accumulated aches of the last several missions. The nicks and scrapes that I always ended up with needed a little more attention, but all I could spare through the fog was a swipe with antibiotic cream before getting into bed.

I can't do this anymore.

That night, I didn't notice the lights coming on in my room for another mission until my door opened. A gentle touch landed on my back as I tried to get up. From outside my dreams, Tara's voice admonished, "Sleep, Gabriel. It's okay. We've got this one. Just sleep."

Sleep...

University of Arizona
Santa Cruz Valley
April 8

"OKAY, Gabriel, let's try it again." Deadeye's voice came fuzzy through an intercom as I stood on the other side of a reinforced window. "Once I count you in, I want you to scan the building and read off where everyone is. You're looking for five targets."

"Copy…" I rotated my wrist to get a better look at the reading on my monitor cuff. I'd slept extra on the nights following the attack on the police station, and the device confirmed what I already knew. Even with a handful of missions in the last few days, my power was functioning at full capacity for today's field calibration test. The lab I stood in had once been well-kept, but time had not been kind to it. The linoleum floors were scuffed, and only half the fluorescent lights buzzed with a sound that set my nerves crawling.

I gave the lights a resentful look before saying, "I can't scan *now*, right?"

"That would be cheating," Deadeye answered. "Wait till I tell you to go; I need to get the field running at full strength before you try to circumvent it. After you scan the building—assuming you succeed—I want you to blast the sensor on the far wall." The green dot of a laser pointer illuminated a target on the wall opposite me.

"I can do that, but—"

"And don't destroy everything."

"That's what I was about to ask." I laughed at her exasperated face as a sigh came through the lab's speaker system. "I'll shield it too."

"*Thank* you. Are you ready?"

I gave my immediate area a final once-over. The room was clear of furniture and equipment, my monitor was functioning as intended, and a vague sense of hope was beginning to stir in my chest. We'd worked on and off at this over the last week, and today it felt like we were closer than ever to achieving our goals.

I squared my shoulders and gave Deadeye a thumbs-up. "Ready."

"Okay, powering up."

I waited, braced like something was going to hit me. The field generator itself—an amalgamation of pillaged xeno tech and custom-made components—sat in the room adjacent to this one. I could still tell the moment it came online. The invisible difference felt like the change in the air that heralded a storm; unseen, heavy, and thick enough that I felt like I could touch it. It wasn't exactly a pleasant feeling, but after a week of testing, I'd gotten accustomed to ignoring it.

"It's running at full capacity, Gabe," Deadeye told me.

"You can begin scanning in five, four"—she held up a hand, fingers ticking down the numbers—"three, two, one. Go ahead."

Okay. Hide-and-seek, but on advanced mode. I took a knee, fingers splayed to stabilize my contact with the floor. An ache built behind my eyes, which closed involuntarily. After a long moment, my power, sluggish as a tortoise waking from hibernation, spilled into the floor and spread through the building.

"Five, you said, right?" I waited to hear Deadeye's affirmation before continuing, "There's Todd and Robin in the upstairs office, Javier's in the printer room, Kaylie's in the downstairs lab, and..." I gave my head a shake as a wave of dizziness washed over me. "And Tim's at his desk."

"Very good," Deadeye said with a sigh. Somehow, I didn't think she was too pleased with how easily I'd located the other engineers. "Okay, go ahead and shoot the thing."

My eyesight wavered as I stood up, and I took a moment to blink my eyes clear of the distortion. The target was a sensor cannibalized from an old monitor cuff, and the cinderblock wall around it already bore the scorch marks from previous tests. Just like I did in practice with Tara, I faced the target and flicked my hand to summon power into it. Ordinarily, there would've been a swell of energy and a matching pulse of warmth down my arm as my power responded. This time, there was—

Nothing.

My eyes went wide, and I tried again.

Nothing.

I lowered my hand, staring as if it—not Deadeye—should answer me. "Did it work? I don't think I'm burned out, but..."

A whoop sounded through the intercom, and I looked up

to see Deadeye raising a fist in the air. "We got it this time!" She ducked out of sight from the window before reappearing with a printout clutched in her hand. "Come look while I turn off the field."

I hurried to the control room. The paper Deadeye had been enthusiastically waving sat on her keyboard, and I took a seat in her desk chair to examine it. Once more, my eyes refused to focus properly, a symptom that resolved—along with the invisible pressure and headache—as the generator powered down in the other room.

"Isn't it cool?" Deadeye demanded as she came through the door.

I raised an eyebrow and passed the paper to her. "You're going to have to spell it out for me. All I see is a graph."

"Right, right, right." She uncapped a dry-erase marker before replicating the graph I'd just seen onto a wall-mounted whiteboard. "Your power—all Shattered power—presents itself within specific energy frequencies, similar to the ones used by the xenos to dampen human emotion and keep all of us like zombies during the occupation."

"Right. That's why Tara's power is too volatile to test with; it's *too* similar."

"Exactly. We've been calibrating to match you instead. Your subtype—the hide-and-seek part, the sensing emotion part—it's here." She stabbed the marker at the highest point along the graph. "Your subtype didn't match the generated frequencies, so you were still able to use it. But then I had you try to use an offensive attack, which operates on a broader spectrum, and here"—she slid the marker to where the line marking my power dropped precipitously—"the field blocked it."

"So…it *did* work. It wasn't a fluke, or me burning out. We

did it." My fingers scrambled to pull up the reading from my monitor cuff. Sure enough, it showed that my power had been functioning fully until the moment that I'd tried to scorch the target. Then it'd dropped, the reading looking for all the world like a failing heartbeat, before returning to normal the moment that Deadeye had turned off the field.

Satisfied, I set the report to print before asking Deadeye, "What do we do now?"

"Now we run more tests," she said. "If we were able to block your offensive capabilities, we might be able to calibrate the frequencies enough to where it'll also block out your subtype." She tapped the marker to where her eyepatch strap crossed her forehead. "When you Shattered, your mind broke. This could un-break it—make it like it'd never happened." Deadeye set the marker aside, a streak of sentiment underlining her voice as she added, "If we'd had something like this when Michael was alive, it might've helped him hold on for longer." She turned to me with a glimmer of tears in her good eye. "Gabriel, we could make it quiet in your head."

Quiet. I turned the word over and over in my mind. I'd wanted to mention the headache and dizziness that I'd experienced while the field was at its strongest, but if this could bring a moment of quiet?

I could deal with the discomfort.

———

BETWEEN DEADEYE'S and my project—now affectionately titled the "Unbreaking Field", my meltdown at the police station, and almost two weeks of silence from Benny, I'd thought my quest to find the Blood Angels' former leader was over. One evening, though, as a rainstorm blew flowers off the palo verde trees and left gold-tattered drifts along the sidewalks, we got good news.

I was on cooking duty with Josephine, stirring a pot of soup while rain pelted the roof. The whir of a motorcycle engine cut off in my sixth sense as Deadeye returned from an errand at St. Augustine's, and a moment later the bay door swung open to admit her.

"Smells good in here," she announced as she came in, hanging an armored jacket on a hook beside the door.

"Don't get too excited," Tara told her as she skidded spoons across the table. "It's just soup."

"Hey," Josephine warned. "*You* try feeding everyone on a public health worker's stipend and see how far you get."

Deadeye sauntered over to taste the spoonful I offered. "Oh, it's good!" She handed the spoon back with a mischievous smile. "Doesn't taste like a low-budget soup at all!"

"Thanks," Josephine and I answered in unison. The off-kilter cadence of our voices sent everyone laughing, as Josephine turned off the burner and lugged the pot to the table.

With Bandit and Caleb summoned, all of us settled in as the rain sheeted down outside. Tara raised an eyebrow toward Deadeye as an errant gust of wind made the bay door rattle. "You rode to St. Augustine's in this?"

Deadeye shook her head, a lock of pink-streaked hair falling in her face as she did. "It wasn't bad on that side of town. Oh!" She bounded from her chair to retrieve a folded set of papers from an inside pocket of the motorcycle jacket. "Benny finally got us that intel on Santana."

I set my spoon down. "Really? I thought he'd forgotten."

"Nah, he doesn't forget things like that." Deadeye

resumed her seat, passing the papers to Bandit. "Actually, he apologized for taking so long. It sounds like he had to call in a few favors in order to find the right people to talk to."

Bandit's eyebrows lowered as he scrutinized the hand-written pages. I resumed eating, my sixth sense providing enough insight to satisfy my immediate curiosity.

Jagged-edged rocks.

Scrub-covered hillsides, breaking into heights bristling with pines.

Numbers shivering into recognizable coordinates.

After a minute, Bandit set the paper to the side. "Son of a bitch never really left Tucson."

Josephine—the only person besides Bandit who'd known Santana as anything more than a piece of history—rolled her eyes. "Doesn't surprise me. He's as stubborn as he is smart. Where is he?"

Deadeye answered for Bandit, pulling over the papers and tapping the handle of her spoon on them. "The Catalinas, like we thought. Up at the top of the canyon, where it's cool enough to survive the summers without air conditioning."

"It's possible down here too," I reminded her. "You just have to—"

"Yeah, yeah, we know," Tara said, waving a hand. "'People lived here for centuries before anyone invented AC.' I like my climate controls, thanks." She shifted to look at Bandit. "Do we have an exact fix on this guy's location?"

He shrugged. "We have coordinates."

"And he might be willing to talk." Deadeye took a bite of soup and swallowed before explaining, "Benny was able to find the guy who drops supplies off for Santana down in the canyon. He left a message with the last supply drop and actually got a response. That's why it took a few extra days."

Josephine looked up from her bowl, dark eyes wide with surprise. "What? Are all of you engineers crazy?"

"Yes," both Deadeye and I answered. She shot me an amused look that sent me chuckling, despite the gravity of our conversation.

"Santana might've been keeping closer tabs on things than we thought." The corner of Bandit's mouth twitched. "That or he's bored and thinks this might be interesting." He balanced an elbow on the table. "Either way, I think we need to go talk with him."

"And not just you, either," Deadeye added. She raised an eyebrow. "According to Benny, Santana wants to talk to Gabriel."

My face heated as everyone at the table looked in my direction.

Great.

"YOU'LL BE FINE HERE?" I asked Tara as she tightened my armor straps in the vehicle bay the following morning. "I'd hate for something to—" I stopped as she held a finger to my lips.

"We'll be fine." The tiredness that we were all feeling had made new lines appear around her cyan eyes. With the new revelations about our power, I couldn't help a stir of worry as she said, "If we don't make some kind of headway, we'll be stuck in this fight until we're all dead." She winked and thumped my shoulder. "And don't they say, 'the enemy of my enemy is my friend'? Go make some friends."

Outside, the moon was still high in the sky. Bandit had

warned that the hike to the coordinates Benny had provided would be almost three hours, and neither he, Caleb, nor I wanted to make that upward trek in daylight. Daytime heat aside, it would be the perfect chance for someone to shoot us from a higher vantage point.

I strapped myself into my seat in the passenger compartment, pulled the screens down, and tried to doze. The all-terrain tires took us easily into the canyon and to the end of the paved road, where a rockslide had obliterated the pavement sometime during the xeno occupation. Stars twinkled faintly overhead as we left the truck at the edge of the road, shrugging weapon straps and backpacks into place and conversing quietly.

"Are we safe, *mijo?*" Bandit asked, his broad-shouldered silhouette dark against the tan side of the truck.

I knelt and put a hand on the ground—just to be sure.

"There's nothing," I said. "We weren't followed, and no one else has any reason to be up here." I squinted through the darkness at the rocky slopes of the mountain above us. "And it would be one hell of a shot for someone to get us all the way down here."

The air was bordering on cold at this altitude and time of night. We hiked in silence as Bandit led the way over the rockslide and up the remains of the road. After half an hour, eroded asphalt turned to gravel under our feet as we left the canyon behind and turned our steps higher into the mountains.

"He really makes this trip up and down every week for supplies?" Caleb murmured as we navigated a set of switchbacks lined with yucca and prickly pear.

Bandit grunted. "If I had to guess, he has a motorcycle hidden near where the road disappears. That'd cut out at least eight miles to and from." He checked our coordinates again on his armband computer. "The more I look at these, the more I think I can guess where we're going." The brim of his hat—worn despite the darkness—tipped toward the ridgeline far above us. "There's a river up that way, or there used to be. It was a good spot for camping; the water didn't ever really dry up."

He led the way again, Caleb and I following as the trail took us upward. As the sky lightened, the rocky grasslands and scrubby oaks gave way to a seam of tall, broad-leafed trees running alongside a creek at the base of a valley. As I paused to take a sip from my water, a stir at the far edge of my range caught my attention. "Hey."

Bandit stopped immediately, turning to look at the craggy rocks peppering the mountainside behind us. His voice came low to my ears. "What is it, *mijo?*"

I stepped closer to him and Caleb, who'd reached for his handgun the moment I'd spoken. "There's something that way," I said, anticipation stirring at the back of my head as I pointed to the right of the path before crouching with a hand in the dust. "There're some bigger rocks, and the creek gets deep. There's something nearby that's like the rocks, but not quite, and..." I frowned, uncertain for a moment before the mental image resolved like a radar sweep refreshing on my surveillance screens. "And there's someone asleep."

Caleb peered at the sky. "Still another half hour till sunrise. Think we have time to get close before they wake up?"

"I think so. There's a side gully near the river." I pointed toward where my power echoed in a gap between rocks. "We can wait there until we're sure it's safe to come out."

We made for the spot I'd found, getting into cover as the

sun crested the eastern edge of the valley. From where we sat, we had a clear view of the river as it flowed between the rocks. The edge of an adobe house could barely be seen, tucked in a corner and almost lost in the overhang of a cliff.

"What do you think?" Caleb asked Bandit.

Bandit was lying on his stomach, sighting his rifle on an open spot between us and the house. He sighed and pushed his hat back to rub his forehead. "I think it would've been a good idea for us to have asked for Logan's help. His accuracy would come in real handy here, if things go badly." He glanced at Caleb. "Not that I don't think you're good; he's just *really* good."

I had to agree with him. Logan's skills extended beyond piloting a Thunderbird—I'd trained him on screens during our time at Base 36, and his rifle skills were almost on par with Bandit's.

Caleb tilted his head to look at the spot Bandit was sighting on. "You can't cover while Gabriel and I go down there?"

Bandit shook his head emphatically. "Even if Santana wants to talk specifically to Gabriel, it's better to have a familiar face to break the ice. He wouldn't recognize you, and I don't want him to panic." He sat back from the rifle and gestured for Caleb to take his place. "I trust you enough to take the shot if it needs to be taken."

AN HOUR OF WATCHING LATER—CALM on the others' part, nervous on mine—Bandit and I walked down the trail leading toward the river. I'd slipped my sunglasses on as we went, the early morning sun high enough that their presence wouldn't raise too much suspicion.

The house came fully into view, tucked beneath the cliff as we rounded a corner. It was a small thing, built of adobe brick with raised garden beds near the door. As Bandit and I approached, a man about Bandit's age—but eight inches shorter and fifty pounds lighter—emerged, brandishing an old-style assault rifle.

You good? Caleb asked in my mind. Clearly, he'd felt me startle.

I kept my eyes on the man as I opened my hands and

held them where they could be seen. *I'm fine. He just startled me. Bandit, is this the guy we're looking for?*

Bandit's response came in the affirmative as he, too, raised his hands. "Santana Ortiz?"

Curt Spanish snapped across the distance between us. "Don't come any closer."

Bandit?

It's okay, mijo.

Santana left the shelter of the rocks and paced forward. His gaze skimmed over me before stopping on Bandit, the angle of his unshaven jaw halfway between surprise and intimidation. "Carlos Espinoza? You're still alive?"

I could almost hear Bandit's sigh of relief as he let his shoulders relax and hands drop. "Yeah, barely." He chuckled. "Not that there haven't been a few close calls."

Santana snorted. "I'll bet." He loosened his grip on the rifle before lowering the weapon to a less threatening position. "I heard you almost lost a leg to those monsters."

Bandit nodded, his face composed even as the memory of a Brute clamping its fangs around his thigh surged through his mind—and mine. I took as cautious a steadying breath as I could, my eyes involuntarily going to him behind my sunglasses. Through the after-echoes of the memory came his voice, perfectly nonchalant. "They were more worried about losing all of me, not just my leg. I got lucky; one of our squad members has healing abilities."

"That's right...I heard about that." Santana turned his gaze toward me, shielding his eyes from the rising sun. "I also heard about some kid with the power to rival humanity's greatest commander." He waved at my sunglasses. "Take those things off, kid. What's your name?"

My heartbeat sped up as I pulled the sunglasses free.

Santana didn't even flinch as the telltale cyan was revealed. "It's Gabriel," I said. "And yeah, it really pissed off the EDF when I decided to stop playing their games." I raised my chin and added, "I'm not sure how informed you've stayed, but Regional Command abandoned everything south of Phoenix last October." I couldn't keep the bitterness out of my voice as I added, "They didn't think it was a place of strategic importance."

The former gang leader rolled his eyes. "Of course not. Why would they? It's nothing but a dry, empty wasteland to them."

"I've never claimed they were *smart*," Bandit said, shifting his weight backward to one foot. "They said they'd come after us for desertion, but they haven't bothered to make good on that threat. They seem content to let the Blood Angels fight it out with whoever stayed."

Santana's face darkened at the mention of the Blood Angels, and something dangerous—betrayal, maybe, or even protectiveness—flickered behind his eyes. "Not a whole lot of honor on either side. That city deserves better." He shifted the rifle to one hand and nodded toward the house. "You'd better come in. And tell whoever's hiding in the bushes to come too."

Bandit's and my surprise ricocheted across to Caleb and back again. *He can see me?* Caleb said. *I thought I was hidden from there.*

I glanced at the edge of the house. A tiny, reflected patch of light caught my eye at the corner of a window—a lens, as out of place against the adobe as the antenna I now noticed at the far edge of the roof. *I think he has a trail cam. Or maybe he just guessed we'd have backup hiding somewhere.*

Could be, Bandit agreed. *He's had to be clever to have lasted this long. Caleb, you'd better come in.*

It was dim and cool inside the house; a benefit of being built halfway into a cliff. Santana set the rifle in a wooden rack alongside two others and gestured at a bench covered with a woven blanket. "Sit wherever you want. I don't get many visitors." He checked a small monitor on a shelf near the rifles, its cables and blinking lights completely incongruous with the otherwise handmade furnishings. "The other people up here tend to stay away—ah." Santana looked up as a shadow crossed the doorway. "Welcome," he said in English.

Caleb kept a hand near his thigh holster as he stepped over the threshold. "You didn't have to switch languages," he said in Spanish. "This works fine for me."

Santana raised a surprised eyebrow. I could almost hear the calculations running in his head, just like they had the first time I'd met Caleb and Tara. "You must be Phantom. Based on the stories, I'd pictured you a little taller."

"Not everyone's as tall as him." Caleb nodded in Bandit's direction, and I had to smother a smile at the memory of my squad commander ducking to enter the dwelling. "Some of us are just average."

Santana laughed. "Yeah, and some of us are shrimps." He propped open the covering over a tiny window, allowing sunlight to stream in and illuminate the white-coated ceiling. "Shouldn't you have someone a little more unhinged as your wingman?"

"Banshee's not unhinged. She hasn't been in years," Caleb said, a hint of frustration through the mind bridge telling me how offensive he found the description of his wife. "And you know that's not why we're here."

"Yeah." Santana leaned against the wall, crossing his arms across a narrow chest with a sigh. "I heard you needed help."

At Bandit's mental urging, I spoke up. "The Blood Angels have been tearing up the city. When the EDF had a foothold, there was sort of peace, but now it's chaos." A flash of memory—Bandit's—caught my mind with the image of a grieving family whose daughter had been caught in crossfire. "We're doing what we can to keep order, but it's hard with opponents who are no better than the xenos."

"That's awfully harsh," Santana said, a challenge clear in both emotions and voice. "You'd better not be coming into my house and talking trash to my face."

"No one's talking trash," Bandit insisted, with a warning glance in my direction. "We're saying that the rules you and I operated under have changed." He leaned forward and gestured at Santana. "You'd never have targeted uninvolved civilians to draw out your opponents. And you *certainly* wouldn't have stooped to something like Brutes to get what you wanted."

Santana sighed, the acquiescence so sudden that I wondered if his ire had been on purpose to get a rise out of Bandit. "True enough. And I hear they're getting desperate now that you've taken that option out of their hands." He took a seat on a crate below the window and gave Bandit a cunning look. "I have a pretty good idea why you're here—that gossipy guy from Augustine's clued me in. I still have plenty of clout down there, or I would with the right people." He shrugged, and even in the simple gesture I could sense the danger that lay under his casual tone. "If I wanted to reclaim the top spot, I could do it."

A shiver went up my spine. Retired he might be, but

there was an edge to Santana that was all too familiar. I blinked hard against the fear creeping in on the heels of old associations, my full attention returning as he said, "Only problem is, I'm comfy up here. And while I *could* come in and remind them how things are meant to go, the idea of getting involved doesn't strike me as hot as it might've years ago." He turned to look at me with a quirked eyebrow. "So convince me. Why should I willingly get into this mess?"

I sighed. Why. Why would *anyone* willingly get involved when hiding was the obviously safer choice? I knew why I'd stayed, but I couldn't answer for anyone else—and now that I came right down to things, I wasn't even certain why *I'd* chosen to fight instead of run. If anything, I was—

"Because we're tired," I said, getting to my feet. Committed to this course of action or not, it felt wrong to try to persuade anyone while sitting on a bench. "My squad's tired. The civilians are tired. Even the Angels are tired." Santana frowned, and I insisted, "Trust me, I *know*."

Careful, Gabe, Caleb warned. *It might not be a good idea to—*

Frustrated now, I turned my right arm palm up and punched the button to disconnect the mind bridge. Both Bandit and Caleb stiffened with surprise as I faced Santana squarely. "The Angel leadership aren't the men you knew in the old days. They're desperate lunatics who keep recruiting teenagers—*kids*—to throw at us. They won't stop, and we *can't*. If things continue like this, we'll keep fighting until we've pounded each other into the ground, and who does that leave? The EDF?" I shook my head, the pain of that betrayal coloring my thoughts red. "They abandoned this territory because they didn't think it was worth their time defending. We disobeyed our orders and stayed to fight, but we're *going to lose.*"

His dark eyes shot up to mine, and stayed there as I continued, "We're outnumbered and outmaneuvered, but we can't back down because innocent people will suffer when we do. And if you know who I am, you've also heard what people are saying about me—about this." I tapped a finger below my left eye. "I'm supposed to be some prodigy with power that could rival the founder of the EDF himself. But fighting this losing battle is taking *everything* I've got."

I looked at the ground, unexpectedly struck by the truth in that statement and unwilling to meet the intensity in Santana's gaze. My next words came out as almost a whisper. "My power's...probably going to kill me sooner or later. It almost did in that cloning facility, and some days I wish it had." Surprise and concern flickered between Bandit and Caleb, but they stayed blessedly quiet as I finished, "At the end of all this, I'm still just a kid trying to save the place where I grew up. And I'm tired."

Silence stretched in the tiny house as my words faded. Finally, Santana gave a resolute nod. "I'll think about it."

SANTANA'S last words stayed with me as we silently made our way out of the valley. Once we were out of range from the tiny house, we stopped. I knelt to refill my hydration pack at the edge of the creek, bracing myself for the push-back from the others—or worse, for them to pry into how honest I'd been.

"Well, that went much better than I'd hoped," Bandit said.

I looked up in surprise. "Really?"

He patted his rifle strap, crisscrossed over his torso. "I had Caleb lined up to shoot him, remember?"

"Oh yeah..." I snapped the filter into place and made sure the connections between straw and pouch were secure before replacing the hydration pouch in my backpack. "I guess under those circumstances it went really well." I settled my backpack straps against my shoulders once more. "Sorry for turning off the mind bridge."

"I was pretty annoyed at first," Caleb admitted. He'd been tense the whole time we'd been walking, but had calmed down once we got into the cover of the trees. "But then I realized you needed to focus."

"Yeah," I confessed. "And it needed to be clear that I was speaking without anyone telling me what to say through comms."

"I *hadn't* thought of that." Bandit took a long drink from his water. "I'm glad Benny smoothed the way for us."

"Think he'll actually come around?" Caleb asked. "I hate to say this, but I think he could really be an asset in taking out the gang from the inside."

"I don't know," Bandit said. "If he does, it'll be on his terms, and in his timing. And we might not like either." He glanced at the sun, now standing halfway in its arc across the sky. "Let's get out of here."

Going downhill was always easier than going up, and we made good time descending from the highest point of the canyon. As we walked, it grew warmer and warmer until I was regretting my decision to not bring a hat.

I wasn't alone in my dislike of the heat. We'd been hiking for an hour and a half, and had just crossed onto the derelict canyon road when Caleb stopped. "Hey, do you hear that?"

"Hear what?" I looked up at the craggy edges of the canyon.

He pointed at a brilliant green clump of cottonwoods. "There's water down there."

"I mean, we *did* just have rain." I wiped my forehead with the edge of my sleeve. "It'll probably flow for another couple days."

"Exactly. We could take a break and cool off."

Bandit checked his watch, then looked at the sky. "We have time." He stepped off the road, his hat disappearing behind a scruffy mesquite. "Come on!"

Caleb raised an eyebrow in my direction. I caught the sentiment even before he voiced it, and bolted off the road as the words left his mouth. "Race you—hey!"

We caught up to Bandit in a matter of seconds, crashing through undergrowth with less precision than a herd of javelina. Within a minute, we stood at the edge of the river. The water flowed gently over a descending granite shelf, pooling in a depression at the feet of the cottonwoods before gurgling onward. A pair of ducks flapped their ungainly way out of the water at our hurried approach. They settled to give us beady-eyed stares from the other side of the waterway.

I threw my pack down in the shade and began tugging the laces on my boots. Caleb joined me a second later, jettisoning his pack and armor before stopping. "It *is* safe, right?"

"You think he'd have dropped his own things if it wasn't?" Bandit said, pulling off his hat and laying his rifle against a tree. "Right, *mijo?*"

I frowned, dug my fingers into the sand, and cast my awareness as far as I could. Nothing stirred in the canyon except birds, animals, and plants. Compared to the hum of the city, it was downright peaceful. "We're fine. There's nothing for miles."

"Good enough for me," Caleb said, yanking his shirt over his head.

I followed suit, glad I'd been wearing gym shorts under my cargo pants. Leaving the rest of my uniform in a pile, I plunged into the water after Caleb and Bandit, diving low and skimming the mica-laden sand to grab Caleb's feet and yank.

He toppled, twisting underwater to haul me to the surface in a grip far stronger than it deserved to be. He didn't see Bandit coming up behind him, and both of our yells turned to bubbles underwater. Surfacing with a laugh, I grabbed Caleb's arm and sent him the image of him diving on Bandit while I took out our commander's feet. Caleb's laugh was almost a cackle as he obeyed, all of us crashing down into the water once more.

We stayed in the water until the chill seeped into our bodies. After a while, Bandit sloshed his way back to our things. "We'd better go soon. I don't want the others to worry about us."

I'd been lying on my stomach on the rocks, letting the warm breeze dry my hair and shorts. Caleb swam underwater across the length of the pool, emerging at the feet of the rocks. "I don't think they'll notice," he answered. "We said we'd be back by dinner, and it's barely noon now." He scrambled to the top of the rock and sat alongside me. The circuits in his arm glinted dully through his skin as he shook water from his short brown hair, and I laughed as I realized why he'd been able to haul me through the water so easily.

"Hey, how come you never mentioned those made you stronger?"

Caleb looked down in surprise. "What? Oh." He turned his arm over to examine the circuits. "I forget. It's not like it makes that much of a difference."

"Says the guy with metal in his arm." I sat up. "You dragged me through the water like I was a guppy."

"Right. Sorry." He opened and closed his hand, the movement alternately revealing and obscuring portions of the metal. "I *do* forget, actually. It's been so long."

"I guess so." I brushed sand from my chest and stomach, glad that we'd be moving on soon. Bandit and I would've been fine in the sun for a while longer, but Caleb was pale enough that he'd certainly burn. Glancing over at the thought, I was struck again by how many times he'd been injured. I'd noticed the scars before, other times he'd been shirtless, but the thought of what it took to get that many still hit me at unexpected moments. "Tara never tried healing those?"

"Sorry?" Caleb blinked, and I realized his mind had been miles away—though, with his mental control, I wasn't sure where. "Oh, you mean the scars." He ran his thumb over the line tracing from hairline to cheekbone—a surgical scar from his time in xeno captivity—and shook his head. "Most of them are from before she gained that ability. After, she was able to seal things right when they happened, and a good thing too." He laughed, but I could tell it was to banish memories. "If she hadn't learned when she did, I'd be dead."

"How—how *did* it happen?" I didn't mean to pry, but I had been wondering for months. The others didn't know, and as far as I could tell, it'd been while he and Tara were absent from the Defense Force.

Caleb's gaze dropped to a jagged mark across his abdomen, knotted and raised against his skin. The memory writhed past his mental walls even without me touching him, and for a moment I saw everything as he'd witnessed it.

The derelict supermarket had looked structurally sound, but its roof creaked ominously as Tara and I sheltered from a violent Midwestern thunderstorm. A rumble from above alerted us to the real danger, as a gust of wind ripped a section of ceiling free.

"Tara, run!" I yelled, shoving her to the side as a mess of ceiling tiles fell. She stumbled clear as a tile struck the back of my head, sending me semiconscious to the floor. The roof groaned again as more pieces gave way, the structure ripping apart under clawing wind. I was just regaining my senses when a piece of twisted metal slammed right through my side and left me pinned.

Helpless. Again.

Energy shot across the building and the mess fell apart as Tara yelled. She dropped to her knees alongside me, blue light enveloping both of us. I screamed as she yanked the metal free, pain shot across my vision in a burst of crimson light, and I fell out of the memory to see Caleb's hand resting on the spot where the metal had impaled him.

"We had no idea that she could be anything more than a force of destruction until that day." He let his hand slide from the scar, and a careful smile crossed his face. "She burned herself out doing it, but she saved my life."

Turning my gaze past the canyon walls, I squinted into the sky. "There's nothing I could do that could ever match that. Not in a million years."

"Don't sell yourself short," Caleb said. "You and Tara—every Shattered I've ever met—you think your power is a curse. But take it from me, it does have its blessings. The number of lives each of you can touch goes far beyond what you think your power should allow."

I blinked hard. "Thanks, Caleb." I wavered for a moment, debating if I should broach the topic of what I'd admitted to Santana. "I—"

"Hey!" Bandit yelled from the shade, his voice breaking the courage I'd mustered. "Let's go!"

Caleb and I splashed out of the water and returned to our things. By the time we'd reassembled our gear, laced our boots, and refilled our hydration packs, the sun was edging toward the west. Bandit cast an eye at the edge of the canyon as we began walking. "It'll be almost dinner by the time we get home."

"I wonder what the others have been doing while we've been gone," I said. A few seconds passed before— "What *do* women do when they're by themselves?"

"Braid each other's hair and talk about us," Caleb said, a smile giving away the humor in his deadpan delivery. "And I hear baking cookies is often a priority."

"Assuming the dough ever makes it to the oven," Bandit commented. "I think Josie's taken a 'cook's tax' off every batch she's ever made."

I chuckled at the mental image. "Maybe they'll have saved some for us. I just hope there's dinner."

"Josephine was going to stay home from the clinic today, so I'd say your chances are good," Bandit reassured me. "She knows today had the chance to go badly, and I think she wanted to be home in case she had to patch any of us up."

"Speaking of," Caleb said. "Not to be rude, sir, but are you planning on marrying her anytime soon?"

If Bandit's hat hadn't been covering his ears, I'm certain they would have glowed red. "I—well—"

"Is there a reason you're delaying?" I asked. He and Josephine had been a couple for almost six months now. Given the circumstances, that was practically a lifetime. "I'm certain she'd say yes, if you asked."

Bandit's steps picked up, and Caleb and I had to hurry to keep pace with him. "It's terrible timing," he insisted. "I can't promise to protect and provide for her for the rest of our lives when there's no certainty that I'd be able to follow through." He waved at the mountain reaches. "If Santana had decided to ambush us, we would've been dead the second we walked into this canyon. I can't ask Josie to live with that risk every day."

"She already does," Caleb said. I didn't think he was being unkind, but Bandit's shoulders still tensed as he said it. "When you commit to someone, you commit even knowing the worst that can happen."

"You and Tara were already married when you joined the resistance, right?" I thought they had been, but the mind bridge tended to blend past and further-past together.

"Yeah, though we didn't have an actual wedding until much later. We got married a couple years out of high school, right before the first blackout hit." Caleb's mental wall flickered, and I caught a flash of a golden-toned, treasured memory—tying a braid of colored thread around Tara's ring finger—before he returned his focus to Bandit. "Sir, Josephine committed to stay when the Medical Corps gave her the opportunity to leave. She's tied to you whether you want her to be or not. You need to ask her."

"I'll help you find a ring," I offered. "There might be places where people would trade for them."

Bandit shot a look at me from under his hat brim and his steps slowed. Finally, he sighed. "I already have one."

Caleb and I exchanged triumphant glances. "You do? Does it fit?"

"I—I don't know." Bandit fished under his shirt. I knew he still wore his dog tags with a St. Michael's medallion hung alongside them, but I hadn't realized there was a second chain beneath his shirt. A simple gold wedding band caught the light as he freed it from his collar. "I think it's too big," he said. "Josie's—" He blinked hard. "Josie's hands are a lot smaller than Maria's were."

I tipped my head to examine the metal more closely. "I'll bet Deadeye and I could help you size it down. She has access to the equipment at the university. If you want us to, that is."

Bandit's gaze softened as he looked from me to the ring. Then, with a deep breath, he tucked it into his shirt once more. "I might take you up on that, *mijo*." His eyes snapped to Caleb. "And not a word from you to *anyone*, you rascal."

Caleb grinned, a rare mischievous light filling his eyes. "Wouldn't dream of it, sir."

WE ARRIVED home as the sun was setting, were greeted by the smells of chili and cornbread, and debriefed with everyone over dinner. It wasn't until everyone departed to bed—or in Deadeye's case, to the office—that the weirdly blended emotions of the long day caught up with me.

I flipped on the light beside my bed and pulled over my notebook. Halfway through recounting the mission into the mountains, my earlier words floated back in to haunt me.

...and I'm tired. I'm tired of feeling like this is a fight we can't win.

My pen halted on the printed lines, and I laid it down.

I didn't think it was that close to the surface, let alone something I'd admit to a stranger.

I closed the notebook and set it on my bedside table before going to the kitchen to make hot chocolate. I wasn't sure how long I stood there, watching the water bubble in the electric kettle, until Deadeye reached around me to turn it off.

"Mind a mile away? Why aren't you in bed?"

I shook my head. "Couldn't sleep. And after everyone goes to bed is the only time it's quiet in here." I tapped my temple before picking up the kettle to add water to my cup. "I'll be honest, I *really* hope we can perfect the Unbreaking Field. It'd be nice to have somewhere to go where things weren't so loud, even if it's a temporary measure."

Deadeye got another mug out of the cupboard and proffered it for me to fill. "At the very least, it'd give you a place to sleep in peace." She plucked a chamomile teabag out of a foil packet and dropped it into her water. "Speaking of, do you want to go outside?"

I looked at the ceiling. "Outside? How come?"

"Change of scenery? Distance?" She gave me a knowing look. "A way to get some of that mess out of your head?"

I gave an exhausted snort. Talking with Deadeye was no Unbreaking Field, but it was better than nothing. The back door snicked closed on my heels as I followed her to the roof. The lights on our sensor system and radio transmitter blinked in a steady on-off-on-off of red and green, the predictability as calming as a heartbeat. Spring was waning, and dust clouded the sky despite the rain from the previous week. Stars winked slowly from between curtains of darkness, their faint light fighting against the floodlights in the parking lot below.

Shattereds die young. And I'm tired already.

I drew my knees to my chest with a shudder, hot chocolate forgotten beside me. That thought had a way of returning at the least desirable moments, and every time it sent a bone-shaking chill through my body. At least this time, the only person who might be in a spot to notice was Deadeye, and she—

"Gabe, what's going on?"

Guess she was paying attention, after all.

"I'm fine, it's just—" I stopped. Now that I was on the edge of the admission that I'd almost made to Caleb this afternoon, I didn't know if I wanted to go through with it. Instead, I gestured beyond our walled yard. "Six months ago, I was ready to die for this place."

"Yeah, it was rough then, between Brutes and gangs." Deadeye laughed shortly. "Not that it's much better now. Feels like we're fighting something in its death throes, and it'll do anything to take us down with it."

"Yeah, exactly. Last year"—I nodded toward the western mountains, beyond which lay the research facility that we'd destroyed the previous year—"I gave up hope of making it out of the cloning facility alive. When I did, I was surprised and relieved. Now..." Another shudder ran through my limbs. "I'm beginning to understand why the Defense Force abandoned this place. I've given everything I've got, but I don't know how long I can keep fighting." The statement was so similar to what I'd told Santana that the rest slipped out without my meaning it to. "I was ready to die defending this region, but now I almost wish I had. I don't love it any less, I'm just so *tired*."

Deadeye had stiffened at my admission, but her posture gradually relaxed into something less alarmed as she thought. After a while, she sighed. "Believe it or not, I understand how you feel. I felt the same, during the war." She leaned back against a braced arm, her voice taking on the cast of memory. "We'd been in conflict for months—going on a year—and we were losing people left and right. Michael was showing signs of burnout—" She stopped and clarified, "Not the 'need to sleep' type, I mean the type that killed him."

I nodded, and she continued, "For the most part, I felt lucky to be alive. But then, every once in a while, we'd be drinking to the victorious dead and I'd be jealous." Her voice turned dark for an instant. "At least the dead weren't suffering any more losses."

"Yeah..." I raised my head to look at Deadeye. "Yeah, exactly." I couldn't help the desperation in my voice as I asked, "How'd you get past it?"

She gave me a crooked smile. "Michael. Who else?" An almost disbelieving laugh escaped her. "Idiot was such an optimist, even at the end. He reminded me that humans are resilient. Determined. Worthy of saving. Even the xenos saw it, in a weird and twisted sort of way. I mean, look at all the stars out there." She waved at the sky. "There's millions of them, and even more planets, but resiliency and the ability to adapt is something that sets humanity apart. If the xenos could value those qualities enough to single out one planet among millions, you and I can decide that one region among thousands is as equally valuable." She sighed. "Even if it *does* cost us everything."

"Maybe so..." I let the words trail away as my awareness expanded into the city. Tucson had always struck me a certain way, in sharp edges silhouetted against a fiery sky, the rumble of distant thunder, and the taste of citrus and salt.

Even before I'd Shattered, I'd always felt like I could reach out and touch the intangible parts of my birthplace.

Being Shattered added another layer to the city. Like a distant lullaby came the sense of parents putting their children to bed. Elsewhere, someone's temper flared, hot against the edges of my mind. Still beyond that came faint strains of music; the sound of ingenuity at work to reclaim the sound of a bygone, happier time. Even wracked by chaos, the city teemed with pockets of life, with determination to thrive in a place that was inhospitable to humanity.

I took a deep breath and shifted to sit cross-legged, the darkness circling my thoughts dissipating like smoke blown in the wind. "It is still beautiful."

Deadeye laughed. "I guess it *has* grown on me—not the place, if you know what I mean." She set her mug down and shivered theatrically. "Heat and dust and too many things that sting and bite—*ach*. But the people; everyone who chooses to stay here has a strong will to live, and I can respect that." She raised an eyebrow. "Resiliency, y'know?"

"Does that go for our enemies too?" I asked before I could think better of it.

"How's that?"

I rotated my cup in my hands. "The Blood Angels. They're...they're not so different from us. I didn't realize it when we were out there." I pointed northwest, where Base 36 lay long abandoned amid the creosote flats of the Gila River Valley. "Back then it was kill or be killed, and more of a black-and-white conflict. But now, here, it's...different. And with every encounter I get more and more convinced." I set the cup down, interlacing my fingers instead. "Deadeye, they're not the same gang that was dead-set on dominating the whole valley with monsters. They're mostly desperate, trapped teenagers with a handful of really messed up guys calling the shots for them. When I was that age—"

"You still are."

I rolled my eyes. "When I was a *kid*, there was the chance of being something other than a scavenger or a gangster. The Defense Force meant stability, both for the region and my own life." I nodded across the city. "Now, their only option is joining the Angels, and that's no real guarantee of a long *or* safe life." I pressed my lips together, the image of a smoking helmet stark against my memory. "Especially not now, with their leaders throwing them at us like they don't matter."

"Maybe there's something to that." Deadeye scooped up her mug and stood, offering me a hand. "It really does seem like it's the leadership that's the issue, but I guess Santana isn't interested in taking back the crown."

I followed her to the edge of the roof and waited my turn for the ladder. "He was hard to read, even for me. I think *if* he intervenes, it'll be for his own purposes." *And in his own timing.* "For right now, I think we're on our own."

"Hey." Deadeye stopped me from walking past with a hand to my chest. "Let's try to keep our hearts fixed on the things we *can* do—and on the people who matter most to us. Focus on the beauty, yeah?" She winked—well, blinked—her good eye. "That's how you keep the fire going, when everything around you wants to smother it."

STAGE TEN

OVER A WEEK and several more tests later, Deadeye and I were growing content with our work. The others who shared the lab space had helped us refine the calibration enough to where the Unbreaking Field—as it was now universally called—could stifle most of my offensive capabilities. We were still chasing the elusive "quiet zone," but everyone was confident that we'd get there eventually.

The rest of the squad were also intrigued, though perhaps less so than Deadeye and myself. I hadn't understood why she herself was so invested until a conversation with Tara after morning practice shed some light on the subject.

"Reneé was really close with Michael before he died." Tara uncapped her water bottle and took a drink. "I don't know if they were just friends or if it was more than that, but

I think that's why she stayed with the EDF when so many of us left. When she looks at you and me..."

"She sees a chance to prevent what happened to him," I finished. I hadn't known what to make of it until now, but the extra information was coming together like the pieces to the puzzle Tara and Caleb had been building on the coffee table this week. "No wonder she's been losing sleep over this." A stir of movement inside the base caught my attention, and I gestured to the bay door. "We'd better wrap up. I think Bandit's about to call for morning lineup."

I was correct. A few minutes later found me with a cup of coffee in hand, listening with amusement as Bandit handed out chores for the day.

"That takes care of kitchen duty..." he mused, crossing an item off on a paper pad. "On patrol for today... Caleb and Tara."

"Again?" Tara complained. "It's hot out!"

Caleb grinned at her. I could tell he was secretly pleased for them to have several uninterrupted hours in each other's company. "You'll be fine, princess. Besides," he added, a touch of grimness filtering through his amusement, "our range is a lot smaller than it used to be, so we won't be out as long."

"True." She slouched in her seat with grudging acceptance painted across her features. "What else, *mon Capitaine?*"

"Don't call me that..." Bandit said as she started sniggering. He crossed another item off the list, then set down the pad with an evil grin. "Reneé, I noticed the office was getting ridiculously cluttered when I went in there the other day. Not that I'm complaining about your creative process, but it's a fire hazard. I want it clean."

I cackled as Deadeye sputtered incredulously into her coffee. *Forget losing sleep, she's been forgetting everything but research.*

My amusement evaporated as Bandit turned to me next. "And *mijo*, I realized that you never finished your Module Three First Aid training."

I snorted. "Finished it? I never started it." I thumped my empty coffee mug onto the table. "In case you forgot, the EDF disowned us, and I didn't have login codes for the online trainings."

"Yeah, I know." Bandit's eyes twinkled with mischief. "But Josephine had all the videos saved. I'll get them set up for you in the med bay."

The others burst into laughter as it became my turn to sputter indignantly. Caleb patted my shoulder as he went past with Tara. "Better get more of that," he said, nodding toward my coffee cup. "If they're the same videos I remember, you'll be snoozing in thirty seconds flat."

My vaguely optimistic attitude lasted as long as it took to pour another cup of coffee, add half-and-half, and open the first video. As the EDF logo appeared in glowing blue and a cheerful female voice began the introduction, I groaned. "There's a reason I didn't start these even when I *had* access, Bandit."

"I know." Bandit's voice held unholy glee as he left the room, calling back, "Let me know when you're done. There's a test."

Muttering under my breath, I slid headphones over my ears and settled in to watch the least interesting CPR presentation ever created. After a while, I took a break. My coffee had long run out, and I paused the training video to get a refill from the kitchen and chat with Bandit as he mopped the floor. Outside, the hum of daily life in the barrio had become a comforting rhythm as I rambled to Bandit about the Unbreaking project—a rhythm that suddenly rang discordant in my senses and forced my words to a halt.

"...and they didn't even notice that the data—"

My voice trailed off, and I focused on the urgency I'd felt drawing near.

"What's wrong?" Bandit asked, setting the mop back in the bucket. His hand drifted toward his holster, worn even in the station. "Something out there?"

"Something, yeah." I dropped to a knee and put a hand to the ground. The barrio snapped into sharp relief, and there, booking it toward us, were two familiar figures.

"It's Caleb and Tara," I said as I regained my feet. My power streaked through the base with an edge of command. ***Deadeye. Living room, now.*** A crash came from the office, mixed with swearing in German as I told Bandit, "Something's wrong."

I was pulling up the mind bridge even as Deadeye's footsteps sounded in the hall. "Syncing," I warned, before throwing the connection wide open.

Darkness ringing a pool of light.

Adrenaline painting the landscape cyan.

Dusty books and the scratching of pencils.

Bougainvillea arching over a turquoise gate.

The suddenness of everyone's combined emotions and memories sent a spasm through my stomach, and I swayed on my feet with my mind splintering into a hundred different moments of others' lives. Bandit's arms wrapped around my chest, steadying me against him as I pulled my senses into my own body.

I've got you, mijo, he reassured me. *Banshee, Phantom, report.*

Not sure, sir. Caleb's mental voice was as unflappable as usual, but an undercurrent of adrenaline ran beneath his thoughts. *There's smoke in the direction of downtown, and something made the ground shake. I thought it was Banshee, but—*

Don't be ridiculous; it's bigger than something I'd do, Tara interrupted. *Gabe, are you ready to receive?*

I'd barely regained my balance, and instinctively reached out to Bandit before saying, *Go for it.*

As soon as the acknowledgment streaked through the bridge, my vision blurred into a memory from Tara—a view down a road, clear to the southern horizon, with a wide column of thick black smoke churning into the sky to the right of it. Together with it came the certain knowledge that *something* had exploded a moment prior, and that neither she nor Caleb had any idea of the cause.

That'll do, Banshee, Bandit said.

I yanked myself back into my own head and locked eyes with him. *I recognize where that is. It's by the rail line. Southwest of here.*

He nodded grimly, letting me go before directing an order at Caleb and Tara. *The two of you, get to an intersection and stay there. We're coming.*

WE THREW our gear into the truck and screeched out of the bay, radio crackling with traffic as Bandit alerted St. Augustine's, the fire department, and the police.

I scrambled into my armor underlay and vest in the back of the truck, doing my best to keep my trepidation out of the mind bridge. The fire department was a barely functioning entity most days, between lack of manpower and lack of infrastructure, and I didn't hold much hope in their ability to do anything against an attack or some other terrible accident. At least, I hoped it was an accident.

What is it? Deadeye asked through the bridge as Tara and Caleb clambered into the truck.

Still don't know, Tara said. She lost her balance as we went over a pothole, and grabbed for a handle on her way to her jump seat. *The smoke's not stopping. Whatever it is, it's big.*

The "what" became clearer as we neared the industrial sector by the railyard. The wails of sirens could be heard in the distance as Deadeye brought the truck to a gravel-scraping halt and we disembarked. Black smoke clouded the sky, and I caught Bandit's order to secure our helmets before he threw his door open. With a tug and a click, my helmet locked into place, and the bio-filter's indicator in my heads-up display flashed green before minimizing in my field of vision.

The air was charged with heat from a massive blaze engulfing what remained of a squat industrial building. Debris lay scattered in a huge radius around the place, pieces of twisted metal and cinderblock thrown dozens of yards into the street. Running figures appeared and disappeared amid the smoke, screams and shouts sounding as something inside the building exploded.

Even before I jumped to the ground, a sickening mix of fear, powerlessness, and pain from the bystanders surged into my sixth sense, and I swore in Spanish before saying aloud, "Sir!"

Bandit's acknowledgment came through my mind, his

voice lost between the roar of flames and crackling of comms. *Report*, mijo.

I closed my eyes against the brightness and let my awareness expand to cover the immediate area. "It's a factory of some kind, sir. The western half of the building's collapsed. Fire throughout, spreading into the intact side of the building. Several victims lying on the ground to the north, and others still in the intact side. There's a crowd gathering; I think they're trying to rescue the people inside." I swallowed hard. The people in the crowd felt familiar, but I couldn't place why—and this frenzied energy could easily be turned on us if we didn't do something quickly. "They're starting to panic, sir; we need to get them under control before we lose more lives."

"Fire department's here!" Deadeye announced. I splintered into her perspective long enough to hear a rush of staticky comms traffic before she added, "They're getting a water supply, but they can't do much with a single truck. Another's on its way, but it's going to take a while."

The wail of another siren subsided nearby as an ambulance turned onto the street. As I followed its progress toward the crowd, I caught a glimpse of sparks being thrown and electricity arcing between the ends of a downed power line. Narrowing my gaze, I could now see a figure crouched nearby, hands sparking with brilliant cyan light as they reached out and...grabbed one of the downed wires.

Electricity...lightning? Shattered lighting? My muscles tensed at the unmistakable Shattered presence, ozone mixing with fear in my sixth sense. *It's her!*

All at once, the familiarity in the crowd made sense. "Sir, they're Blood Angels!"

For a heartbeat, everyone froze.

"You're sure?" Bandit asked, his voice iron.

"I'm certain, sir. Their Shattered is here, at least two of the people inside are members, and—" I caught my breath and tried my best not to let my panic spill over into the others. "Sir, the whole crowd is affiliated! This facility must belong to them!"

Both Deadeye and Tara swore at the same time. Caleb did too, in his head.

A yawning pit opened in my stomach. *Guys, what are we going to do?*

For a few seconds, everything was a churning mess of uncertainty, resentment, anger, and frustration. Then— *Those who live in this region are resilient. Determined. Worthy of saving*—Deadeye's words from earlier came through my mind. Maybe she was thinking about it, herself. *Does this count for our enemies too?*

I glanced at the spot where I'd seen the Shattered. She was gone, but the power line no longer arced raw electricity into the environment.

Maybe this time, we can actually do what we were meant to do, and save lives.

As the thought ran through my head and across to the others', a woman broke away from the crowd and ran to us, her hands open and pleading. "Help us! I don't care who you are. They'll die, please help us!"

I was about to step forward and translate when a question and confirmation went between Caleb and Tara faster than I could track. Before either of them spoke, I knew what they'd decided—what all of us had decided.

"Doesn't matter if they're affiliated, or even full members," Tara said to the rest of us. She stripped off her reinforced gloves and blue light began glowing between her fingers. "We have to help." Without another word, she took to her heels, Caleb behind her as they ran toward the burning building. A shield burst into life over them as they went, its light clearing a path through the crowd into the smoke.

Bandit swore again, the single word carrying resignation and determination all at once. *Stay safe, you two. We'll get things under control out here. Mijo, survivors are where?*

I dropped to a crouch, energy pulsing through both hands into the ground as my awareness plunged into the veil of smoke surrounding the building. It was a metal-sided warehouse—its girders jumbled and roof caving almost to the floor—with a rectangle of cinderblocks forming an office to the south. Inside, my power sketched the visuals of several reddish blobs, fear painting their outlines white.

Two in the back room; there's a window on the south side. I scrambled to my feet and broke into a sprint as the third figure resolved itself as male, terrified, and small. *And there's a kid in the middle! Tara!*

Tara's shield glowed through the smoke, and I homed in on her and Caleb as another burst of blue light flared deep in the building. A girder rumbled and slid from a half-collapsed wall in response, a shift in the smoke marking its path. The heat was almost unbearable, and my heads-up display began scrolling warnings in lurid red across the top half of my vision.

Temperature advisory. *No kidding.*

My shield merged with Tara's as I caught up to her and Caleb, the combined power enough to bring the violent blinking in my helmet down to a steady flash.

Where are the survivors? Caleb asked, fear pulsing

through his mind as he cast a glance at the partially caved-in roof.

I pushed the image of the three survivors into their minds before sending a streak of light to mark a metal door in the intact cinderblock wall. *Other side of this. I think the roof only collapsed on this side. The kid's—*

All three of us jumped as the noise of something exploding on the other side of the warehouse reached our ears.

The three of you need to hurry! Bandit shouted through the mind bridge. *The bystanders said there's propane in there. It could blow at any moment!*

Tara growled and sent a blast of power at the door. It burst open under the impact, and she and Caleb bolted inside. *We'll get the ones in the back. Get the kid, Gabe.*

The blue of their shield disappeared into the darkness, and I followed long enough to find the door to what I now recognized was a bathroom. Inside, the smoke had yet to bank all the way to the ground, and the chaos from outside was shockingly distant. Water pooled on the floor, each footfall making a splash as I scanned through the stalls.

There.

A whimper drifted through the strangely quiet space, changing rapidly to a frightened wail as I pushed the last stall door open to reveal a skinny kid—seven or so—huddled between the toilet and the wall. The world stretched, snapped, and for a moment I saw myself as he did—a forbidding armored figure, anonymous in a helmet, standing within a bubble of brilliant light.

My stomach sank.

"Hey." I knelt in front of him and switched to Spanish. "Hey, I didn't mean to scare you. I'm sorry."

The kid shrank even farther behind the toilet, tucking his knees to his chest and burying his face in them with a terrified whine.

"Look, look." Every warning scrolling across my heads-up display said that taking my helmet off was a stupid idea, but my hands still went to the releases. The helmet slid free, and I set it on the floor beside me with a splash. My shield flickered out, leaving both of us in the dark.

"Hey. I know you're scared. This is really scary, but I'm here to get you out." Shuffling forward on my knees, I managed to get hands around the kid's arms and hauled him from behind the toilet. "C'mon, buddy. Let's get going."

I could tell the moment that the boy's fear shifted to trust. In a split second, he went from resisting my grasp to clinging to the straps of my armor. Skinny legs wrapped around my waist, and he buried his face against my shoulder with a relieved wail.

"It's okay," I reassured him, one hand going to cradle the back of his head. His hair was wet, probably from the puddles of water, and an idea stirred at the realization. "Here, let's do this—" I pried him away from my chest long enough to scoop my helmet from the floor and tug it over his head. "Okay, there you go. Hold on tight."

The helmet bobbled as the kid nodded and renewed his grip on my armor. As he did, the building filled with an earth-shattering crash.

Gabriel, run! Tara shouted. *We're already out, don't worry about us!*

I lurched to my feet, the kid's weight pulling me off-balance before he clung to me tighter. The smoke was banked farther down the walls now, and I was forced to move in a half-crouch that reminded me of a Brute's lumbering gait as we made our way out of the bathroom and into the office hallway. Beyond the door I'd entered through, flames glowed a terrifying orange.

"Hold on!"

My shield winked into existence over us, and I pushed as much power as I could into it before taking a deep breath and bolting into the factory. As soon as I stepped out the door, smoke enveloped the shield. I had to rely on the faintly glowing path revealed by my sixth sense to retrace my steps out of the building, charging through flames with the piercing knowledge that at any second, the shield could fail and leave both of us with lungs full of toxic smoke. The thought added extra speed to my movement, footsteps thundering in my ears before we broke out of the smoke and were in the open air once more.

Bandit was the first person to greet my vision, tension in every line of his shoulders and relief breaking through the mind bridge as I staggered to a halt. "Gabriel!"

"I'm okay," I gasped, letting my shield dissipate and the kid spill into the arms of several bystanders. Frantic, relieved Spanish flew between the onlookers as I collapsed to my hands and knees, coughing and retching in a desperate effort to breathe clearly.

"Hey, back off! Give him some space!" A water bottle came into my periphery, and Bandit urged, "Take it easy, *mijo*. Breathe."

The plastic crinkled as I took the water, and I drained the bottle. "Thanks," I gasped. My limbs shook, and I let myself drop to the pavement.

"Stay here," Bandit ordered. "I'm getting the medics."

He said something else to someone over my head, but his

departing words were lost as another wave of coughing started.

The kid's okay, I reassured myself, relieved despite whose turf we were on. *I'm okay. We're going to be okay. This I can do.*

I groaned and rolled to my side as the coughing subsided, blinking through watering eyes at the sky—a sky that became charged with heat and smoke as something within the factory exploded.

Or maybe not.

STAGE ELEVEN

SOUND OFF! Bandit shouted through the mind bridge.

We're good, Tara said grimly. She was holding a shield over several bystanders while pouring power into someone lying on the ground. *This guy's in rough shape, though.*

I'm fine. A flash of awareness from Deadeye showed that another company of firefighters had arrived and were hurrying past with a hose. Annoyance spiked from her as they were forced to skirt several men whose posture and clothing marked them as active members of the Blood Angels.

I struggled to my feet. *I'm okay too. Deadeye, there's—*

I see them, she replied. *You'd think they'd man up and make themselves useful instead of standing around watching. I'll handle them.*

My lungs felt a little clearer as I pulled my helmet—

abandoned by the bystanders as they rushed the boy I'd saved away—over my head and locked it in place. Filtered air rushed past my face and my thoughts cleared. I skirted the edge of the crowd to come up behind Deadeye as she strode over to the group of men. *I've got your six.*

"Hey!" she snapped. "This is an emergency scene, and you're blocking the firefighters from doing their jobs. Either start being helpful or beat it."

One of the men leered at her. "You going to make us? We're just making sure everyone's interests are being protected." His hand crept toward a holster at his side. "Though if you have issues with that..."

He stopped talking as I shifted my feet behind Deadeye. A warm swell of energy filled my palm, and I turned it upward to show him a plasma ball ready to launch. "Don't," I ordered. My voice sounded deeper than usual when distorted through my helmet filters, and it was gratifying to see his bronze skin turn a shade lighter. "You heard her. Walk. Away."

"Okay, okay! Geez!" He stepped back. The others followed suit, though I noticed some glancing at the spot where I'd initially noticed the lightning wielder. As they retreated to the stoop of a building across the street, I cast my awareness wider. The feeling of ozone that marked her presence was gone, but so was any hint of electricity from the downed lines. Which reminded me...

Bandit, be advised that the downed electrical lines are no longer live, I said through the mind bridge. *I think the Shattered took care of them for us.* I turned to face the burning building as two Medical Corps paramedics rushed past with a gurney, pushing through the crowd surrounding Tara and the injured man.

Is she still here? Bandit asked, caution sparking in his voice.

No, she scampered. I closed my eyes and envisioned the area as if seen through a satellite map, Deadeye stepping closer to steady me. Fire roiled from the western side of the building, and now I could hear a high whistling noise that reminded me of the times when Deadeye left the teakettle running. *She's gone, and the other active Blood Angels are keeping their distances. I think they're afraid of what we'll—* the teakettle whistling built to a shriek—"TARA, SHIELD!"

From inside the bridge, I felt her obey immediately. And not a moment too soon. A thunderous shockwave went through my chest, and my vision flared white as frantic red warnings flashed into my heads-up display. "Again?" I shouted—mostly to Deadeye, but I'd take any answer. "What happened?"

"Propane tanks!" a firefighter yelled. "The pressure releases must've broken." His helmet angled toward the fire, then at me, and I caught a thread of consideration before he said, "All this water's just sliding off the sheet metal; we can't get it down into the building to cool things off. Are you able to help break it up?"

I paused on that. "We can't move stuff, but—hey, Tara?"

"What?"

"The firefighters need help moving roofing sections so the water can get to the fire." The memory Caleb had shared a few days ago sprang to mind, and I projected the image of a building falling apart into the bridge. *Can you do something like this? Do you have enough juice?*

I'll help, Caleb said. The thought of a roof collapsing had sent his fear skyrocketing for a moment, but all I could sense now was determination. *If we take it slow, it'll be fine.*

Let's try. Tara stepped away from the paramedics to take his hand. She squared her shoulders and faced the burning building, blue streaks shooting down her legs and into the ground. A second later, cyan light illuminated the inside of the smoke cloud, and a crash sounded within.

"You'd better help them," Deadeye said aloud. "You can't do much from here."

"You'll be okay with—" I glanced at the stoop where the Blood Angels had retreated to.

"I'll be fine. Just let them try something." Deadeye slapped my shoulder. "Go! We need to get things under control, or we'll end up looking even stupider than them."

I jogged to join Tara and Caleb, conscious as I did that people were now moving out of my way, rather than obstructing my path. Another sheet of metal shivered and broke in two, falling in a shower of sparks as Tara took a deep breath.

"It's working, but it's slow," she said. "It'd be so much easier if we could move the pieces, but this is the best I can do."

I frowned at the building. The piece she'd broken was tipping on a pile of debris, and I focused on expanding a shield immediately below it. With a grinding screech that was quickly lost in the roar of flames, the metal sheet tipped, slid, and settled far below the tangle of steel that had once been part of the factory roof. A stream of water immediately filled the vacated space, and the smoke turned whitish as the temperature lowered.

"That'll do it," Caleb said. I couldn't see past his helmet visor, but the threads of blue lacing his and Tara's fingers proved that he was amplifying her power. "If you can lift them enough with a shield for her to break them, we might be able to do something."

Pace yourselves, Bandit cut in. I hadn't realized he was listening through the mind bridge, but he'd turned from a conversation with the newly arrived police to stare pointedly in our direction. *This is going to take a while to get under control.*

I DID my best to listen to Bandit, but the next hour dragged on and on as Tara and I used her destructive subtype, shields, and small-scale vortexes to break apart the debris enough for the firefighters' hoses to have an effect. After forty-five minutes, I had to let the mind bridge go.

Sorry. I blinked against the pain in my right eye that heralded impending burnout. *I can keep doing this or keep comms, but not both.*

It's fine, Bandit said tersely. *We survived without comms in the past; we'll be okay now.*

Another fifteen minutes and two mini vortexes later, the pain had lanced through my eye and deep into my head. We'd moved closer to the building, firefighters and residents of the barrio combining forces to try to smother the flames by any means. I thought we were done for when something flared up with a gout of brand-new flames. Before I had time to shield, a smaller piece of sheet metal rose into the air, flipped on the short axis, and dropped onto the newborn fire, snuffing it with an extinguishing *whumph.*

"Thanks!" Tara gasped.

"Wasn't me." I'd been crouched, trying to recover some energy. Now I turned to scan the slowly diminishing crowd, and a fading trace of blue caught my eye. "Him!"

The man I'd pointed out gave a sheepish sigh and approached, pulling off sunglasses to reveal eyes that—based off his bronze complexion—had once been dark brown, but were now as bright cyan as my own. He was easily a decade older than Bandit, thickset, with skin weathered from years in the sun. "Sorry," he said in Spanish. "I didn't want to get in your way. And given where my loyalty's stood all these months, I didn't think you'd want me here."

"Don't be so sure," Bandit said. "They're wearing themselves out; we could use any help you want to offer."

The old guy shrugged agreement. "I'll do my best." He nodded to me. "You pulled my nephew out of there. It's the least I can do."

He stepped back from Bandit and unbuttoned the cuffs on his worn-out denim shirt. The lines framing his eyes deepened, and his face tightened with concentration as he extended both hands in the direction of the building. Blue light shimmered down his forearms and streaked to form pools under a toppled I-beam. The metal moved with a grating sound and came to rest on the floor, empty space immediately filling with steam as the firefighters hit it with a water stream. I let out a relieved sigh, my shoulders relaxing with the realization that Tara and I might not have to dismantle the entire building by ourselves.

Bandit gave a surprised grunt of his own. "Telekinetic?"

"I guess," the man said. "Things move where I want them to move."

"Huh. The gang never recruited you?"

The man laughed at that. "They didn't know." He cast a sideways glance at the empty stoop where the Blood Angels had been sulking. "I've only had it for a year, but when you work construction your whole life, you learn to use whatever tools you have available."

Bandit passed me a water bottle before continuing his conversation with the new Shattered. It was apparent by now that the factory—a refinery for jojoba seed oil—had served enough Blood Angel interests that most of the staff had familial or social connections with the gang. I only hoped enough of their associates had witnessed the incident and our response to it to get their stories straight when they went home.

After another hour, my water bottle was empty and my power almost gone. Many of the bystanders had dispersed, though a few still milled around in a busybody sort of way. The firefighters were picking through the smoking rubble for hot spots, and I was sitting on the bumper of the fire engine when a disturbing rumble caught the edge of my diminished senses.

A gasoline-powered engine. The feel of red-tinged ghetto Spanish. *Blood Angels.*

My heart sank, but there was no helping the facts. *We just embarrassed them by fixing a problem they couldn't solve themselves. There's no way they'd let us get away without some show of force.*

I'd taken off my helmet, so the warning had to come in an undignified shout. "Sir! Contact! Gas-powered truck on our nine!"

I had time to see Bandit's head swivel and his hand go to his holster before the truck screeched into sight. I was halfway to the others when a handful of men piled out. No posturing this time; they'd drawn their weapons and had them trained on us before I could take another step.

My eyes flicked between gang leaders, first responders,

my friends, and the wrecked building. Even without them having the drop on us, this could go so, so badly.

I have to do something. Images of death streaked through my mind, and I fought against a rising wave of futile panic. *This will all be pointless if we're forced to fight here; I have to do something!*

Power traced the Blood Angels' anger and frustration in a glowing spiderweb of emotion. There was no time to think, no time to consider if I had the reserve *or* the knowledge to do what needed to be done.

My hands shot out, twisting in the air as I pictured myself grabbing all the threads and holding them tight, sealing everything with a single word.

FREEZE.

For a heartbeat, nothing happened. Then, muscles locked, hands froze on triggers, and the Blood Angels stopped in their tracks as their bodies betrayed them—caught in the grasp of Shattered power guided by iron resolve.

The world around me dulled, everything shrinking to a silent battle of wills between me and the handful of armed men. I staggered for a moment, then dropped to a knee and one hand on the asphalt. For a moment, I thought I'd lose control, that the bullets would fly and more deaths would reverberate through the already shell-shocked barrio. Then, the world stilled, and I held the twisting threads secure.

"I can't hold them forever," I warned Tara as she and Caleb ran to me. A drop of blood hit the ground as I raised my head, and I lifted a trembling hand to my face. When had my nose started bleeding? "They're fighting it, and I don't know how long I can last."

"I didn't even think you *could* do this," Tara commented. My vision was going foggy, every bit of concentration focused on the Blood Angels as she reassured me, "We'll help you; just don't let go."

Over the next few minutes, the police managed to disarm and cuff all but one of the Blood Angels—men I now recognized as leadership in the gang hierarchy. I gratefully released my hold to allow the police to walk their captives to the cruisers, relief catching at my heart. *Maybe this time, nobody has to die.*

Then, a horrible tearing pain ripped through my nerves. I screamed with pain as the man who I'd intimidated on Deadeye's behalf jerked free of my power's grasp. His grip tightened on his gun, and he spun to point the weapon straight at me.

My every muscle tightened, and the breath caught in my lungs.

A single shot rang out.

At the edge of the crowd, a short, wiry guy with a red bandana around his upper arm lowered his handgun as the Blood Angel slid to the ground.

I bit back another cry as the sudden death made me double over. Tara was instantly at my side. "Is that..."

"That's Santana," Caleb said grimly, getting an arm around my torso to keep me upright. "And he's making an entrance in style."

Bandit pushed through the crowd, his long stride taking him past us to Santana. I blinked through a growing fog, nausea and dizziness making my head spin as the two men stopped to face each other at the edge of the debris field.

"Took you long enough," Bandit said. Despite his even tone, every word rang out over the hushed crowd. "I wouldn't have waited."

"I'm not you." Santana holstered the gun, but the rest of

his posture barely changed. "And thank God I'm not; your people are crazy. Only the certifiably insane would run into a burning building to save their enemies, then refuse to retaliate when their own lives were in danger." His piercing gaze swept over all of us, lingering for a moment on me. Respect stirred behind his eyes, and he held out his hand to Bandit. "I can get behind something like that."

I didn't hear the rest of their conversation. Shudders ran through my limbs, and before I had the chance to warn anyone, I'd fainted into Tara's arms.

STAGE TWELVE

Station Somewhere
Santa Cruz Valley
May 1

IT WAS A WHIRLWIND WEEKEND. According to Benny— and heaven only knew how *he'd* found out—the fracas that ensued after the factory fire left several more Blood Angel hotheads dead, a community leader shot, and Santana in control of what remained of the gang once the rest of their leadership had fled or been imprisoned.

Methodology aside, his pull with the fractured gang—old guard and teenagers alike—was undeniable. He took up residence on the south side of the city, adamantly refusing our offers of supplies and insisting he'd be fine. "I said I'd help you. I didn't say I'd take your help."

A few days later, Deadeye and I were working on the truck with the bay door open when a car approached the station. I'd been lying on the floor and noticed the vehicle coming from a distance away, but hadn't thought anything of it until the noise registered in my ears.

"Gasoline engine," I muttered as I slid from under the truck. "Deadeye?"

She didn't pull her head out of the side compartment. "What?"

I laid a hand on her back and transmitted the memory of what I'd heard. *Car outside. A gas-powered one.*

A muffled curse came from the compartment, and Deadeye squirmed out. She dropped a pair of wire clamps in the toolbox and ordered, "Get the others."

I obeyed immediately, glad that my suspicion was shared. The door between bay and living room swung in my wake as I burst through it, and Bandit looked up in surprise from the reports he'd been compiling on the table.

"What's going on, *mijo?*"

I explained over my shoulder as I crossed the hall toward the medical bay. Within a minute, all of us were outside, waiting with varied degrees of unease as a young man assisted an elderly woman out of the back seat of the vehicle.

I swallowed hard at the sight of a woman on the shorter, plumper side, carrying a cardboard shoebox. Though there wasn't much similarity in her face, the physique and demeanor reminded me enough of my *abuela* that a stab of loss went through my heart. She came directly up the driveway, stopping a few feet away as Bandit said in English, "Ma'am, please don't come any closer. Can we help you?"

"So suspicious," she said, bright black eyes flicking between him and the rest of us. "Is that how your mother raised you to treat your elders?"

I couldn't help snickering at Bandit's offended stammer. "Well, no, but—"

"Easy, *mijo*," she said. "I'm not here to hurt you. I just wanted to come and say thank you—to all of you." She looked past him, and I knew I wasn't imagining her stare lingering on me. "For so many months, I've prayed for peace to be restored, and your courage and willingness to compromise have finally seen it done." Amusement touched her voice. "I'd never have expected it of you, Carlos."

Bandit's eyes narrowed, and I caught a jolt of recognition before he hoarsely said, "Tía Gloria?"

"Oh, you *do* recognize me! I didn't think you would after all these years." She beamed and reached up to pat his shoulder. "Santana always talked about you, and not often good things! I'm glad you boys managed to work things out between you. And you, my dear!" She turned to Josephine, passing her the shoebox with a kiss on the cheek. "You've grown so beautiful! Your brother was never this good looking."

Laughter flickered from Tara as Josephine's face turned pink. Some of the tension in my shoulders relaxed as the woman addressed the rest of us. "If you're available, I'd like to have you all come to dinner this weekend. I haven't had a party in so long, and I'd like to express my thanks properly." She gave us an amused smile as we all looked at each other in panic. "Oh, don't worry; you don't have to say yes now. I'll send someone on Thursday to find out how many to expect. Just think about it!"

With that, she turned back to the car, accepting her driver's help into the passenger seat. The kid slammed the door and hurried to the other side of the car with a surly look at all of us. Given the edge of a red bandana sneaking out from under his T-shirt sleeve, I understood why.

"See you Saturday!" Tía Gloria—I'd decided to give her

the honorific until I learned why she had left Bandit and Josephine so flustered—waved cheerily from the window as they pulled away, leaving all of us in a befuddled cluster on the driveway.

Tara's laugh carried relief as well as mirth. "Well that went—well." She elbowed Bandit as we began heading inside. "Why'd she have you in such a sweat?"

"Yeah…" I pushed open the living room door. "Who *was* that?"

Bandit dropped into his chair. His words came out stiff as he said, "Tía Gloria is the closest thing any of the old-school gangbangers had to a matriarch. She's Santana's aunt —well, she's not really his aunt, but she practically raised him—and everyone else just naturally called her 'Tía' as well."

Josephine wrapped her arms around his shoulders, leaning her chin against his head. "Back in the day, her home was neutral turf; even more sacred than a church. If you needed a place to lay low, medical attention, a square meal, that's where you went."

Deadeye whistled. "Gang matriarch." She flopped onto the couch. "And she's asking us to dinner? Why?" Suspicion made her good eye narrow, and she sat up halfway. "What's she playing at?"

Bandit shook his head incredulously. "I don't know."

Caleb opened the shoebox and peered inside. "Well, I'm no judge, but all I got from her was 'tamales and warm hugs.'" He raised an eyebrow in my direction. "Gabe?"

I joined him at the other end of the table. The box was filled with *pan dulce* in all different shapes and sizes— including some I'd thought were doomed to stay childhood memories. I picked up a *cochito* and took a bite, speaking around a mouthful of molasses and spices. "I think she was telling the truth. The only hostility was from her driver, and he's a Blood Angel. Makes sense for him not to trust us, but *she* was on the level."

The others stared at me for a long moment as I took another bite.

"So, you trust her?" Caleb asked.

"I'm eating the food she gave us, aren't I?"

Deadeye got up to inspect the pastries, picking one and taking an experimental bite. She made a surprised, pleased noise as Tara said, "So, she's inviting us to dinner. What happens if we say no?"

Both Bandit and Josephine stiffened and shook their heads. "Uh-uh," Josephine said. "Not only is it rude, but it could undo whatever progress we've made."

"Santana might've gotten rid of the ones who only had bloodshed on their minds, but that's a long way from actual peace," Bandit said. "Tía Gloria commands a higher level of respect. There was no way she'd have helped us without Santana's approval, but now that he likes us, she's either our biggest asset or greatest enemy."

"He's right," I said through a mouthful of food. "Trust me, I grew up around women like her. Matriarchs rule their clans, no matter what side of the law they run on. If she wanted to, she could turn every Blood Angel and half the barrios against us." I swallowed the pastry and did my best to sound confident in the face of yet another unknown. "Like it or not, we can't risk offending her."

"Great." Deadeye leaned against the counter. "So, what are we wearing?"

———

"BANDIT, we're going to have to go inside at some point." Tara shot me an amused look before speaking again into her comm set. "If anyone's watching us—"

"They are," I said, looking out the passenger side window. The house we'd been given directions to wasn't far from Station Somewhere, in a neighborhood where water ran close to the surface. It sat several hundred feet from the road, a graceful adobe building screened by layers of old-growth mesquite trees. *Luminaria* lined the twisting drive-way, the lack of flickering inside the paper bags an indication of battery-powered lights instead of proper flames.

"Well, they'll know by now that we're sitting outside, too scared to go in." Tara raised an eyebrow, even though Bandit was in the passenger compartment and unable to see her. "Somehow, I don't think that's the image we need to present."

Bandit's response was halfway between a growl and a sigh. "All right, all right! Let's go, everyone."

The truck vibrated slightly as the back hatch opened, and Caleb's face appeared in Tara's window. "Ready?"

Tara pulled her comm set out of her ear and dropped it into the console between our seats. "Let's get this party started."

I dropped my own comms and clambered from the truck, falling in step beside Caleb and Tara as they followed the others toward the house. I hadn't realized how used to our uniforms I'd gotten—the waistband of my new jeans rode differently against my stomach than my cargo pants did, and I had to stop myself from tugging at it.

Beside me, Tara smoothed the fluttering edges of her

blouse over her hips. "I don't like this," she muttered, quiet enough for just Caleb and I to hear.

"Me neither," he agreed from the other side of her, his eyes hard against the steadiness of his voice.

"I don't like it either. But at least it's pretty." I pointed up as we walked under the arching limbs of an ancient tree. Tiny lights twinkled in the branches. "Not many other places we've fought in have had mood lighting."

Tara cast a glance up, and her expression softened as she reached to take Caleb's hand. "It's been a long time since we've gotten a date," she told him. "I guess this is the closest we're going to get to one, huh?"

"I guess so." A cautious smile spread over Caleb's face as Bandit and Josephine stopped on the porch ahead of us. He bent to kiss Tara's temple. "Might as well try to enjoy it."

I'd expected a Blood Angel to meet us with a weapon in their hand. Instead, the magenta-painted door swung open and Tía Gloria greeted Bandit with a squealed, "You came! I didn't know what to think when Octavio said how suspicious you'd been."

"I talked them into it," Josephine said with a smile, returning Tía Gloria's affectionate hug and adding, "Thank you so much for the invitation...it's a treat to have an evening off from cooking."

Tía Gloria laughed and beckoned us inside. "Come in, come in! Make yourselves at home."

The entryway was low-ceilinged, sunken a step below the rest of the floor and illuminated with lamps in the corners. Beyond, I could feel a corridor leading to the back-yard, another leading to a kitchen filled with steam, and movement as staff—or family members—went between the two. The others followed Tía Gloria down the hall, not real-izing that they'd left me to trail behind.

I took a step forward to catch up and stopped, stunned.

I'd expected Blood Angels to be here, and they were. No surprise there. Over a dozen presences were marked in reddish light by my power, both inside the house and in the yard. What surprised me was the familiarity of one person in particular.

Ozone.

Lightning.

Fire and fury and piercing helplessness—coming toward me?

I barely had time to register the Shattered's approach before a girl with curly blonde hair and suntanned skin hurried around the corner. She stopped short as soon as she saw me. Recognition sparked in her eyes, even as both of us froze.

"You." My voice hushed. "I know you."

The girl's hand closed into a fist, and a fragment of elec-tricity darted between her fingertips. "No you don't." Her voice came out with a hard edge. "No one does. Now get out of my way."

I realized I was still standing in the entryway, effectively blocking the door. Too surprised to do more than stare, I took a step to the side, a jolt of electricity catching my shoulder amid a waft of a citrusy smell as the Shattered shoved past me and out the door.

She's my age. I tracked the girl's presence across the front yard, her pace increasing until my power coolly informed me that she was running into the darkened city. *I knew she was young, but I didn't think she was my age.* I shivered, skin tingling with residual electricity. *How long has she been fighting?*

"Gabriel!" Tara's voice floated down the hallway. A moment later she appeared, eyes wide with concern. "I thought you were right behind us."

"Coming." I shook off my surprise and followed Tara to a wide patio strung with fairy lights and filled with tension.

Bandit and Josephine were talking with Santana in the center of the patio, Deadeye and Caleb standing a few paces away and eyeing the dozen or so Blood Angels—both old guard and newcomers—who'd taken up positions behind their newly appointed leader. If it hadn't been for the aromas of freshly steamed tamales, I'd have assumed this was a hostage negotiation instead of a casual dinner gathering.

I slowed my steps as I approached and quickly swept my power through the area surrounding the house, just to be safe. As I did, someone dropped a dish—or something—in the kitchen, and I couldn't help but jump at the breaking-glass noise. A flash of blue went across my vision. With a sickening feeling, I realized my eyes had reacted to my surprise and were now almost certainly glowing. *Dammit.*

One of the Blood Angels started back, reaching for what I assumed was a holster hidden in his waistband. "Boss, look out!"

Santana's head snapped up, his eyes piercing mine. The other Blood Angels' exclamations were lost in Bandit's deep voice asking, "Gabriel?"

I held my open hands out in front of me. "I promise, sir, it's nothing. The noise just—" I nodded toward the kitchen, face warming with embarrassment. I could practically hear the snickers now...*stupid kid, jumping at nothing*. My shoulders slumped and I looked at the ground. "It's nothing, sir."

Bandit frowned. "Take a seat, *mijo.*"

I let my hands fall, the urge to apologize too strong to keep quiet. "Bandit—"

"You heard him." The speaker was a broad-shouldered man with a tattoo crawling up his neck. "Sit down, freak."

"Hey!" Bandit's and Tara's voices sounded in unison, and urgency spiked from Caleb.

"You're one to talk about freaks," Tara snapped. "We're not the ones who spent months trying to take over the valley with monsters doing our dirty work."

"No, you just twitch your fingers at something, and it explodes." The man spat in her direction. "You're not just a freak, you're a killer!"

"Speaks the man who happily pulled the trigger any time he was ordered to," Santana said without turning his head. "No matter who was at the receiving end. Remind me why I let you come, again?"

I think I know why the other Shattered left... I thought. If that's how this group feels about Shattereds, she wouldn't be safe here.

"He's telling the truth. The EDF's full of killers, and some of them *are* freaks." A younger man hadn't stopped eyeing me from the moment I'd walked onto the porch. "That one killed my brother."

My breath caught with a stab of pain as the Blood Angel's loss and grief—magnified over sleepless nights and twisted by guilt—slammed through my chest. An image of a kid with bronze skin lurched to the forefront of my mind, my memories superimposing blood over his face like the last time I'd seen him, dead by my hand at the police station.

"He was only sixteen." The man's dark eyes flashed with

unshed tears, face turning red. "And you left him in the dirt with a hole right through his head!"

He shoved past the others, reaching for his hip, as Bandit threw an arm in front of me and a shield winked into place around Tara and Caleb. In my periphery, Deadeye's hand had also gone to her waistband—though where she'd hidden a weapon, I had no idea. Power coupled with despair surged through my veins, my heart rebelling even as I began searching for the best attack strategy.

WHACK!

The sound of a sandal hitting flesh resounded through the yard.

All of us—Blood Angels and squad alike—stood in stunned silence as Tía Gloria drew herself to her full height and demanded in Spanish, "What is this you've brought into my house?" She shook the sandal in the face of the man who'd accused me. "You've spent your whole life chasing violence, and *now* you'll cry when your brother follows your footsteps and suffers the consequences? You have more blood on your hands than he ever did, but he paid for your mistakes!"

"Tía—" Santana began, taking a half step forward before she pointed the sandal in his direction.

"No! Not in my house." She swept her gaze over the entire group, eyes flickering to each person before she announced, "You're carrying a gun, and so are you! You know the rules!"

The Blood Angels she'd singled out looked uneasily away as Tía Gloria turned a fierce gaze on Bandit. "You as well. Get rid of them, all of you. And you!" She pursed her lips, clearly unintimidated by the glowing blue bubble surrounding Caleb and Tara. "No Shattered powers at my table." The sandal made a slapping sound as she dropped it to the patio floor. "You're here tonight to eat together and *listen* to each other. Settling your differences with violence will not happen here." Her strength swept over me as she stamped her foot back into her shoe. "Not in my house."

Santana turned to face his men. "You heard her." His voice filled with as much adamance as Tía Gloria's. "Get rid of them. Now."

They started dispersing, some with sheepish looks and others with dark muttering, as Santana turned to Bandit with a half-smile. "Maybe we should have a seat."

Bandit's hand finally went away from his hip, and the slant of his shoulders relaxed. "Sounds good to me. I need to put something in the truck first, though." He gave a stern look to Deadeye, who rolled her eyes. "You too."

"Um, sir?" I held up my wrist as he passed, tapping my shirt sleeve over the monitor cuff with a questioning look. "Do you want..."

Bandit's brow furrowed, and he shook his head. "They're on edge as it is," he murmured. "Let's not remind them of the other things you're able to do." He touched my arm and gently guided it downwards. "I think Gloria broke the tension for us. Let's wait and see how things go."

Old Fort Lowell
Santa Cruz Valley
May 5

I HADN'T THOUGHT I'd be able to eat much, not after the welcome we'd received from our dining partners. I'd also expected Bandit to have me sit with Deadeye like we'd previously discussed, to make sure she would have someone close by who spoke Spanish. Instead, he surprised me by pulling Deadeye aside and changing our planned seating so that I'd be closer to him.

He's not Papa, I told myself as Tía Gloria's helpers brought out pans of tamales and bowls of beans, rice, and salsa. *He'd probably be upset if I even thought of him that way, after losing his own son.* Still, the warm feeling of being wanted, even chosen, stayed as we began eating. Josephine and Tía Gloria were doing an admirable job keeping conversation going at their table while Bandit and Santana reminisced about the "bad old days."

I wished I'd been able to bring my notebook or voice recorder along. The world of their generation was so distant from my experiences, but they talked about it like it had only been a few months ago. *It's a pity that me recording the conversation wouldn't go over well.*

I was halfway through my food before I realized there was more to Santana's nonchalance than met the eye. He was nervous, but not in the sense of someone who was about to throw a grenade or pull a gun. Keeping my eyes on the table, I let my senses expand as much as I dared, checking first the back yard, then the surrounding area for any threats.

Nothing out there that shouldn't be. I focused on the Blood Angels in and around the house. *And nothing there either beyond the usual cynicism and distrust.* Finally, I zeroed in on Santana. There it was again; nervousness, anger, even fear of something—or someone—that I couldn't pinpoint. *He's hiding something. I thought this evening was to bury the hatchet between us, but maybe there's something else going on.*

Taking a deep breath, I considered my options for alerting the others. Caleb and Tara were at the other end of the long table, having what I considered a passably normal conversation with two of Santana's lieutenants. Josephine and Tía Gloria were laughing over something. As Bandit and Santana began comparing notes on a conflict we'd fought against the Blood Angels earlier in the year, I made up my mind.

Unbuttoning my sleeve, I carefully slid it up far enough to expose the screen on my monitor. I'd practiced enough with the controls that it was the work of a breath to select a name from the list and drop straight into the head of the squad member I'd selected. Lines of code spiraled around me, humming through my mind before—

Gabe? Deadeye stiffened across the patio before hurriedly composing her sharp features. *What's wrong?*

Were you writing software in your head? I thought over the code I'd seen—or maybe heard. *Is that what you do when you're bored?*

Shut up, Gabe. It was always odd hearing her thoughts without an accent. *I can't speak a word of Spanish, and these guys know it. What else am I supposed to do?*

I quickly explained what I'd felt from Santana, finishing with, *And I think something else happened, or is about to happen, and he's not sure how to tell Bandit about it. If I had to guess, I'd say he's going to ask us for a favor. It would explain why he and Tía Gloria called us here.*

Interesting. I'll see if I can figure anything out. She gave me a thin smile with a razor's edge in it. *And if I can't, I'll ask.*

Reassured now, I nodded my agreement and terminated the link. Bandit hadn't noticed me fiddling with my shirt cuff, and I was able to safely return to eavesdropping. Even though we weren't on the verge of a firefight anymore, the atmosphere was still tense at the other tables. As soon as the meal was over, the brother of the kid I'd killed approached Santana with the request to wait by their vehicles.

"We did what you asked, okay?" The man gave me a chilling look before turning his attention to his leader. "Take as long as you need to, but we'll be out by the truck." He cast another hostile glance toward me. "And we'll watch your back."

Santana waved tiredly at his men as a handful—almost half of whom he'd brought with him—retreated. "Thanks."

He rubbed his forehead with a sigh as the gate closed behind them. "And to think, those were the ones I thought would benefit *most* from meeting you face-to-face. Guess I was wrong."

"It opened the door a little further," Bandit said. He looked up as the others came to join us at the central table, along with the Blood Angel lieutenants who'd been talking with Caleb and Tara. "Sorry they didn't stick around, Tía."

Gloria took a vacated seat near the kitchen door. "This evening was to break the ice between you." She eyed the gate through which the disgruntled gang members had departed. "And to weed out the ones that can't learn to work with others."

Deadeye nodded her approval as she sat beside Josephine. "That's the best thing I've heard all night." She leaned an elbow on the table and addressed Santana, "But there's something else going on, too. Isn't there?" She gave a deferential nod to Tía Gloria. "Thank you for opening your home. We all greatly appreciate it. But what's going on here?"

Santana raised an eyebrow first at Deadeye, then at me. He gave a short, bitter laugh. "You've been reading my mail, kid."

"Oh, don't flatter him too much," Tara said from her seat at the end of the table. "He's talented and all, but nobody with your type of influence would call us here just to make nice." She drummed her fingers on the tabletop. "You need us for something, which means things are going wrong."

"She's right," I said as Santana turned his attention to me. "You weren't bothered by the possibility of us getting into a fight, so it's not that. And the longer you've talked, the more nervous you've gotten." I tried to emulate Bandit's tone from a time when he'd chastised Judge for being too squirrely while on mission. "There's something you're not telling us that has you worried." I narrowed my senses, certain now of what I'd been feeling. "And you feel threatened, but not by us."

He laughed. "That's crazy, how you do that. But you're right. There *is* some stuff going down, but it's all tied together and I'm not sure how to explain without just putting it all out there."

"In that case, I'd recommend just putting it out there," Bandit said. "If something's going on, we need to know. What's wrong?"

Santana sighed with resignation. "I found out some stuff today—new stuff. Or maybe it's old stuff, and I'm behind on getting the whole picture." His face had gone drawn with worry, the dark areas beneath his eyes now more pronounced. "You ever heard of anything called the 'Vanguard Project'?"

I shook my head, the movement mimicked by the others around the table. Only Deadeye nodded. "A project Regional was working on had a name like that. Does this have something to do with the lab we trashed last year?"

Santana gave her a measuring look. "You knew it was more than a cloning facility?"

"Sort of," I said, sitting up straighter in my chair. "We found out about the research into Shattered abilities a while ago. We've been continuing some of it on our own, with help from the university. Do you—"

He held up a hand. I sat back and shut my mouth as he said, "I don't know much about that. The data I came across today is encrypted, and the only ones with the key are in the wind."

Deadeye chuckled. "I'll say it's encrypted, 'specially if it's from that facility. I dropped a data bomb into the system when we attacked, and when I scramble something, it stays scrambled."

"I'll take your word for it. What's bothering me is the stuff I *could* read, which spelled out where the information came from and how my predecessors got it." Santana halted, staring at the table until a rapid admonition in Spanish from Tía Gloria made him look Bandit in the eye. "You told me that your superiors gave the order to abandon this region because of the conflict with us, but that's not exactly true. Regional Command *agreed* to leave in exchange for us staying confined to the Santa Cruz Valley. And they knew about the cloning setup, but were content to let us keep it if we let them have access to the other labs in the facility."

A hush had settled over the table.

"I knew it," Deadeye muttered. "Didn't I say I wouldn't put it past them?"

"They told us it was because they couldn't keep wasting resources in a losing battle," Josephine said softly. "They knew what would happen to civilians if they left, and they still agreed to this? For the sake of research?"

"The filthy little vipers," Tara spat. "Accepting a loss is one thing, but *collaborating?*"

"They knew about that lab all along—that's why they sent troops after us so quickly when we trashed it." Bandit's voice stayed level, but I could feel the anger twisting through his emotions. "And now that research is in the hands of scientists who answer to no one."

"That we know of," I said, a sense of dread yawning in my stomach. "What if those guys *didn't* go rogue? What if they just went underground before someone higher up got wind of what they were doing?"

"It would make sense if someone was trying for a power grab." Bandit rubbed his chin. "It bothered me last year that Central Command didn't intervene after we lost Judge, but now I wonder if they never knew in the first place."

"Exactly," Santana said. "That's what I'm worried about. The name I said earlier—the Vanguard Project—it's a code name for a group that's setting up shop in the city." He sighed. "They don't claim any affiliation with the EDF, but there's Defense Force fingerprints all over them. From what it sounds like, this group came to an agreement with my predecessors, to the tune of 'stay out of our way and we'll stay out of yours.'" His face twisted with frustration. "It's like this whole region is destined to become their own private testing ground."

Bandit buried his face in his palm with a groan. "I'll bet that's why no one's noticed the solar grid being neglected, or the water treatment plants failing, or the supplies no longer making it in. Regional—or *whoever* is behind this—is trying to cover their tracks by wiping the city off the map."

"Oh, don't get me wrong; I didn't mind the fighting. Conflict is in this region's DNA—has been for decades. But there were some things you didn't do." Santana tapped the table for emphasis. "You didn't put your people in harm's way unnecessarily. You held a healthy respect for your adversaries. You didn't sacrifice the long-term for short-term gains. Those guys who *were* in charge around here—" He swore. "They brought this whole thing down on us by making deals with the devil. And my guess is they're going to run straight to their friends in the Vanguard Project, now that I've stirred them up."

"...And you want us to help track them down. That's why you called us here, isn't it?" Bandit glanced at me as he said it, and I gave a quick nod.

"Well, yeah," Santana admitted. "I stuck my neck out by getting involved, and I don't *ever* do things for free. Until this morning, I'd planned on asking you to help me deal with the last few bad apples and calling it good between us once you did. You'd go your way, I'd go mine, and we'd see each other on a battlefield someday. But now—" He leaned back in his chair with a halfhearted laugh. "I assumed that I'd flip the rug and send a few roaches flying. Instead, I found a rattler coiled under the mat."

"Sucks, doesn't it?" Bandit said with a chuckle. "Be careful; you'll end up a public servant with the way you're going."

"When hell freezes over, El Bandito." Santana shrugged. "But I don't mind working with you for a while. It's better for everyone if we can get this place back on the radar."

"And what do your guys say?" Deadeye asked, sweeping a piercing look around the table. "We were fighting tooth and nail last year; you ready to give this a chance?"

"Most of us weren't happy with the EDF presence, but we didn't mind y'all," one of Santana's lieutenants commented. "You treated us like people, even when we didn't give you a choice except to keep fighting." He nodded at the other Blood Angels who'd stayed to talk. "Some of us deserted once we realized there could be bigger problems to worry about, but you never had that chance."

"We did, and we took it," Bandit said. His presence hummed in my Shattered sense with something alert and calculating, the same assuredness that made him a reliable commander. "And it's what got us here." He leveled his attention at Santana. "Where are your 'cockroaches' now?"

By the look on Santana's face, he didn't know and it was bothering him more than he wanted to let on. I was on the verge of saying it, just to prove that I could, when he admitted, "We can't find them, *or* the Vanguard Project." He tilted his head to concede, "I have some leads that I'm working on, but it's going to be difficult to flush them out. This city's full of places to hide. That's where I'd hoped you'd come in."

To my surprise, the last part had been directed at Deadeye. She raised an eyebrow and laughed. "Me?"

"Yeah, you. Between you and him"—he stabbed a finger in my direction—"we're miles better off when it comes to finding people who don't want to be found. And as for the rest of you...you're much better trained and equipped to deal with this kind of operation than we are."

"And don't forget it," Tara said.

I turned to look at her and Caleb as they sat at the end of the table. Caleb hadn't said a single thing during this whole discussion, and the expression on his face was guarded enough that I knew something was bothering him deep inside.

I made a mental note to check on him later, as Tara continued, "You're a force to be reckoned with, and God knows we've tangled enough times to know each other's strengths. But this type of thing is exactly how we've spent most of the last decade."

"She's right," Bandit said. "And I'll add this: if we do this, we're doing it by the book. I know, I know." He held up a hand as a few people—including Deadeye—made irritated sounds. "We're not affiliated with the EDF anymore, and maybe we don't want to be at this point. But these last few months have seen us walk closer and closer to a line that I don't want to cross."

To my surprise, several of the Blood Angels were nodding as Bandit continued, "We're trying to restore order in this region, and we're never going to do that if we become as ruthless as the guys we're trying to take out." He nodded at Santana. "We'll help you. Let's just pray that we're not about to walk into something worse than any of us expected."

"No kidding," Santana said. "You and your squad have 'liability' stamped all over you." His gaze shifted to me, and I had the unsettling feeling that a warning lay behind his words. "If someone affiliated with your side *is* trying to squash this region, I'm certain they'll waste no time in removing that liability once and for all."

AFTER THE ROCKY start to dinner, and the unsettling revelations of the following conversation, we returned to Station Somewhere with silence rattling through the truck. Things were never completely quiet as everyone's emotions filtered through the edges of my mind—Bandit's deep-seated concern, Deadeye's irritation that someone else had gotten their hands on the lost facility data, a sense of betrayal from Josephine, and Tara's renewed frustration toward the EDF. By the time we all got to bed, I had a decent idea of how everyone was feeling about the new threat against us.

All except one.

"You didn't say much in that meeting. It's not like you," I said to Caleb the following day. He and I had lugged a box of saved shell casings out of storage, and were separating the damaged ones from the ones we could still use. "You're usually on top of stuff like that—almost as much as Bandit—

but you didn't say anything. Even when they started planning logistics. What's going on?"

In the safety of the station, Caleb's emotions were less guarded. Wariness, concern, and fear flicked through before he sighed and shook his head. "I know we'd already been warned about the rogue scientists, and we already suspected there was more to the 'retreat' order last October, but it hits differently when the info's coming through someone who's hearing it for the first time." He tossed a dented casing into a box. "And all this has the potential to bring up a lot of things that I wanted to leave buried."

"I'm not sure I—oh." I winced as the implications dropped into my head. "Do you mean the..." I nodded at his augmented arm.

"Yeah." Caleb flexed the fingers of his left hand before closing them into a fist that held a bit of a tremor. "After I got back, plenty of folks were curious about this. They wanted to see if it'd changed me beyond what was obvious, if the exposure meant I was another step closer to Shattering, if... Well, here." He opened his hand and nodded to it. "I'll show you."

"You sure?" I set aside the bowl I'd been sorting through. "If you don't want to..."

"Easier than explaining."

"Okay." I reached across the table to wrap my fingers around his. Almost as soon as I did, a new voice jumped into my head, and I was in Caleb's past.

"Amazing."

I gritted my teeth as a tingle of electricity wove through my skin, my fingers closing around the grip meter of their own volition. The device flashed its reading back to us; almost twice as strong as it had been when they tested my other hand. A cramp ran up my arm, and I had to stifle a groan.

"Can you turn that off? Please?"

"What? Oh." The scientist looked up in surprise, pushing thin-rimmed glasses up his nose. "Sorry, sure."

He disconnected the electrode and my fingers fell slack. "Amazing," he repeated softly. "The things that science can accomplish. If only we knew how they'd done it."

I pulled my sleeve down to completely block his view of the alien circuitry embedded beneath my skin. "Can't say I share your enthusiasm. I saw how they did it, and I don't ever want it to happen again."

"Yes, yes, of course," he said. "But I can't help but wonder"—he looked at me with intensity growing in his mild blue eyes—"if this is possible, what else could be?"

Caleb pulled his hand away, returning both of us to the kitchen table. "I spent a lot of hours in the lab after recovering. It gave me a good chance to get a read on the guys in the research departments—the same ones who I'd guess are heading this 'Vanguard Project' now. There's a super thin line between genius innovator and boundary-pushing lunatic, and now I'm worried that they crossed it a long time ago."

I'd be scared too, I thought. The fine, thin scars that etched Caleb's skin in too many places to count had always been a mute reminder of how seriously to take his concerns. Today, I almost regretted hearing more of their story out loud.

"I understand. And you're right, it makes sense to be worried. You don't have to say anything else; I was just wondering." I plonked another repurposed ammo can on the table before going to the kitchen. Reaching into the cupboard, I took down two coffee mugs before pausing. After a moment's thought, I swapped one of the coffee cups for a glass of orange juice and joined Caleb at the table.

The frown creasing his forehead smoothed as I set the glass at his elbow. "Thanks."

"No problem."

We worked in silence for a while, the plinking of metal on metal a comforting rhythm that helped dispel the heaviness of our earlier conversation. After a bit, Caleb walked past the coffee pot to refill his glass at the sink. As he sat back down, I asked, "Did you always avoid coffee?"

He shook his head with a laugh. "In high school and college, it was practically all I lived on. That and packaged noodles."

"What changed?"

"When you've lived through what I did, you tend to avoid anything that changes how much control you have over your body." He winced. "I tried coffee once after they rescued me. The caffeine sped my heart rate up and caused a panic attack."

"Oh." I looked at the table. "Is that why you refused sedation when you got your bio interface reactivated?"

"Yeah. I mean, it hurt, but at least I knew and could control what was happening." The shell casings rattled as Caleb swept a handful off the table. "It wasn't like that, other times. The xenos used dampener fields to keep prisoners under control—like the ones they had in civilian population centers, but more powerful. I could shake them off sometimes, but most of the time I wasn't even able to move. It was like my brain couldn't tell my body to respond." His brow furrowed. "I've tried to avoid anything like that ever since."

"Sounds horrible," I whispered. *The generator for the Unbreaking Field must've been one like that. No wonder he didn't want Tara anywhere near it.* On our most recent test, we'd managed to deafen my sixth sense down to strong emotions only, but the results had been almost instant nausea and dizziness and we'd immediately halted the test. The mere *concept* of a field so powerful as to render someone physically incapable of moving was enough to make my muscles tense in protest. I shook away the thought and told him, "I know I've said it before, but I'm sorry. That shouldn't have happened to you."

"Yeah." Caleb tossed another handful of metal into the "keep" bin, his movement slowing as he released the casings. "I shouldn't have survived. Others didn't." A thread of black guilt slithered from behind his mental walls, and his gaze dropped to the tabletop. "I just got lucky."

"Or," I said, dropping a casing with a decisive clink, "the thing that kept you alive was there all along, and it's kept you fighting even after getting rescued. Your spirit's stronger than most, and you care about others. That's something that didn't diminish *or* increase because of what happened to you."

"I guess so."

"You said once that you were only in this to protect others from what happened to you," I reminded him. "But all of us, we're with you. If these guys are out to dig up stuff that should've stayed dead, or continue something that never should've begun, I'll go with you to the ends of the earth to make sure they're stopped."

Caleb let out a breath, the sound as much determination as it was gratitude. His fingers curled into a fist, steady this time, as his eyes finally met mine. "Thanks, Gabe."

STAGE FOURTEEN

Station Somewhere
Santa Cruz Valley
May 10

TO MY GROWING CONCERN, finding the former Blood Angel leadership took us longer than we expected. The days that followed saw us spreading out across the valley to follow up on the leads Santana had mentioned, but with little to show for our efforts.

I'd begun to worry that our quarry was gone for good, until a girl with skinny limbs and shifty eyes came one morning to see Josephine. I made myself scarce as Bandit joined them in the bay, but enough of the gist came through their emotions that I went to find the others—Tara in the kitchen, Deadeye in the office going through surveillance data, and Caleb watering the plants.

After a few minutes, I felt the rush of movement as the girl scurried down the street. When Bandit and Josephine turned to come inside, all four of us were crowded around the back bay doors.

"Well?" Tara asked, stepping aside to let Bandit through. "Anything?"

"Something," he said. The springtime sun had climbed halfway into the sky and the trees were casting dappled shadows across a pair of ancient picnic tables. He crossed the yard with long strides and sat on the end of one of the tables. "Not all the younger Blood Angels stayed when Santana took over; plenty took the chance to scatter. That was one of them."

"By the looks of her, she's been living in the open," Josephine said. "There's a camp out in what used to be a park, and she's got friends out there. Well." A shadow crossed her face. "As much of 'friends' as an addict really has."

All of us nodded. Despite how difficult it was to get regular supplies, the number of illicit substances hadn't decreased. "Why'd she come to us?" I asked. The image that had been at the front of Josephine's mind for a split second had been somewhere far south, deep in the area that had once been exclusively Blood Angel turf. "We're way off the beaten path from there."

Josephine picked up the watering can that Caleb had abandoned and began trickling water into the rows of vegetables. "One of her friends recently disappeared; a Shattered who'd just come into his power." She sighed. "She said someone from their old group—another Shattered, it sounded like—came to the camp, and he left with her."

Tara and I exchanged concerned looks.

"The girl with the lightning?" Deadeye asked. At our nods, she swore before adding, "I thought she split when

Santana took over. Didn't you say she left that night at Gloria's?"

I nodded. "I guess she went back to the other side. The leftover leadership who allied with the Vanguard Project. They might've been the ones who'd known her for longer." The memory of our chance meeting at Gloria's hadn't left me alone for days, and something compelled me to add, "I wish there was something we could do to get her to come back."

"Going after someone who doesn't want to be helped isn't going to result in anything but heartbreak," Tara reminded me. "I get why she left. Too many people are unsettled by us, and unsettled people can be dangerous. It's better to be around people who know you, even if they're bad news, than it is to be alone."

"It makes me nervous that they're reaching out to another Shattered," Josephine said. "And a new one at that. Trying to rebuild their forces, maybe?"

"I hadn't thought of that." My knee bounced in an irregular rhythm as I said, "We need to find them before they regroup. And I'll bet if we find one faction, we'll find both."

"Did that girl have any idea where they've holed up?" Caleb asked.

Bandit answered as Josephine shook her head. "We got a general area, and that was it. She wasn't the most forthcoming... I think Santana's guys might've been through that camp and were a little more direct in their questions than she felt comfortable with."

"She knew me from the clinic," Josephine added. "I've seen her a few times around there. I think that's why she came to us instead of going to Santana."

"Poor kid. Did you at least send her out with some food?" Deadeye asked, earning a surprised look from Caleb.

Josephine snorted. "Of course I did. Who do you think I am?" She set down the watering can. "It took guts for her to come up here, but at least now we know where to look for those sons of bitches."

"Sure do." Bandit tipped his head to look at Deadeye and me. "Think we can narrow it down?"

I stood up, the urge to do something humming in my veins. "I need a map."

IN THE END, it took all four of us to reduce the area marked by the girl to a single square mile of city. The next afternoon, Tara rode with Caleb to the police station and picked up a drive containing every report, rumor, and frame of surveillance imagery from the barrio. I wasn't certain the data would help us, but we'd worked solo for so long that having another interested agency on our side came as a profound relief.

Deadeye and I spent the day in the office, eating granola bars and overlaying different outdated satellite maps to better figure out which buildings might be large and well situated enough to house the dozen or so Blood Angel leaders that had escaped Santana's takeover. It'd been months since I'd done the job the EDF had originally trained me to do, and it was refreshing to be matching my wits against computers. I'd ruled out a five-plex and an abandoned dollar store, and we were working on the next grid section when something totally unexpected swept through the station.

Surprise.

Love.

Joy.

I dropped my pen with a clatter onto the keyboard and buried my head in my hands, happy tears burning my eyes. While there were many instances where I hated my powers, the ability to feel others' joy was something I'd *never* take for granted.

Deadeye stopped what she was doing to cautiously touch my back. "You okay? What's wrong?"

"Nothing." I sniffed away tears with a growing smile. "But Bandit just asked Josephine to marry him, out in the kitchen."

Deadeye dropped her tablet on the crowded desk and ran out of the room. I followed close on her heels, emerging from the hallway as the couple were mid-kiss. They broke apart at Deadeye's long, warbling whistle, and Josephine's laughter echoed through Station Somewhere. "You stop."

I hadn't thought the timing could be any better, when Tara's voice came from the bay door and proved me wrong in perfect fashion. "Stop what?" Her confusion broke into excitement when she saw Josephine and Bandit still hugging each other. "You did it?"

Behind her, Caleb was beaming. "That's one way to boost morale, sir."

Everyone started laughing at Bandit's stammered explanation that this was *not* why he'd picked now to pop the question, before Josephine pushed in front of him to eagerly show everyone the ring on her hand. Coos and admiration filled the kitchen from the other women, and within minutes the talk had shifted from immediate peril to weddings and dresses.

Bandit and I exchanged a clandestine nod across the

room. As unexpected as his timing had been, the event itself hadn't been a total surprise. After our talk while returning from the mountains, he'd let me help him resize the ring he'd been saving. Chances were, Josephine wouldn't wear it often with how messy her job could get, but the happy squeals and chatter were worth every hour of work we'd put in.

My writing hand ended up cramped from the many stories that circulated the dinner table that night, most of them centered on Bandit and Josephine's shared teenage years. As the women—still occupied in reminiscence—began cleaning up, Bandit, Caleb, and I retreated to the living area to put the new data from the police onto our big screen. There wasn't much new information. Police reports were patchy, and surveillance footage almost nonexistent. Still, the information was enough to underscore the area that Deadeye and I had pinpointed during our work that afternoon.

"Looks right, sir," Caleb said to Bandit as he highlighted a few city blocks on the map. "At least, it's close enough that we can pass it to Santana for his guys to look into." He turned as I made a surprised noise. "What, you thought I was going to recommend you waltz in there to look for yourself?"

"...I mean, yeah?" I gestured at my monitor, its indicator lights glowing a comfortable green. "I'm running hot right now; I could do it."

"Nope." Caleb shook his head. "No way. It seems like they're either recruiting or targeting Shattereds, and you'd be a prime target. I'm happy to let Santana's guys do the rest of the legwork for this thing."

Bandit powered the screen down and pulled the updated drive from the computer held by brackets to the wall beside it. "There's no reason for us to do all the recon for this operation. I'll get this to Santana tomorrow," he told Caleb, "or you and Tara can. What we need to figure out is how we're going to get these guys without immediately killing them all."

"I wondered if you meant it when you said you were going by the book," Caleb said, leaning against the base of the couch. "I guess technically, we do have a no-kill option if the police are going to have any involvement. Though I'd hate to be whoever has to decide what to do with them once we *do* get them."

"That's for someone else to decide. I'm not keen on being judge, jury, and executioner." Bandit pocketed the drive and sat as well, giving me an interested look as he did. "Though, speaking of Judge, I'm wondering if you're able to repeat that crowd control thing you did the other week."

"Oh yeah, I was going to ask about that as well," Caleb agreed. "You haven't ever been able to freeze someone like that, have you?"

"Nope." I'd been sitting with my back against the coffee table, but now I scooted to sit cross-legged facing them. "I've only been able to do single commands, and even then it's a fifty-fifty chance that they resist the order. This *was* more like what Judge could do, which makes a little more sense, given his subtype—"

I abruptly closed my mouth on the rest of what I'd been about to say. I'd only figured out in recent months how close Judge's mental control subtype had been to full telepathy, and he'd never forgive me if I let it slip now. Instead, I settled for, "There are enough similarities between what he could do and what I did that I might be able to do it again if I practiced."

Based on the quizzical nod Bandit gave me, I guessed that my hesitation hadn't escaped his notice. Thankfully, he didn't call me out on my evasion.

"I imagine it's not something you could master in time to use against these guys," Caleb said. He looked over his shoulder as a peal of laughter sounded through the kitchen before returning his attention to me. "It looked like it drained you pretty fast."

I nodded, wishing he wasn't right. "Any time I try something new, it takes a lot more out of me. I don't know if we can rely on it for this." I frowned at a new thought. "And I'm not sure how I'm supposed to practice. I don't mind seeing your memories—at least, it's something we've all had to get comfortable with—but controlling your actions feels dirty and underhanded."

"We're used to it," Bandit said matter-of-factly. "How do you think Alexi learned?"

Caleb laughed. "Didn't he make you dump a bag of flour on the sarge once?"

Bandit rolled his eyes. "A bowl, but you're not that far off. That was after *he'd* dumped a cup of water on the guy's head."

A laugh burst out of me. "A what?"

"Water, followed by flour," Caleb explained with a grin. "It's called 'antiquing.' We were scrubbing the floor for another hour after that."

"As long as you keep the flour in the kitchen, I'll let you try it with me sometime," Bandit told me. "Sometime when we're not planning a full-scale raid. For now, let's assume you *don't* have a future as a puppet master, and make our plans to reflect that." He looked up as Josephine and Tara dropped into seats on the couch. "All done?"

"Done, yeah." Tara scooted to sit behind Caleb, her hands dropping to rub his shoulders. "Movie?"

"Movie?" Caleb asked, craning his neck to look up at her. "What about 'planning'? You want to go blind into this?"

"We were going blind into ninety percent of our deployments last year, until Gabe's subtype developed enough to give us early warning." She leaned against the arm of the couch, reaching down to ruffle his hair. "Besides, it's a special night."

"It is," Deadeye agreed from the kitchen, the staccato rattling of popcorn kernels punctuating her words. "And besides, we can't plan anything until we find exactly where they're holed up."

Deadeye's endorsement—or maybe the popcorn—was enough to tip the scales in favor of a movie. Josephine and Tara decided on the film, and everyone settled in as the opening titles rolled on a story of a girl hidden in a tower and a thief hidden in a devil-may-care persona. I stayed on the floor, sprawling on my stomach with a pillow under my chest and warmth in my heart.

I did my best to capture the moment in my notebook that night, telling the story of the evening as if I were relating it to someone who hadn't been there to witness it. Judge came to mind more than once—most likely due to my earlier conversation with Bandit and Caleb—and after a while, my writing became something like a one-sided conversation with the deceased Shattered.

"You probably knew how Bandit felt about Josephine," I said out loud. "I know you were aware of what we were thinking, even if you did a really good job of hiding it. I just wish you'd been there to see them kiss that first time. You'd have given them such grief, but you would've loved seeing them so happy."

I closed the notebook and smoothed the cover. "I managed to pull off a stunt like what you used to do, the other week. It was weird, but I think I understand how to do it now. And if I can learn what you could do, that means you most likely knew how I do the empath thing." An impressed chuckle punctuated the realization. "Heck, you probably could've worn the command helmet yourself and saved me the trouble."

My pen clicked closed, and I clipped it to the coiled metal spine of the notebook. It was getting late, and I wanted to get at least a few hours of sleep. "I understand why you hid it, though. Michael was the only other telepath I've ever heard of, and you were there to see what happened to him. If you'd let the truth be known, they'd have put you in Command with no choice but to go by the book with everyone watching your every move." The image of Judge stuffed into the command room came to mind, and I snorted a quiet laugh. "You'd have hated that even more than your secrets coming to light."

Sharp edges of grief ate into the amusement. "All that caution, and you're still gone." I sniffed, uncertain if the prickle in my nose was tears or frustration. "Now there's nobody to rile up Deadeye, and watching movies isn't the same without everyone yelling at you to shut up with the obscure trivia." I closed my fist over the power making my fingers tremble. "I know I have the memories you shared, but it just isn't the same as hearing your obnoxious voice."

That night when I laid out my gear, I pulled a heather-grey T-shirt from the top drawer in my closet. The design on the front was a goose holding a knife in its beak—one of Judge's favorites. The material was soft against my fingertips as I put it atop my folded cargo pants for tomorrow. *Memory isn't the same,* I thought as I lay down. *But at least it's better than nothing.*

STAGE FIFTEEN

SOLAR PANELS WERE MY NEMESIS. Bandit insisted he couldn't hear the drone they made, but both Deadeye and I swore that you could tell how old a panel was by how loud it buzzed. Tara and Caleb had left that morning to drop off our reconnaissance notes with Santana, which left Deadeye, Bandit, and myself to hunt through abandoned neighborhoods for functioning solar panels to supplement our station reserve. I didn't mind the job, but it was still tedious to reconnect and test each panel before lowering them for Bandit to load into the truck.

"All I'm saying is that if Elrond had thrown Isildur into the lava, everyone could've been saved a lot of trouble." Deadeye squinted against the glare coming off the panels, face pinching around her eyepatch strap and a bead of sweat running down her temple.

I locked my leg around a strut and passed her a pair of pliers. "Maybe so, but it's not really in keeping with his character." After we'd watched the Lord of the Rings films, Caleb had lent me his tablet to read the source material. The resultant disagreements between him, Deadeye, and myself had made for excellent dinnertime conversation. "And the elves had a pretty bad track record for recognizing threats or taking them seriously."

Deadeye gave a sardonic laugh. "If you call welcoming Sauron as a master craftsman a 'bad track record.'" She clamped several wires before reattaching a plastic cover. "But seriously, the lava was right there. If he'd just manned up, the ring wouldn't have gotten lost in the river, Gollum wouldn't have found it, the hobbits would've never had it in the first place..."

"Deadeye?" Bandit said from the ground.

"Hmm?"

"Shut up."

I suppressed a laugh as Deadeye subsided, her annoyed muttering switching to German. Bandit's patience was long-lasting, but even he had limits and I could feel his tension rising with each minute our squad was separated.

I rubbed sweat off my forehead with a glance at the sky. We'd made an early start this morning, with an eye toward being home before it got warm outside. Even with that precaution, I could feel the sun beating on the back of my neck as Deadeye and I lowered the last panel.

"That's all for today!" Deadeye called to Bandit. "There might be some other good ones up here, but I don't want to bite off more than we can chew. And I want to get back before the others."

Bandit acknowledged with a wave before ducking into

the cab of the truck. As I focused on him, I caught a stir of interest as the radio crackled, then a sudden, sharp surge in his emotions.

The contentment I'd been feeling soured in my stomach. "Reneé, something's wrong," I warned. "Bandit's talking to someone on the radio and he's worried about something."

Deadeye swore. Her hands sped up, rope whisking against her palms, and the solar panel came to rest on the ground with a thump.

Both of us scrambled down from the solar array and hurried to the truck, right as Bandit emerged from the cab. His face was tense under his hat brim, anxiety and fear running through his words as he explained in a clipped tone, "That was Dispatch. Something's happened to Caleb and Tara."

A chill spread through my spine. *We're too late. Vanguard made their move first.*

THE CITY FLEW by in a blur a few minutes later, our hard-won solar panels forgotten in the dusty parking lot. I had the mind bridge open with Deadeye, who sat across from me in the back of the truck as we sped toward St. Augustine's. Her face flickered through a myriad of emotions as I silently translated the Spanish-language conversation occurring in comms between Bandit and the dispatcher.

Caleb and Tara didn't even make it to Santana. The Blood Angels found them fighting it out with someone—the dispatcher doesn't know exactly who, but she thinks it's the guys we were trying to find.

Deadeye's eye narrowed under her eyepatch strap. *Dammit, they couldn't have waited two days? We would've had them!* She looked sharply at me. *What happened to the attackers?*

I clicked the mic button on my comms set and asked Bandit, waiting for the answer before shaking my head at Deadeye. *They got away. The Blood Angels barely made it out alive themselves. The attackers were using some kind of weapons the dispatcher couldn't describe. All she knows is they were packing some serious firepower.*

They didn't have anything like that before. I understood the implications even before Deadeye said it. *Someone supplied them.*

I nodded without a word as Bandit and the dispatcher kept talking. The drive across the city to St. Augustine's was only twenty minutes, but each heartbeat felt like it lasted an hour. After relaying the pertinent details of the conversation, I turned off the mind bridge and rested my head against the shaking compartment wall. *I knew I should've insisted on scouting things myself. Maybe if I had, we would've known about these new weapons. Instead, we wasted days scrubbing through those stupid maps and trying to play nice with everyone.*

Lost in my whirling thoughts, it was only as we arrived at St. Augustine's that I sat up and paid attention to my surroundings. Once I did, I was flabbergasted by what I found. "Bandit, heads up," I warned, holding down my mic button. "There're a bunch of Blood Angels here—Santana's guys. They must've stayed after getting Caleb and Tara here."

He took a deep breath—I could hear it rasp against his mic—and the truck bounced as he stepped down. "Let's hope they're planning to stay peaceful."

Midday sun flooded the passenger compartment. The

first person to greet us was Logan, who returned Bandit's handshake as Deadeye closed the truck hatch. "You got here fast."

"Yeah," Bandit answered tersely. "Where are they?"

"Surgery."

Anxiety skyrocketed my heart rate. "Both of them?"

"No, just Tara." Logan led us through double doors into the lobby. "She's in good hands, but we can't get close enough to Caleb to see if he's hurt. He looks like he's ready to snap."

Bandit swore under his breath. "He'll need help. *Mijo*, can you find him?"

I projected my awareness through the halls of the hospital, Deadeye taking hold of my sleeve to keep me from running into anyone. Ahead of us, a handful of Blood Angels milled around a set of double doors, one presence among them standing out in cyan so bright it was almost white. Even at this distance, I could tell it was Caleb—and he wasn't even trying to hide his emotions.

"Found him. And you're right, Logan, he's a mess." I snapped back into myself and turned my forearm palm-up, preselecting Caleb's name from the comms program in my monitor. "We need to get everyone away from him."

"You got it," Bandit answered. "Reneé?"

"*Ja?*"

"Go find your gossipy informant." Bandit's words had filled with sharp edges, closely matching the urgency and guilt flooding his mind. "Of anyone, he'll know what's going on. And I want to hear it from someone unaffiliated with either side."

"Copy that." Deadeye veered off down a side corridor,

her spine straight and footsteps determined as she disappeared.

The Blood Angels at the end of the hall had noticed our approach. They parted ranks to reveal Caleb leaning against a wall, clutching a bloody gauze pad to his temple. His helmet rested on the floor at his feet, the rest of his armor filthy with blood and dirt. A dangerous light glinted in his silvery eyes, and I knew it would only take a single wrong noise, word, or accidental touch to send all that panic streaking out in violence.

I quickened my pace to shove through the Blood Angels. "Caleb!"

He turned the full force of that dangerous look on me for a terrifying instant before shock and recognition ran through his expression. "Gabriel." He blinked hard. "You heard—"

"We heard." Without another word, I flicked on the mind bridge. The world blurred, snapped, and stabilized into a whirl of gunfire and cyan flashing. *What happened?*

I didn't even need to ask. I could see it all in the moments he was dwelling on.

Happiness, such happiness, at Tara sounding more like herself today than she had for weeks. Then, there was a crash from a nearby house, screaming and shouts, and the weight of my gun swinging to the ready. Blue Shattered power arced across the street, contrasted by ruby flashes from a type of weapon I knew all too well.

"Tara, run!"

Pain exploded in my back, something froze my muscles, and my forward momentum betrayed me into the pavement. My helmet hit the ground with a crack, and I heard Tara scream.

We were powerless.

Powerless.

At that word, something sickening tugged on our combined emotions. The floor opened out from under me, and I fell deep into a memory that had been locked far, far away in the depths of Caleb's mind.

Cold. Cold, cold, cold—darkness.

Darkness. It was never dark here. Why was it dark? Could I move?

Then, a flare of blue. Electrical popping and gunfire. Voices—not the unearthly xeno chatter, but the honest-to-God sounds of furious humans.

"Found him!"

"Hurry, get over here!"

"Kill that device; get him out of it!"

A woman yelled, the sound ripping me out of the last remnants of the fog that'd imprisoned my mind. I knew that voice.

"Banshee, he's alive!"

The ground shook in response.

Something—someone grabbed me. Fiery pain jolted through my body and I tried to scream, but my voice had worn itself out long ago. My limbs spasmed, and I thrashed against the person holding me before someone else called my name.

Hey, buddy. I got you. You're safe now. *The new voice was harsh at the edges, calm in the center, heavily accented, and clear in my mind.* You're safe n—

All the lights turned on at once. The voice vanished from my head, and I found myself unable to move again.

"Caleb!" I tore myself out of the memory with a panicked yell. Reality shimmered, resolving into the dingy white of the St. Augustine's hallway. Caleb and I were both crumpled on the floor. By the shocked looks on the faces around us, we'd collapsed with little to no warning.

I struggled to my knees, rolling Caleb over and pulling him to sit against the wall. *Hey. Hey! You're not there. It's not real. This isn't real!*

Caleb's arms shook as he drew his knees to his chest and buried his face against them. I knelt beside him with my hand on his shoulder.

"Caleb," I said aloud. "Breathe." In my head, I counted down, projecting the numbers into his mind. His shoulders shuddered up, then down as I counted again, talking him through each moment. *They came for you. That's what you're remembering. They got you out. You're not powerless now. Breathe.*

I counted breaths. I don't know for how long.

Eventually, Caleb's shuddering calmed and his breathing became more even.

It's always there, Gabe. His eyes were exhausted by the time he finally opened them, a lost look filling the greyness. *I can't get rid of it.*

I know. But there's more to life than this, remember? My fingers gripped the shoulder strap of his armor as I poured memories into him—hiking on a misty fall day, happy dogs bounding after a ball, laughter at a prank well executed, getting a good grade on a test, the clinking of soda bottles around a beach campfire, Tara's smile—all moments I'd seen through the mind bridge. *There's more to life than what's locked inside your head.*

Thanks, buddy. Caleb's arms loosened around his knees and he took a deep breath and let it out. I could already feel his usual control returning—or maybe he was trying to distract himself—as he said, *They were using EDF weapons modified with xeno tech.* An image of Blood Angel armor flicked through his mind, pulses of red light flashing from the muzzles of weapons that looked awfully familiar to anyone who'd gone through the EDF's basic training course. *They had us backed into a corner. There was nothing I could do.*

I sat back on my heels, letting my hand fall from his shoulder. We'd been looking for certain confirmation of who our enemies were, but... *I didn't think the EDF used xeno tech.*

We didn't. Not during the war. He sighed. *The xenos' weapons were difficult to modify, and regular rounds were just as effective against them. But I know someone in R&D was converting our arsenal. This has got to be Vanguard's doing—they're the only ones around here who would've had access to EDF tech.* Caleb let his legs slide farther from his chest, resting an arm atop his knees as Bandit set a plastic cup of water next to him. *Thanks,* he said without looking up.

I didn't bother reminding him to speak aloud. *What happened to Tara?*

The answer came in an instant, as clear in my mind as though I'd experienced it myself. A lightning bolt had streaked out of a clear sky, the energy overloading Tara's shield before Caleb could get enough physical contact to amplify her power. Before either of them could respond, several shots had found their marks.

I pulled her into cover, and returned fire. The cup crinkled in Caleb's grip, and he set it down before closing his hand into a fist. *They got me too, but I think it was a stunner. At least, it didn't permanently hurt me. If Santana's guys hadn't shown up, we'd probably be dead.* He leaned his head against the wall. Helplessness surged behind his eyes as he confessed, *I don't know what to do. When I get hurt, she's always there to help. Now she's in trouble, and I'm useless.*

You're not useless. You saved her life.

Caleb gave a tiny smile, but I could tell he wasn't buying it as Bandit came to crouch in front of us. "Just got done talking to the docs. They say she'll be okay."

"What about the—" Caleb gestured at his abdomen. I knew what he was talking about—based off the memories he'd dumped into me, at least one shot had impacted below Tara's armor.

Bandit's tone stayed reassuring, though I could feel the undercurrent of worry behind his words. "They're saying those modified weapons were a blessing in disguise. Your attackers had the frequency dialed to make it more of a stunning shot than a killing blow. The only one that did any real damage was here." He patted his stomach, a little to the right of the midline. "That was a conventional bullet, and they think it barely nicked her liver."

Even after the first aid training I'd received, I wasn't certain if a liver puncture was a survivable thing. Caleb's cautious sigh of relief, and the knowledge flooding the mind bridge, was enough reassurance that I didn't need to ask out loud.

"Did they say how surgery's going?"

"She'll be through it in another hour or so, and they want to keep an eye on her here for the next twenty-four hours at least." Bandit shifted his leg to pull a slim tablet out of his pocket. "You left this in truck. I don't know if you want it."

Caleb took the tablet without a word, stuffing it into a cargo pocket. *It's nice of him,* he said for my ears only. *But I can't read at a time like this. Not until I see she's safe for myself.* He opened and closed his fist, the harsh industrial lighting catching the scars running along his forearm. *If she dies—*

She won't, I interrupted. *She's got a fire in her soul.*

If she dies, I don't know what I'll do. Caleb reached across and turned my wrist to face him, eyes flickering until he found the button to turn off the mind bridge. The connection fizzled out and he stood, pocketing the gauze that had fallen from his temple.

"Thanks, guys. I'm going to take a walk. Gabe"—he locked eyes with me in a way that was at once apologetic and determined—"will you find me if anything happens?"

I nodded, turning away as Caleb's footsteps faded. The Blood Angels had moved around the corner, taking up residence in a waiting area off the main hall. At some point—I assumed while I'd been distracted in the mind bridge—Logan had also drifted away. I was opening my mouth to ask after him when Bandit said, "I asked Logan to get Josephine from downtown."

"How'd you know?"

"You had that look that said you were checking everyone's whereabouts, but couldn't find someone. The deeper in your subtype you are, the more it shows on your face." Bandit pulled a navy bandana from his pocket and wiped his forehead. "I don't know if you noticed, but Santana's also here."

I frowned and turned my attention to the next room. Sure enough, Santana's wiry, focused energy stood out among the others. "That was awfully fast."

"Pretty sure he was right behind us. He's as pissed as we are that these guys got the jump on us before we had the chance to take them out. Reneé went to go find that informant of hers, assuming he hasn't disappeared into the ductwork." Bandit's eyes searched the ceiling, like he could command Benny to appear out of thin air. "Once she finds him and Josie gets back with Logan, we all need to talk."

"Okay..." I looked down the hall. The doors of the chapel stood open, calling me in. There wasn't anything I could do about Caleb, Tara, or our immediate predicament, but maybe I could do something about the exhaustion clawing at my heart. "Sir, is it all right if I take a minute until Josephine gets here? I think I also need to take a walk, or"—I lowered my voice, uncertain why I felt sheepish saying it out loud—"or maybe pray."

"Sure, *mijo.*" Bandit looked up as a surgical tech came around the corner with an expression that said she was looking for someone. "I'll send someone to find you once we're ready to regroup."

STAGE SIXTEEN

CHANTING in Latin fell on my ears as I stepped through the carved wooden doors of the chapel. I couldn't see where the music was coming from, but the tinny quality to the deeper tones made me suspect there was an old speaker system hidden nearby.

I took a seat in one of the unoccupied pews, my chest aching after the last half hour of distress. Another, similar pain spasmed through my left arm, and I winced and brought it to my chest with a quiet groan. If Caleb's memory was to be trusted, I'd just witnessed the moment when his squad rescued him from xeno imprisonment—but it still didn't make sense as to why the physical pain had crossed over.

It was all too much.

I sank to my knees with my clasped hands resting on the back of the pew in front of me. The prayers that tumbled from my lips made no sense at first, caught in a half-Spanish, half-English stream of frustration and weakness, but soon the pressure on my heart decreased until I was able to make sense of my words.

"Every time we make headway, something always comes to shove us down again. It *was* the Blood Angels. Now there are these crazy scientists. And they're not just coming after me—I could handle it if they were. Now, they're after all of us." I tightened my hands against each other, frustration sharpening my voice. "And on top of all of that, the power I never asked for is going to kill me eventually. At this point I wish it would hurry up and get it over with."

"At least then it would stop hurting." The unexpected reply came from behind me. "But I don't think that's what you actually want."

I jumped to my feet, destructive force surging to my fingertips as I whirled on the man standing in the chapel entrance. He took a startled step back, a grey and black rosary falling from his hands as he raised them. "Sorry, I didn't mean to scare you."

"Who are you? Why didn't I—" I glanced between him and the door. There would've been no deceiving him about who I was, not with cyan flickering between my fingers. I let the energy go with a sigh. "What did you say?"

He knelt to pick up the rosary. "May I join you?"

"Um. Sure." I stepped farther along the pew and took a seat as the man knelt in prayer for a long minute. Closing my eyes as well, I let my sixth sense focus on him.

Nothing.

It was as if he didn't exist.

I opened my eyes, to be sure I hadn't made a mistake. He still looked the same—head bowed in prayer, black hair cut neatly around his ears, golden tan skin. As I watched in disbelief, he raised his head and sat beside me. "Thank you." He extended his hand. "I'm Diego, a chaplain here. And you must be—"

"Gabriel." I shook his hand, still baffled. "I couldn't feel you at all, either coming up behind me or just now."

He shrugged. "I wouldn't think too much about it. I was made easy to overlook for a reason. I wasn't sure why I was supposed to come down here, but then I heard you praying. It's a heavy load you've been carrying, isn't it?"

I hadn't meant to tell him. I didn't plan on everything— the fearful past, the discovery of my shortened lifespan, and the terrible sense of futility that had encompassed the last six months—to come pouring out in a rush of anger and hope- lessness.

"If I could go back, I would've stayed hidden in the library and never come out. At least then I wouldn't have— wouldn't have—" I swallowed hard against the tears fighting their way into my eyes. *Dammit.*

"Wouldn't have what? Wouldn't have seen your friends declare their love for each other? Wouldn't have seen the humanity in your adversaries and sought peace instead of war? Wouldn't have found the family you never thought possible? No." Diego shook his head. "There's more to this story than just the pain it's caused you. I've been stationed here since the invasion, and I've learned some things over the years. Sometimes, it takes more courage to live than to give up on your life." Diego looked directly at me, eyes deep wells of compassion and certainty. "And Gabriel, I think you have more courage than you know."

Hurried footsteps echoed in the corridor outside the chapel. I could tell it was Deadeye long before her pink-streaked hair appeared around the doorframe. "Bandit says we need to talk."

The aching in my chest had disappeared as I stood up, though I had no idea why. There was no way the few minutes here in the chapel should've settled my nerves as fast as they had—not after everything that had just happened —but they *had*.

"Wait, here." Diego pulled the rosary from his pocket and pressed it into my hand. The paracord knotted between jet beads was rough against my palm as I closed my fingers over it. "The Psalmist writes, 'He will cover you with his feathers, and under his wings you shall take refuge'. May the Lord be a refuge for you when the world grows too loud."

"Thank you." I slid the rosary into the pocket on my thigh, where it rested alongside the pen I usually fidgeted with. "And—thank you for talking."

FROM THE CONFERENCE room on the eighth floor, I could see the whole city. My notebook lay in front of me, the pages covered in doodles and messy notes from where I'd attempted to organize the information Caleb had relayed through the mind bridge. He'd seemed in control as he walked in the conference room door, but I could tell that the memories he'd just relived were weighing heavily. Traces of tears marked his face, and he looked exhausted as he finished giving his account of the ambush.

"We weren't given the opportunity to counter anything.

And the weaponry they were packing wasn't like anything we've fought before. It's even more powerful than what the xenos had." He leaned his elbows on the table and buried his head in his hands. A pang of discomfort ran through me at the helplessness in his voice as he said, "Between rogue scientists and turncoat gang members carrying experimental weapons, it's practically Area 51 out here."

Area 51? I wrote the name down in my notes with a question mark next to it. Maybe Bandit would explain if I asked him later.

"Well, at least we don't have aliens to contend with anymore," Santana quipped, spinning his pocketknife on the table. "What bothers *me* is that you were attacked practically on my front doorstep. I'm certain that timing and placement was on purpose; they know we're on the same page and wanted to send all of us a message." He slapped his palm over the knife and brought it to a halt. "I know I said you guys were a liability, but I didn't realize they wanted to take you out *this* badly."

"They have an axe to grind," Bandit said. "We trashed a facility that held a lot of value to both factions, between the Brutes and whatever else Vanguard was getting up to." He sighed and rubbed his forehead. "I feel like they've buried their differences to come after us. And Vanguard doesn't seem to have any issue with supplying their new recruits with firepower."

"Sure, then they won't have to get their precious hands dirty or send anyone *they* care about into harm's way." Deadeye hunkered over the table beside me, hands busy with a pencil and scrap of paper. "They're all cowards at heart."

"Not that there's anything we can do about it. Just like

before, we're stuck fighting an enemy who's holding all the cards." My shoulders tensed and I pushed my notebook aside, the horrible feeling of powerlessness from Caleb's memories resurging and making my words come out almost frantic. "Except now it's worse. This time, they know everything about us—our strengths, our weaknesses—and they're going to keep hitting us where it hurts."

THERE WAS MORE to the discussion, but after another half hour I stopped being able to pay attention. Between the frantic journey across town, Caleb's memories, and the emotional release I'd experienced in the chapel, I was wiped. I finally passed my notebook over to Deadeye and rested my head on the table, numb to everything except the exhaustion overtaking my mind and body.

It wasn't until Deadeye tapped my shoulder that I realized the meeting had concluded. Caleb and Bandit had already left, and Santana was in the corner talking in rapid Spanish on a cell phone.

"You ready to go?" Deadeye asked, returning my notebook. "They said Tara's awake and we can go see her."

I shook the heaviness from my limbs and got to my feet, patting my pockets to make sure I had everything I'd arrived with. "Yeah—they're okay with it?"

"Bandit and Caleb already headed down," she said as we exited the room and waited for the elevator. "I just had to finish up the last of the notes. I figured you could look over everything once we get home, or I can share the memory if you want a blow-by-blow."

"Thanks," I said, and meant it. "Sorry, I—"

Deadeye flapped a hand at me. "Don't apologize. I could

tell you were tired. And it's no trouble; I just picked up the notes where you left off." She laughed. "Though, did you realize you switched from English to Spanish halfway through?"

"No. Really?" I flipped open my notebook as the elevator took us downward. Sure enough, the notes I'd been taking during the meeting on the eighth floor started in English, then merged into Spanish after I'd scribbled my question about "Area 51."

"Sorry. Guess I'm more tired than I realized." I sighed. "I really wish we'd been able to get the Unbreaking Field to work without making me feel like I'm sick or burned out. It would've been nice to hide in there after a day like this."

"I know..." Deadeye made an irritable sound as we turned a corner to approach the surgical wing. "There must be something we're missing. Getting it to match your subtype shouldn't also give you burnout symptoms. It's a pity, but I don't know when we're going to be able to work on it again. While you were in the chapel, I called Todd at the lab and asked him to move the generator into storage and lock it up."

"Yeah, that makes sense." *Not that it makes me feel any better.* I closed the notebook and tucked it under my arm. As I did, the scrap of paper Deadeye had been drawing on floated free, revealing a cartoony image that was undeniably Judge chasing a goose. "What's this?" I laughed, scooping the paper from the floor.

"Oh, that's where that went," Deadeye commented as she punched a code into the keypad beside the surgical wing's doors. "It's just a doodle; you can keep it."

"Thanks." I slid the drawing into my pocket as the doors

opened with a rush of cool air and antiseptic smells. "Hang on, how did you know the code to get in here?"

"I didn't, but people never change." Deadeye jabbed her finger at the ceiling. "Somebody wrote the code on the doorframe."

"That's..."

"Terrible security, I know. But it's so, so easy to exploit."

I whistled softly. "Sometimes you scare me. I'm glad I'm on your side."

Deadeye's only answer was a snort as she brushed aside a curtain and strode to join the others in the recovery unit. Tara's face was pale and lined with pain, but the adoration in her eyes as she looked up at Caleb warmed my heart. He was lifting a plastic water cup away from her lips, his other hand securely behind her head. Josephine was dwarfed by the height of the IV pole beside the bed, contrasted by Bandit's constant, protective presence at the edge of the room.

"Gabriel," Tara croaked as Deadeye took a seat on the end of the bed. Relief muddled past the pain and fogginess surrounding her, and she weakly beckoned me closer. "You're okay, you're safe. I was sure they'd be going after you too."

"Yeah..." I sat on the opposite side of the bed from Deadeye, taking care that I wasn't jostling anyone. "They probably will. But, hey"—I frowned, willing every doomful thought out of my mind—"you took a bullet through the guts. Worry about me later."

"We'll take care of things for now," Bandit said, his protective presence shifting as he came to stand beside us. "You focus on getting better."

"We'll hold the line." Deadeye patted a spot on the bed where I assumed Tara's foot hid beneath the blankets. "Rest for now, Banshee." Her affectionate tone turned mischievous. "We've still got a wedding to plan, and Josephine'll get married in her scrubs if we don't do something about it."

THEY KEPT TARA THAT NIGHT, and another after that. By noon of the third day, she was home, propped up in bed and protesting us fussing over her. I'd thought she and Deadeye were joking when they talked about wedding planning—like it was some kind of wishful thing to distract them from the danger looming over our heads—but it soon became clear how much I'd underestimated feminine priorities. They turned Bandit out of the station a few days later, sending him and Caleb on patrol while Josephine tried on the dresses they'd acquired.

They'd only been thinking about this for a week. Where they'd gotten not one, but several wedding dresses, I had yet to discover. I didn't have the chance to ask, either. I'd been relegated to the kitchen and was feeding pasta dough through a hand-cranked machine while sauce bubbled on the stove behind me. Between the giggles and flashes of emotion making their way down the hall, I gathered things weren't going well long before Tara and Deadeye came into the living area.

"I told you it wouldn't work," Tara said with a teasing grin, lowering herself gingerly to the couch as Deadeye stormed past to whirl a spoon through the tomato sauce. "You always guess sizes wrong, and I don't think either of us has enough skill to alter it that much." She gestured at her own figure, all fiery energy in a compact frame. "We can't even use me as a dressmaker's dummy. Not enough curves. Right, Gabe?"

I shook my head with wide eyes, almost catching my thumb in the pasta machine. "I'm not going *near* that discussion. Ask Caleb."

Both women laughed at that. Deadeye's annoyance faded to mild irritation as she stirred the sauce at a more reflective pace. "Well, I tried. She might end up getting married in her scrubs, after all."

"Maybe." Tara leaned back with a groan. She'd been quiet about how much pain she was in, but I could feel it sneaking through the outskirts of her voice. "Especially with how uncertain things are. At least we tried."

"I meant to ask, and I hope it's not rude..." I stopped cranking the pasta machine and leaned on the counter so Tara could see my face. "Why are you so focused on this? We have enemies after our heads; why are we talking about wedding dresses? For that matter, why are we having a wedding at all instead of just having a priest marry them?"

"Gabriel, I'm surprised," Deadeye began. "Of all the people, I'd think you—"

Tara held up a hand. "No, hold on. Gabe, have you ever been to a wedding?"

I shook my head, grateful that she'd stopped Deadeye before my face *really* turned red. "My parents never took me to any when I was a kid, and I avoided big gatherings once I was older." *Not to mention that I didn't have friends who would've invited me.* "I promise, I'm not trying to be obnoxious; I just don't understand."

"If we only thought about the threats, we'd have gone insane a long time ago." Tara shifted positions with a wince. "Some things have a way of bringing hope into dark situations. Babies are one thing." She gave a half-laugh that didn't have the bite I'd expected, given what I knew her abilities had cost her. "Weddings are another."

"Birthdays," Deadeye added from near the stove. "Pranks. Movie nights!" She grinned at me. "You understand those last two things, but I guess you've never experienced a new baby or a wedding."

"I guess not," I said. "But I think I understand? It's like how everyone felt when Bandit proposed. But why the extra stuff? The—" I waved at a dress that had been too big, now lying like a deflated marshmallow on the dining table. "The *that*. Does it help make things more hopeful?"

"Well, it's fun, which makes so many things more bearable." Tara's hand went to her stomach, and discomfort crossed her face. Her painkillers must've been wearing off. "Don't worry, we haven't forgotten about the threats. Why do you think Bandit's been out so much? He's trying to get ahead of this before it catches us unawares again."

I nodded, heart a little more settled at the thought. *At least someone is taking things seriously.* "Okay, then."

A rustle of fabric announced Josephine's reappearance. "Think this will work?"

All three of us looked up to see her petite form almost hidden by a bundle of frilly fabric. Once she'd unfurled the armful, it turned out to be a white *folklórico* dress with brilliant red accents.

Deadeye rounded the counter as Tara whistled approvingly. "That'll fit you, for certain. I didn't know you'd kept any of them."

Josephine's smile held years of nostalgia as she brushed a hand over the red ruffles at the bottom of the skirt. Now that I was looking closer, I recognized the colors and pattern from a picture pinned to the wall above her desk.

"I got rid of most of them when I joined the Force. This was the only one I kept." She held the ornate dress to her torso. "It still fits, or will with only a little work. Do you think it'll be all right? I mean, it's not traditional for a wedding, but—"

Tara reached up to touch Josephine's elbow. "It's still white, sweetheart. And in this day and age, I think that's all that matters. Besides"—she winked—"I think Carlos would still marry you, even if you were wearing a biohazard suit."

STAGE SEVENTEEN

"THE WHITE DOVE of the Desert, they used to call it," I said to Caleb as we stood outside the Mission San Xavier del Bac. "I never went to Mass here, but my parents used to talk about it." I stuffed my hands in my pockets—I was wearing jeans again, determined to get used to how uncomfortable they felt—and looked at the twin whitewashed towers atop the adobe structure. "It's one of the oldest buildings in the region. I'm still amazed it survived the xenos."

"And the Blood Angels," Caleb commented. He tugged at the cuffs on his jacket, a dark olive dress uniform from the EDF's earliest days. "Or were they more likely to leave a holy site alone?"

I shrugged, biting back a laugh as Deadeye almost lost her balance on a stepladder, from which she was tacking bougainvillea branches to a wooden arch outside the church.

Tara sat on a bench nearby, beautiful in a dress almost as pink as the flowers. Her face was still lined with pain, and she couldn't stand for long periods of time, but she'd insisted on being here nonetheless.

"The Blood Angels are Catholic," I said. "At least, most of them were. There are some things you *really* don't mess with."

"Hey, come help over here!" Deadeye yelled, stepladder wobbling beneath her.

Caleb laughed and went to help, leaving me to my contemplation of the mission. Guests were beginning to arrive, most in Defense Force or Medical Corps uniforms with a handful in civilian clothes. Thirty attendees was a pitiful number compared to how weddings had been in the past, but I didn't mind how few people were here. This would be a very emotional event, and nothing made me cry faster than secondhand joy.

The thought stayed with me as I stood in the back of the baroque chapel alongside Logan. The rest of the squad sat near the front, Tara remaining in her seat as the rest of the congregation followed the sit-stand-kneel pattern of a tradi-tional Mass. As the priest went through the wedding service, I had to fight back tears.

I hadn't thought about how much I'd missed this, I thought, reaching into my pocket and letting the beads of my newly acquired rosary brush my fingertips. The rise and fall of voices united in a psalm was enough to see me step away from Logan and quietly make my way to join the rest of the squad.

Tears began leaking from my eyes as Bandit and Josephine came to stand before the priest. Josephine had pinned her curls into a knot at the back of her head, and the hibiscus blossom tucked behind her ear complemented the red accents on her dress. Bandit, like Caleb, had pulled his old uniform out of storage. Unlike Caleb, he'd left his rank insignia on the sleeves and shoulders, a double silver bar reminding everyone that he'd earned the right to command others through hell or high water.

I swallowed hard against the lump in my throat as both Bandit and Josephine firmly answered "I am" when asked if they were willing to accept the responsibility of raising future children. A warm feeling spread through my chest. *They'll make wonderful parents.*

I blinked away the tears and looked over at Tara and Caleb, standing in the place reserved for witnesses. Caleb's hand was under Tara's elbow, supporting her as she leaned slightly into him. The words of holy vows whispered around me, their weight as powerful as any shared memory. For a moment, peace formed a shield against the struggle of the last several months, and my heart settled in the stillness.

I think I understand what you meant, Tara. This does make things lighter.

A FEW HOURS LATER, twilight saw us gathered beneath the wide porch at Tía Gloria's house. Never a woman to be refused, she'd volunteered her home for the wedding dinner and we'd considered it best to agree. Tonight, the tension that had marked our first visit was gone—replaced by laughter, good food, and reggaeton thumping from a speaker system.

Bandit sat with his arm wrapped around Josephine's shoulders, occasionally breaking from his conversations to kiss her like the years of waiting had passed in a heartbeat. She practically glowed from within, both of them exuding so much unfiltered joy that everyone on the porch was drawn irresistibly to their table over and over again.

After a long day of preparation and planning, I was happy to stay at the edge of the well-wishers. For whatever reason, this wedding was serving to bury the last bits of hostility between us and the higher-ranking Blood Angels, and Santana himself sat at the table nearest Bandit and Josephine. By the time dessert was served, the happy chatter had turned to reminiscence. I'd been sitting with Tara and Caleb, but the shift in conversation piqued my interest enough that I got up to approach Bandit.

"Sir? Is it okay if I grab my notebook?" I'd changed back into my cargo pants, and my pen clicked as I pulled it free. "I left it in the truck, and this is too good to miss."

The lines around Bandit's eyes deepened with his smile —though, to be fair, he'd hardly stopped smiling the entire evening. "Sure, *mijo*. I don't mind, and I don't think anyone else will notice." He winked. "There are some hair-raising stories in this group of people."

"I'll try to be unbiased," I promised with a smile. "Be right back."

The others didn't notice as I rounded the edge of the patio. Tara had fallen asleep against Caleb's shoulder as he talked with Logan, and Deadeye was comparing notes with Benny about something. The fairy lights draped in the mesquite tree brushed my hair and left a sparkling after-image against my eyelids as I slipped through a side gate and made my way toward the truck.

It was dark outside the walled yard. The last time we'd been here, there'd been *luminaria* lining the driveway, but tonight the curving gravel strip lay cold and grey under the night sky. A breeze brushed warm against my skin, and my boots crunched pleasantly into the gravel before a strange sound caught my attention.

Static?

I tipped my head upward to scan the skyline for electrical poles. Just like the solar panels, they sometimes made a buzzing sound that Bandit always laughed at me for being able to hear. The noise didn't dissipate as I turned a full circle, but no telltale sources presented themselves.

I shook my head, but the static only built. Nervous now, I stopped shy of the vehicles parked in the driveway and crouched to touch the ground. In my mind's eye, the satellite image of the house and driveway became overlaid with the branches of a swiftly growing root system. Bandit, Josephine, and the others stood out as blue glowing outlines, the figures of the others distinct orangey blobs scattered in and around the house. Even the usual Blood Angel sentries could be seen, cagey as ever as they surrounded the house.

Surrounded.

I shut my physical eyes and focused my power on the sentries. Most of the time, they struck me as being bored. Now, however...

Understanding clicked into place and my heart skipped a beat as the static hum grew louder. I whirled to my feet, an energy ball coalescing in my palm as I did. Before I could release it, a flash of ruby light came from behind the hood of the closest truck, and my vision flashed white and red as pain spread through my chest.

The figures I'd mistaken for sentries were running forward now, the barrels of their weapons glowing the same unfamiliar ruby hue as the light that had struck me. My ears were ringing, but cleared enough for me to hear the static hum change to resemble something sharply recognizable.

Lightning.

I screamed as another shot found its mark on my stomach, twinned with a blue wall of force that knocked me off my feet. My head hit the ground with a crack, and a starburst of light exploded in my vision. Voices came from a distance, Spanish mixing with English and muffled through helmets.

"He's down! Hurry!"

My sight cleared in time for me to see several dark figures converging on me. One grabbed my wrist, bearing it to the ground as I thrashed and leaning against me with their whole weight. "Here, I got him! Get it in!"

Something stung the outside of my arm, and a startled yelp escaped my mouth. A harried male voice said, "It's in! Hey, hold him!"

"I can't!" A girl's voice, frantic and more than a little scared. "He's too strong!"

I *knew* that voice.

LET GO!

With a furious yell and a wrench that tore at my shoulder, I yanked an arm free and sent an energy bolt into thin air. The girl swore, her voice distorting through a wave of dizziness. A shout came from somewhere else, and even through the confusion unfolding in my head I could sense the chaos stirring in the house behind us.

"They know something's up; let's go!"

"We can't, he's still conscious!" the man insisted. "It'll take a minute to kick in; someone buy us some time!"

My awareness was getting foggy, cyan collecting in the corners of my vision as my limbs grew heavy. The last thing I heard was weapons' fire and someone yelling my name before blackness and silence enveloped me.

————

CONSCIOUSNESS RETURNED with the scratching of sand trapped behind my eyelids and a horrendous headache. I took a slow breath, my chest expanding freely in a way that was never possible under my armor. Cold air brushed bare skin as I took another breath, bringing with it the understanding that both my shirt and the jacket I'd been wearing over it were gone. Something soft and scratchy circled my wrists, holding them fast to—

My eyes snapped open despite the grittiness.

I was lying on a bed like the ones at St. Augustine's, my wrists bound against the metal rails with Velcro restraints. An IV catheter was taped into the crook of my elbow, cold fluid draining into my arm from a bag hanging on a hook above my head.

Blinking slowly, I took in the rest of the room. It could've been any industrial office were it not for the bed I was bound to; windowless, painted soulless tan, and lined with cupboards on one side. A screen hung on the opposite wall from the cupboards, displaying layers of scrolling data like that from my missing monitor cuff.

Data coming from...where?

I peered down to see a pattern of round dots—sensors of some kind—stuck across my chest and stomach. My power stirred sluggishly as I called on it, my surroundings coming into focus agonizingly slowly. There was a hallway outside the door to this room, toppled furniture in the next room over, and several presences ranging throughout the building. As I tried to focus on the nearest person, a warning stab of pain went through my right eye.

Burnout?

I frowned at the screen and tried to think. The crippling headache pulsing through my skull reminded me of the last few moments of consciousness I'd experienced. *They drugged me. My power must've been fighting it in my sleep.* Fearful now, I tugged at the restraints, wondering if my hands could narrow enough to slip free.

The thought "what then?" crossed my mind, and I stopped pulling.

Even if I could break loose, I can't find my way out without my powers, let alone fight off however many of them there are here. I shivered, more than just the cold sending chills across my skin. Alone. Burned out. Helpless.

Cold, glittering light, flash of red, panicked immobility—

A fist tensed against the restraint—and against Caleb's memories. I closed my eyes and took a measured breath. *Calm down, Gabriel. Breathe. You have to keep it together if you're going to get out of this one.*

Four counts in. Four counts out. Repeat.

I still had my eyes closed when the door opened.

"This wasn't my idea."

I opened my eyes to see the Blood Angel Shattered holding a tray of food with a sullen expression. Now the voice I'd heard as I lost consciousness made sense, and I glared up at her with my initial fear forgotten.

"You." Now that we were face-to-face and I didn't have much left to lose, all I could feel was anger. "You had a perfect opportunity to take off, to start a new life that *didn't* involve terrorizing people, and you went back to *this*? I gave you chance after chance to run—why didn't you take it?"

She slapped the tray down on the counter, irritation and resentment clear in her cyan eyes. "Keep your power out of my head. I'm just here to make sure you eat." This part she said with a glare at the door. "Like I said, this wasn't my idea."

I allowed myself a small stir of satisfaction. The part of my sixth sense that was still active informed me that my angry questioning had found a mark. Somehow, somewhere, there was regret looming in her mind. *Finally*.

"How exactly is that supposed to work?" I nodded at my bound wrists. "I can't do *anything* like this. Unless you're planning on feeding me?"

By the look on her face, that was *exactly* what she'd been told to do—and she didn't like it one bit. "Shut up. I'll let you have a hand free, if you promise you'll behave."

I was on the verge of another smart remark, and never mind the consequences, when Tara's first lesson on burnout flashed through my mind. Shattered abilities took longer to regenerate on an empty stomach, and I needed to be at full strength to escape—especially given who my opponent was.

"Fine," I muttered. "I won't try anything. Just let me feed myself."

The girl considered me for a long moment, then undid the Velcro holding my right wrist against the metal bed railing. "There. Don't—"

"I won't." My muscles had cramped, and I stifled a groan as I worked the kinks out of my arm and shoulder. "Thank you."

"Don't be silly; I'm not doing you any favors." A flash of emotion—guilt this time—came from her. "I just don't want to feed you like a baby." She set the tray on the bed where I could reach. Handing me a fork, she dragged a folding chair from the corner of the room and sat, her silence more disconcerting than hostility would have been.

My manners weren't nearly as good as Abuela would

have wanted, eating with my nondominant hand. After the fourth time I missed a noodle with a clumsy stab, the girl stood up with a huff. "Seriously?"

"What?" I looked up as she leaned over me to undo the left restraint, catching a hint of something citrusy as her hair whisked past my face. "You never stopped to consider that I might not be right-handed?"

She resumed her seat with a frown stamped across her face. Even with my attention deliberately elsewhere, I knew when the questions began burning at the back of her mind. And for that matter, I could tell what some of them were. Finally, I dropped the fork on the tray. "It was last year."

Her face turned bright pink, and mental walls to rival Caleb's slammed across her emotions. "What?"

"When I Shattered. Last year." The monitor dots prickled against my skin as I stretched my shoulders. "I think you were there. That day at the rail line near Picacho Peak?"

If memory served, she'd been among the Blood Angels captured—then suspiciously released—by Regional Command. *Come to think of it, that might've been when the two factions struck their deal.*

"You've barely had your power for a year?" she asked, eyes wide with disbelief. "And you've gotten this far since then?"

"Less than a year. It was last August." I winced as another sensor pinched. I was starting to wonder if there was more than adhesive holding them in place. "I had good teachers. And I'm not sure how long it takes others to learn, but I guess it was faster for me." I decided to risk asking, "When did *you* Shatter?"

She was silent for a long time. I was beginning to think I'd overstepped—and was about to get shocked for my curiosity—when she said, "It's been almost three years." She glanced at me. "I was sixteen."

"Oh." I twisted the edge of the blanket covering my legs. "That's...that's young. Were you alone?"

Something flashed past her walls, helplessness that I almost recognized, before, "Yeah." She tipped her chin up angrily. "Not that it mattered."

I think it did.

Some of my thoughts must've come across my face, because her expression morphed back to the hard, expressionless mask it had been when we encountered each other at Tía Gloria's. "I turned out fine, thank you. Maybe I didn't have such great teachers, but I still learned." She got up to grab my hand, cinching the restraint painfully tight and securing my wrist against the bed rail before repeating the process with my other arm. "The Angels saved me."

"Call it that if you want." I knew I shouldn't say it, but some part of me was grateful that she'd let down her guard even a little bit. *Maybe there's still hope for her.* "But even if they helped you once, you aren't anything but a weapon for their allies now. Loyalty's supposed to work both ways, you know. This—" I nodded at her. "This just seems like you do their bidding, like some kind of servant."

I wasn't braced for the sting of electricity that made my muscles seize and left a metallic taste in my mouth. As the sensation faded on the echoes of the door slamming, something else made its way through the pain.

Tears. She's upset?

Tara's reminder rang loud in my mind. *Going after someone who doesn't want to be helped isn't going to result in anything but heartbreak.*

I clenched a fist, my muscles tensing against the

restraints. *I have to try. She might not realize it, but she's just as trapped as I am.*

I DID my best to sleep that afternoon, and by that evening, my power was regenerated. I spent the next hour mentally mapping the area, the knowledge that I would only have one opportunity to get away weighing like a rock in my stomach. By five o'clock, I'd concluded this was the derelict medical complex a few miles south of where Los Diablos had captured me—too far from Station Somewhere for anyone from the squad to hear me, but close enough that I could get there on my own if I was able to escape this facility.

With my awareness so heavily invested in my surroundings, it was easy to notice when several new arrivals made themselves known during the afternoon. Shockingly cold to my Shattered senses, they gave me the impression of glistening metal and white light, sharpened words, and the sense of control so brittle that crimson violence would certainly spill if it was lost.

I shivered. These newcomers felt like Caleb's nightmares in physical form. *I didn't think Vanguard would already be so different from the rest of the EDF. I need to get out of here.*

The Shattered returned to give me dinner at six, every expression screaming that she'd rather be anywhere but in my presence. She did release my dominant hand for me to feed myself, but my attempts at conversation were met with stony glares. After a few tries, I resigned myself to eating in silence.

I noticed the others coming down the hallway before she

did—the original gang members and those who had once been EDF got along about as well as cats and dogs, and these three were arguing even as they approached. They opened the door; a pair of tattooed men who'd once been Blood Angels and a man whose regulation haircut was starting to grow out. The former Defense Force man was wearing a navy medical jacket like what Josephine had worn at Base 36. He pulled a pair of gloves out of his pocket and eyed the monitor screen.

"Well, that didn't take long. I think I understand why they're so worried." He rounded the bed with a curt command to the girl. "Get that back around his wrist, kid."

"The *kid* has a name, whitecoat," she said, slim fingers moving to secure my wrist to the bed. "Believe it or not, some of us freaks do have souls."

Somehow, I felt like that remark was directed at me.

"Sorry. Sierra, is it?" The man didn't wait to hear her answer as he twisted a second line into a juncture on the tubing between my arm and the saline bag. "Sierra, I'm going to have you hang around while we do this. Just in case things go sour."

The relief of having had a day without interference vanished in a cold sweat. "Do what?" I asked, praying my voice had stayed steady.

"Oh, we don't want you bringing the building down on our heads, or trying to read our minds." The medication pump attached to the IV pole beeped, and I looked up to see him pulling an opaque cover off a new, small IV bag. The liquid inside looked clear, innocuous, but I knew from helping Josephine that appearances could be deceiving. "It's only a temporary measure, but"—cold fluid began flowing down the tubing—"at least it'll keep you quiet."

"Wait—" I yanked at the restraints, cyan swirling under my skin. "What are you—"

The man made an urgent gesture, and one of the gang members drew a handgun with startling speed and a panicked expression.

"Stop!" the girl—Sierra—yelled. She planted a blue-glowing hand on my chest, leaning into it and pressing sensors deeper into my skin as she ground out, "Don't. Move." She gestured toward the door with her free hand and leveled a stern look at the doctor. "Get out, all of you. I can handle him. You can do whatever else you need to after he's sleeping."

While I guessed the former Defense Force man had some experience with Shattereds, it was obvious that the two others didn't. They practically shoved him out the door, stumbling and cursing in their hurry to get out themselves.

"Don't move," Sierra repeated, this time with a hint of pleading as she turned her attention to me. "It'll only be a minute till it takes effect, and all you'll do is sleep. They only want you to stay quiet. Just don't—" She swallowed hard. "Don't try to fight your way free. I'd have to kill you, and—" Reluctance hummed in the narrow space between us as her fingers tensed. "Don't. Just don't."

I wanted to argue, but my eyelids were getting heavy. "I'm not...going to try anything." My power pulsed, slug-gishly trying to fight the forces overtaking my nervous system. Drawing a deep breath, I forced out the prematurely honest words, "I don't want to hurt you, Sierra. I never did."

"What?" Her eyes widened. As sleep overtook me, I heard her whisper, "Why?"

CHURNING red against white light and glittering metal. Caleb's memories? *No, this isn't that. This isn't there.*

Cold, professional voices; clinical even in the middle of an argument. *I can hear them. How? I'm asleep, right?*

"We can't keep sedating him. This isn't a long-term solution. See?" A bright light shone into my eye. "His power's eating up the Versed like it's nothing. Eighteen hours of this and he should be out cold, but he's barely even asleep!"

A slam of something—a cabinet door?

"You think I don't know that?" A shadow moved across my eyelids. "It's not ideal, but it's the best thing we've got. I don't care how much he needs or what combo we have to try, we *can't* risk moving him until they're ready for containment."

Spanish from the hallway. Silence from the two in the room.

Then, "Dude, if they find out..."

The head of the bed angled backward, and I couldn't stop my head from flopping to the side as gloved hands repositioned me.

"Shh!" A sheet rough with industrial detergent slid over my torso. "You realize what those gangbangers would do if they knew? They think they're going to get him all to themselves once this is done, and they'll be pissed when they realize it's not going to happen."

"Yeah. They're crazy, man. I mean, look at him." Gloved fingers encircled my wrist, checking the pulse before tightening restraints. "He's just a kid!"

"Not *just* a kid," the first voice warned. "If not for him, they'd still be top dogs around here. You should've seen the looks on their faces when the docs said we needed him alive." The man's voice dropped. "Doesn't matter how cooperative they've been; they want him dead."

"Yeah, well, Kartchner will kill us *both* if something happens to him now."

Darkness on the heels of a switch being flipped. Something beeped softly, and the sensors kept skewering into my skin. It was cold, so cold, and even this moment of clarity was fading with the voices as they retreated down the hall.

They're afraid. Of me, of their allies.

But more afraid of their superiors than anything else.

I'm asleep—right?

Miramonte Neighborhood
Santa Cruz Valley
May 24

MUDDLED dreams gave way to unconsciousness, broken only by shocking, searing pain. My eyes snapped open to dizzying brightness and the sight of several former Blood Angels. One ripped a sensor from my chest and I jerked away with a startled yelp. My eyes refused to focus and my power was sluggish, as slow to wake as a tortoise from hibernation. Still halfway asleep, I shied away from the man holding my shoulder, only at that point realizing that my hands were free.

"Where—what—"

"Hold still, kid," he said in gruff Spanish.

Another sensor ripped free with more energy than care. I twisted my head to see it land with a *plink* alongside several others in a tray on the counter. Blood glistened on tiny metal teeth, and matching stickiness welled in several places on my chest.

"It's time to go," one of the others informed me. "They've got your new home all ready for you."

The brightness of the room faded to predawn darkness as I was hustled into the hallway. Each footstep echoed down the corridor, its shining linoleum marred with skid marks and scratches from years of abuse. The darkened shapes of several more former gang members blocked our entrance to the next hallway, and a new voice asked, "They're ready to move him?"

One of the men supporting me spat on the floor. "Yeah, finally. And the sooner they give him back, the better."

A deep sigh came from the men blocking our way. "Yeah...about that. Sounds like plans changed, and they'll need him on a permanent basis."

Someone cursed behind me. "Permanent? I've got a score to settle with this freak!"

"Well, Vanguard said they needed him 'alive.'" Foreboding circled the edges of my consciousness as the shadowy figures drew nearer. "I don't recall them saying *how* alive."

Someone laughed, a broken, hopeless sound that pierced my heart as my arms were pinned behind me. "That's more like it."

There was a crack, and my vision exploded with white light as a fist hit my temple. Before I had time to react, something drove into my stomach with the force of a sledgehammer.

I doubled over, gasping in shock as my weight pulled the man behind me off-balance. He spat out a curse and shoved me to the floor. The air rushed out of my lungs for a second painful moment as I hit the ground, my reflexes still too slow to catch myself. A fiery spurt of pain went through my ribs as a kick landed with all the force of frustration released.

"Not so tough now, are you?" someone said, the glow of a flashlight hitting my face. Another hard strike landed on my lower back. Awful, instantaneous pain spread through my torso as he added, "And to think, all it took to get you down was a little night-night juice."

Cruel laughter sounded in my ears, the emotion flooding my system with cold, horrible helplessness. A burning sensation streaked across my ribs, and a muffled, high-pitched whine escaped from behind the arm I'd wrapped to guard my head.

"Oh, he's crying." Rough hands dragged my arm away from my face, light stinging my blurry eyes. "Guess their wildcat's just a kid after all."

I'd been like this before.

Rain pounding against the library roof.

A roll of thunder, answered by another concussive noise from inside the building.

The Blood Angels flooded my safe haven, tearing apart my belongings in search of the supplies I'd already delivered to the convent. I threw myself flat, frantically reaching for the knife I'd hidden under the couch. A boot thudded onto my hand, and the gangster twisted his foot to send white-hot agony shooting up my arm.

"What's going on?" A girl's voice cut through the harsh laughter, her sleepy presence outlined in cyan at the edge of the room.

Someone had the decency to sound guilty. "Sierra."

A hard hand shoved my face into the floor before releasing. I curled around my injured ribs with a whimper, side growing sticky with blood from a gash across two of them.

From above, someone else said, "Docs wanted him moved, finally. They didn't say what condition he needed to be in when he arrived."

"Are you crazy? Don't you know what he's capable of?"

Humiliated tears streamed down my face as I bit the inside of my cheek to keep from screaming.

"Cute. He thinks he can fight back." The gangster crouched to look me in the face. "When are you going to learn, kid? Nobody puts over anything on the Angels."

I'd been powerless then.

But now—

I took a deep breath, then another. The Gabriel of two years ago had curled into a ball and endured the pain, afraid of taking action. But I wasn't him. Not anymore.

"You screwed up." I pushed myself to an elbow, then my knees, gasping at the pain that shot through my chest. Adrenaline finally overpowered the drugs in my system as I said, "I'm not a kid anymore. And you left my hands free."

Power bloomed in my core, and I didn't waste a moment before letting it loose. Cyan light exploded outward, the wave knocking everyone back as I regained my feet with trembling limbs.

The man who'd been holding my arms pulled a gun from his waistband and snapped several shots in my direction. They pinged harmlessly off the shield that blinked into life around me, its light filling the corners of the desolate room with eerie blue. The other men were slower to react, getting to their feet with groans. One man's hand went to his chest, and he winced and swore as he drew his handgun.

My own ribs burned, with a deeper ache pulsing in my lower back. I did my best to ignore it and settle into the guarded stance Caleb had taught me. I needed to end this fast, or the pain from my injuries would overwhelm my concentration and I'd be a goner. *Keep it together.* A thread of hope darted through the edges of my mind. *Maybe I can get out of this.*

I dragged in a painful breath and sent an energy ball directly at the man who'd first awoken me. The force of the blast knocked him into the wall, his head cracking into the cinderblocks before he crumpled to the floor. The shock of his death sounded strangely through my head, freezing my limbs and sending me staggering.

Across the room, Sierra yelled. Any trace of sleepiness had vanished from her presence, and her eyes glowed with a blue so bright it was almost white. Burning, blinding energy coursed up through the unshielded ground and through my feet. With muscles locked and my mouth open in a soundless scream, I toppled—and another wave of power burst out of my body.

Sierra's yell was cut off, and the electricity locking my limbs evaporated. I regained my feet with difficulty, my relief disappearing in panic as several more men charged into the room. The weapons in their hands were familiar shapes, but bore markings that—in the glow of my shield—were the color of old blood.

"Stand down!" someone yelled, the timbre of his voice undercut with fear.

I gritted my teeth against a wave of pain and sent power through the ground, like Tara often did and Sierra just had. The linoleum buckled and heaved under my opponents' feet, sending them stumbling.

Ruby light cracked overhead, and I involuntarily ducked the bolt as a fragment of Caleb's memories arrested my mind. Shaking off the terror, I launched a blast of energy to counter the next shot from the hybrid xeno weapons. A ceiling tile dropped in the aftershock, then another, as one of the men screamed, "It's coming down!"

He lowered his weapon and dashed around me, his foot catching on the linoleum and sending him sprawling over a body crumpled in the hallway. The person he'd tripped on moaned and rolled over, and with an unexpected pang of regret, I realized it was Sierra. Blood darkened her blonde hair and ran down the side of her face as her comrade pulled her up, her confusion and dizziness potent enough to make my stomach turn.

The building shuddered, and a doorframe buckled. A chunk of the ceiling impacted my shield as the roof began dipping toward the floor.

"Stand down, stand down!" the man near Sierra yelled. He'd wrapped an arm around her torso to keep her upright, pleading replacing the anger in his voice. "You'll kill us all!"

Determined. Resilient. Still worth saving.

The unexpected emotion was enough to throw my concentration, and for a moment, my shield winked out.

One of the others noticed my hesitation. He dove, catching my knees and slamming me to the floor. The impact against my shoulder did nothing to soften the pain that exploded in my ribs, and my groan came out more as a sob.

"Surrender," the man demanded, wedging his knee into the small of my back and twisting my arms behind me. "Before we all get killed."

My voice rasped over vocal cords worn out by containing screams. "Okay."

MY CAPTORS WEREN'T careful of my injuries. Within

moments of surrendering, I'd been handcuffed, blindfolded, gagged, and carried bodily out of the building. A truck waited outside; one of the gas-powered vehicles they'd operated out of as Blood Angels. Fresh air hit my face before the door slammed shut, the warmth reminding me how close we were to the full fury of summer.

My power was ebbing after the onslaught of sedatives, pain, and overuse, but I focused as much as I could in the direction of Station Somewhere as we sped away. Now that the adrenaline from the fight was gone, all I was left with was pain and regret. There was little chance of my getting anyone's attention at this distance, but I had to try.

I'm alive.

I'm fighting.

Does anyone hear me?

Finally, like a tiny flame flickering across a darkened field, a response. Silent tears, lingering pain, the tension of a sleepless night broken by surprise and recognition.

Gabriel?

Tara! I turned my head toward the sense of her. It was faint, even the whisper fading as the distance between us stretched. *I'm alive.* I pushed the words in her direction, imbuing them with as much of my will as I could. *I'm alive.*

I thought she might've understood, but the flame that marked her presence vanished into the darkness of the city. Exhausted, I stifled a moan as the truck bumped over something.

"Shut up," one of my captors muttered, a boot prodding my injured side.

I bit the inside of my cheek to muffle another moan. After that I stayed still, as my waning power tracked our progress through the predawn city. We were going south, that much I could tell, but beyond that I was lost. *How's anyone going to find me? Will they even know where to look?*

"Look alive, everyone," someone warned in Spanish as the truck slowed to turn a corner. "They're not going to be happy with what happened."

"It's not my fault," one of the others argued. I thought I recognized the voice as the man who'd rushed to tend to Sierra. "I told them antagonizing him was a bad idea."

They fell into arguing over what story to spin for Vanguard as the driver navigated the outskirts of a large industrial campus. My power reserve ebbed lower and lower as I strained to triangulate my position, range shrinking until I could barely keep track of the area immediately outside the truck.

We came to a rolling stop amid sheer, echoing concrete— a loading dock of some kind—and the truck bounced with the exit of its passengers.

I couldn't make out what was said between the personnel who came out of the Vanguard building and my captors, but the sudden anger from the newcomers communicated everything I needed to know. The icy lethality I'd felt from them earlier was even more apparent today, and even less contained.

I huddled in the corner of the truck, numb to everything but terror as the *snap, snap, snap* of weapons' fire shattered the dawn. The panicked voices of men who'd once been Blood Angels fell off one by one. Their presences vanished from the edges of my mind, punches of death reverberating through my stomach and sending twists of nausea up my throat. In the cab, Sierra cried out—equal parts fear and fury in her voice.

Finally, the weapons' fire halted, and I knew with a

growing sense of anxiety that Sierra and I were the only two left alive of those who'd arrived at the industrial complex.

"You and you, take your squad and go back to their base," someone ordered with the curt edge of an officer in his voice. "Clean it out completely. I don't want any of them left to come after us later."

Several voices snapped out acknowledgments, and the sound of boots thudded past the truck. "Sir?" someone called from the cab. "Their Shattered's alive, but she's hurt. What should we do?"

The officer's voice was crisp, like he'd anticipated this question. "Get her inside. The docs said..."

His voice trailed out of my hearing, leaving me faintly worried about what I'd overheard. Before the implications could sink in, a sharp intake of breath and string of curse words heralded the arrival of someone else to the foot of the truck.

"They weren't kidding when they said he was in bad shape... Hey! Someone get a gurney over here!" A firm hand touched my shoulder, and I recoiled with a muffled whimper. "I knew something like this would happen. I *told* them not to leave him alone."

THE NEXT SEVERAL hours blurred into fluorescent lights and clinical voices as medical staff tended to my injuries. The lights glinted off the tiny teeth of new sensors as they bit into my chest and back, a nervous technician putting an adhesive cover over each before moving on to the next. I wasn't certain at what point my power finally blinked out, only that the pressure against my mind had morphed into a featureless void. The staff left me alone after finishing their ministrations, though the scrape of a chair outside the door warned me of the presence of guards.

With my hands free at last, I undid the hidden zippered pocket at the outside seam of my cargo pants and pulled my recorder free. With a cautious glance at the strip of light beneath the door, I clicked on the device and took a careful breath.

"Well, I'm alive," I whispered, throat grating on even the quiet words. "I'm not sure why or how, but I'm alive. It's—" I looked at the clock over the door, its ticking unsteady like its batteries were wearing down. "It's just after ten in the morning, and they've left me alone." I ran a hand across the regulation T-shirt the medical staff had provided me with. It was rough against my fingertips, but at least now the sensors, bruises, and bandages weren't visible.

"They say I broke a few of my ribs, and I have something close to twenty stitches—I think. I lost count while they were putting them in." The medic doing the stitches had done her best to numb things, but I'd still felt the needle as the gash over my ribs was sutured shut. Bruises had already begun showing through my skin, dark and ugly under the bronze. "And something's wrong with my kidneys too—at least, there was blood when they took a urine sample and my back really hurts."

I shifted positions against the raised head of the bed and winced. Between stitches, cracked ribs, lower back pain, and the headache that came with burnout, I hadn't put up a fuss when the medics administered a painkiller through a newly placed IV. My vision was getting swimmy, but the pain was finally subsiding to something I could *almost* ignore. "Given all the injuries, I don't think I could get out of here on my own, even if I managed to escape the guards."

Up to now, things had been easy enough to say. Straight-forward, like the narratives Bandit insisted we write for each incident. I swallowed hard before continuing, "I don't know what's going to happen to me. Vanguard patched me up like they want me to recover, but that only makes me more scared." I shuddered as a crimson flash blinked through my brain and was gone—a fragment from Caleb's memories. "And whatever they're up to here, they don't want anyone knowing about it." The orders I'd overheard the officer giving took on new meaning as I stammered, "Th-they *killed* the rest of the Blood Angels—all of them but Sierra."

Dammit. I hadn't meant to say her name.

Metal scraped against linoleum, and a murmur of voices could be heard in the hall. My tongue froze to the roof of my mouth as counterintelligence training ricocheted through my head. *Don't give them anything they can use against you.*

I stared at the recorder's blinking light with new eyes. I'd been speaking Spanish, yes, but that was no real guarantee of privacy. *They could take this and use it against me.* I shook my head, vision swimming with painkiller fog. *I can't trust my thoughts with anyone*—the recorder's plastic housing creaked as I tightened my grip—*or anything.*

Once decided, my fingers couldn't move fast enough, fumbling over the tiny buttons in my haste to delete every story, personal log note, and conversation I'd collected in the last two weeks. Only when the indicator lights flashed their test pattern of green-red-green did I stuff the device into my pocket and slowly exhale.

Gone. All of it.

I lowered my head to my knees, drawn up to my chest despite the pain. It was dark behind my closed eyelids, the silent space in my head an echoing void.

It's so quiet in there.

After Judge's death, I'd gone into the desert and burnt myself out on purpose. Then, the silence had been welcome. Now, it made me feel untethered, drifting aimlessly through space and time with nothing to hold on to—almost as though the silence itself could overwhelm.

May He be a refuge to you when the world grows too loud.

The chaplain's words at St. Augustine's.

I dug in the opposite pocket where I'd put the rosary he'd given me. Rough paracord met my fingers, and I closed a hand over it like it was the only thing tying me to reality. The words that spilled from my lips toward heaven weren't polished or beautiful, but on their heels came peace beyond anything I'd hoped to find.

Finally, I fell asleep. Even surrounded by enemies and uncertainty, I fell asleep, and—if the clocks were to be believed—stayed so for almost a day. My dreams remained peaceful, unmarred by nightmares or worries. When I woke, it was with a moment of calm before the hands of the clock and my own mental calculation made me realize that something was horribly wrong.

It was still too quiet in my head.

THE "QUIET ZONE," Deadeye had called it. The goal we'd been working toward for months, the final realization of our calibration of the Unbreaking Field.

I hadn't expected it would feel so...empty.

"How are you doing it?" I demanded, pain shooting through my chest and radiating down my legs as I stood in the hallway outside my room. For all the security I knew the EDF was capable of, the door hadn't been locked, and the troopers on either side had almost stumbled over each other to get out of my way. Luckily for them—and me, not that I'd ever admit it—one of the doctors from yesterday had been coming down the hall.

He stepped back, one hand raised as if to ward off an attack, "Nothing! We haven't done anything to you."

"Not *me*," I snapped. "My power!" If I'd been uncertain earlier of what was going on, the physical symptoms now setting in were a clear indicator. My vision was distorting, my stomach churned, and my head ached like I'd been burned out for hours, just like it had during our calibration tests at the university. "I've been asleep for over a day; there's no way I should still be burned out. What did you do?"

"Leave him alone."

This new voice was level, stern, and came from behind me. I turned my head to see a lanky, brown-haired man approaching with another pair of troopers behind him. His eyes were mild blue behind a pair of thin-framed glasses, but every stride was filled with authority. Even worse, I'd seen him before, in Caleb's memories.

That must be—

"Dr. Kartchner." The man I'd been intimidating scuttled forward. "I was about to call you. He—"

"Yeah, 'he.'" I turned to face my new opponent, ribs protesting and my shirt catching on the edges of bandages as I moved. "'He' is wanting answers. Now."

The scientist stopped in front of me and crossed his arms. "Understandable. But you'll get your answers when we've had ours. Let's go."

One of the troopers grabbed my arm. I stifled a hiss at the stab of pain that went through my chest and, on instinct, flicked my free hand to summon an energy ball. Just like when we'd had our first success with the Unbreaking Field, nothing happened. My shoulders slumped, and a sinking feeling went through my stomach.

"Well, perhaps I don't need to ask to get my answers," Dr. Kartchner said with a satisfied smile. He nodded in the direction from which he'd come. "Bring him this way."

A LAB OCCUPIED the other end of the hallway, nonskid grey flooring meeting dingy white paint and speckled ceiling tiles. A procedural table took up most of the floor, its shining metal surfaces and clean lines more foreboding than any dark hallway. One wall was filled with a waist-high window, opening into a control room that glowed with monitors. Another, larger monitor occupied the opposite wall, displaying an array of jittering lines and flowing wavelengths.

As the troopers marched me past the screen, I caught sight of my own name beside a data set. The line indicating my power dipped and flickered, its usual peaks flattened like a failing heartbeat.

It's true, then. I swallowed at the sight of the datasets, familiar after months of working with similar readings in the university lab with Deadeye. *How'd they get their hands on the device? I thought we had it locked up?*

"Recognize it?" Dr. Kartchner said behind me. "We have you to thank for calibrating the generator. Well, you *and* Ms. Ziegler. We'd never have gotten as far as this without your help."

Dismay made my voice stretch thin. "The schematics... the data..."

"Ours." He raised an eyebrow. "And both of you were kind enough to swallow the story of fugitive researchers hook, line, and sinker while the deep science division set up operations here." He glanced pointedly at the top of the monitor, where a sleek blue globe surrounded in laurel leaves glowed proudly against the dark background.

The Earth Defense Force's insignia.

I'd once been proud to wear that emblem, proud to raise

my right hand and swear to defend this planet from threats terrestrial and alien. Now, however...

Betrayal smacked me in the stomach, almost as painful as a death. "So someone in the EDF *is* behind this."

"Someone," the scientist agreed. "But not everyone. For that matter, I doubt most of Central Command would appreciate what we're doing. Not that they know—there's a reason it's called 'deep science,' after all." He nodded to a chair in the corner of the room. "Have a seat, please."

I dropped into the chair, "helped" by the troopers. One raised his voice over the rumble of an air handler to ask, "Sir? Need us to stay?"

"No." Dr. Kartchner was rummaging through a drawer below the window. "Given his injuries, I don't think he's much of a threat. You can go; I'll call you if I need you." He pulled a stool over with his foot and set a tray down on a rolling table. A paper packet peeled open to reveal a collection of blood draw tubes. "Your arm, please?"

It wasn't a request, but I complied anyway. Maybe it was insanity, but the people I'd once trusted had turned on this place—on *me*—and I wanted to know why. As blood began flowing into one rainbow-topped tube after another, I finally got my voice under control. "Why? Why me? Why this?"

"We've been keeping a close eye on you, Gabriel. Hardly anyone develops their power entirely in the field, and so far, no one has developed a subtype like yours." The researcher swapped out a filled tube for one containing bright blue reagent. "I had hoped to study your abilities when you first Shattered, but instead of cooperating you ran back to this godforsaken place."

Anger pulsed deep in my core. "It's *not* godforsaken," I

said from between gritted teeth. "It's home. And at least I had enough courage to fight for it."

He snorted and pressed gauze into my arm before withdrawing the catheter. "Courage, yes. A quality your predecessor had in spades. You and he are very similar, and not just in personality." Dr. Kartchner wound a length of bandage around my arm to hold the gauze in place. "Those similarities have given us some very interesting ideas with regards to Shattered power."

I tugged my arm away the moment his hold loosened. "I've heard about your curiosity from someone who experienced it firsthand. I'm not interested."

Dr. Kartchner chuckled softly. "You must be talking about Lt. Fletcher. You can't deny that the xenos had some pretty good ideas, but this isn't about that. *My* interest has always been Shattered abilities, specifically how they're awakened." His voice had taken on a note like what I was used to hearing from Deadeye—the cadence of a scientist whose mind was completely wrapped up in a project. "That's why you're here. Given that we have a field that's fine-tuned to someone who's already Shattered, we can create scenarios that'll let us reconstruct how your Shattering happened." He smiled. "And if we can quantify it, we'll be another step closer to repeating it in others."

A shock went through my chest. "WHAT?"

"Oh yes." He pulled off his glasses and closed them, placing them in his coat pocket. "Think about it. We could induce Shattering under controlled conditions, even tailor subtypes to the individual. No more relying on people suddenly breaking in the field. No more lives ruined by untrained Shattereds with no control of their power." He tilted his head to look at me. "No more lives unnecessarily lost."

My chest painfully expanded as I took a long breath. My thoughts spun as images of the Shattereds I'd known—Tara, Judge, Sierra, even the Blood Angel who'd died several months ago—flashed in and out of my mind's eye. *We could have families of our own. Our lifespans might increase. There would be fewer deaths, and maybe the world wouldn't look at us like something to be feared.*

The hope almost ached. "You could do that?"

"*We* could, if we worked together." He spread his hands wide; an invitation. "You could help us pioneer this new technology; be on the cusp of the greatest scientific discovery of our time." His voice dropped. "So many people could be saved, Gabriel, if you only help us."

I turned the idea over and over in my mind, letting it unfurl in the muffled emptiness where my Shattered power normally filled the void. *Maybe...maybe there's a chance I could fix all of this, if I say yes.*

"I won't lie, it sounds really good. To be able to live a life without fear and help others do the same. It's all I've wanted, ever since the occupation ended." The words came quickly, though instinct warned me to temper the hope. *I have to know for sure.*

With a quick glance at the monitor, I reached out for my power. During our testing, I'd been able to break through the field's parameters with my empathic subtype even if my offensive capabilities were stifled. Surely this would be no different. After a long moment, cyan bloomed behind my eyes and a fragile tendril of power snaked through my mind, lending a tiny glimpse into the man's emotions.

Greed.

Control.

I frowned and pressed further. "I'd like to say yes, except..."

Fanaticism.

Manipulation.

Dr. Kartchner's eyes flicked to the monitor, then widened in shock. The line depicting my power was steadily creeping upward.

"You're...you're *lying.*" I could tell for certain now, the thread wrapping clearly around his emotions and painting the sickening truth into my consciousness. "It shouldn't surprise me. I saw what you did to the Blood Angels after they delivered me here. You don't care about your allies once they've served their purpose, and I can't believe you have Shattereds' best interests at heart." An angry edge roughened my voice as I got painfully to my feet. "I might not love everything my power entails, but there's no way in hell I'm letting you mess with it."

The doctor smacked a button on the wall. A chime sounded overhead, and the door flew open to admit the troopers. Within a few seconds, my hands were twisted behind me, the cut across my ribs burning with each breath. Power still wove through my head, and I cautiously began gathering it into my core. I'd been able to break the "quiet zone." Maybe now I could fight my way free.

"I suppose I shouldn't be surprised," Dr. Kartchner commented with a sigh. He replaced his glasses on his face and turned to the monitor, inspecting first it, then me with the clinical interest of a child burning ants on the sidewalk. "But I have to say I'm still disappointed."

He adjusted a setting on a console to the right of the screen, and a wave of nausea struck me. The power I'd gathered vanished, and my knees buckled. I closed my eyes, breath coming in carefully measured increments until the nausea subsided. After the brief input from my sixth sense, the silence was once again deafening.

When I opened my eyes, the line on the monitor had flattened completely, and something malicious had appeared in the blue of Dr. Kartchner's eyes. "This isn't a fight you're going to win, Gabriel. The faster you learn that, the easier it'll be for everyone."

THEY GAVE me a few days to recover, if you could call it that. A glass cubicle had been constructed in one of the other procedural rooms, and the Vanguard staff kept pulling me into it as if I were a lab rat—drawing blood, measuring biometrics, and suggesting I test my abilities against the field's parameters.

After the attempts to coerce me failed, their tones turned ugly. I learned why the sensors embedded in my skin had metal teeth after a bone-rattling shock startled me out of an argument with one of the technicians.

"I'm patient, but even my patience has limits, Gabriel," Dr. Kartchner said through the intercom. "Cooperation really is your best option here."

I threw a rude gesture in his direction. As I did, the pain of another shock put me on the ground—and in that moment, a burst of cyan filled the pod. Sound and sense flooded my mind, and the facility snapped into place around me. Blue light collected in the corners of my vision as I pushed myself to my knees, exhilarated and energized despite the pain in the moment of my abilities returning.

There's no time. They'll block it any moment; I need to hurry.

I flexed a hand, willing power to swell into my fingers. Nothing came, but my senses sharpened even more. In a flash, I'd mapped the layout of the building. The lab here, humming with air handlers and computers. The procedural room across the hall, chrome and glass and sterile air. The generator itself, like a solid block of iron in a room by itself. A maze of corridors—this building was bigger than I'd originally assumed—peppered with the amorphous silvery forms of Vanguard staff and troopers. A girl—Sierra—alone in a room, bright cyan in my senses. A prisoner? Compliant? I had no idea, there was—

No time.

My sixth sense skipped over Sierra, speeding through the concrete-and-steel edges of the building to stretch as far beyond the Unbreaking Field as possible. There. The outside air, golden with late-May sunlight.

A surge of triumph came. *I knew I'd be able to break through. I wonder if I can*—I pulled the power in, gritted my teeth through another shock, and *yelled* as hard as I could.

HELP!

Something tightened on my senses like a damp towel snuffing out a candle. I doubled over and collapsed on the floor, consumed by nausea and a debilitating headache as the world went silent once more.

I pushed myself up on shaking arms. *I did it. I can still break free.*

On the heels of the triumphant thought came another, guilt-filled and sickening. *What have I just handed them?*

I didn't have long to wonder. Dr. Kartchner's voice came through the pod intercom a moment later. "Thank you,

Gabriel. That was extremely insightful. I think we're done for today." His voice took on a detached tone as one of the troopers unlocked the pod door. "I think we're going to have them give you something to help you sleep tonight...it'll give you a chance to rest up for the next phase of testing."

Sure enough, a technician with a green stripe on her sleeve appeared as my escorts returned me to "my" room. The medication pump beeped as she input a series of numbers into its depths and connected a set of tubing to the port in my arm while I sat unwillingly on the bed.

"This'll kick in after a few minutes," she told me, depressing the plunger on a syringe filled with clear liquid. "It's not going to knock you out fast; just make you sleepy."

Before I could even contemplate resisting, she was unscrewing the syringe from the port and throwing it away. The lights clicked off in her wake, there was a murmur of voices outside, then quiet.

Too much quiet.

They weren't prepared for me to break through the field, I realized in the stillness as I lay down and curled into a ball. *It gave them more data, but I wonder... I wonder if I could do it again.*

I let the idea play out in my mind, planning for the next time my power rallied. The sense of control should have instilled confidence, but only anxiety greeted me as I thought. I wasn't sure what adjustment had been made to the Unbreaking Field's frequencies in the wake of my temporary success, but every muscle in my body was aching like I'd been in a fight for my life. Based on how constant the nausea and dizziness had been over the last several days, I had every expectation that this new pain was here to stay.

I still have to try, but what's it going to do to me next time?

I sat up with difficulty and pulled the rosary from my pocket. Fragments of a psalm skittered past the shattered edges of my mind, half remembered despite the fog muddling my thoughts.

"Though I walk through the shadow of death, I will fear no evil..." The words turned over in my head as the sedative took hold, leaving bone-deep exhaustion, foggy thoughts, and silence. Finally, my eyes closed, and I drifted away.

"Get him, Gabe!" Deadeye cheered from the other side of the table.

Caleb and I had agreed to arm wrestle over who would clean up the dishes, a mistake I'd never made since. Even using his non-augmented arm, he was still stronger than me. He winked after slamming my arm to the tabletop, a compassionate light shining in his eyes. "You wash. I'll dry."

I came to long enough to feel someone repositioning my limbs.

"He's fighting it."

"Not that it'll do him any good."

"There's not a chance he could get in touch with the others, is there? I don't want Banshee tearing down the place with us still in it."

"Nah, Kartchner said they've finally gotten it dialed in so that he can't use his subtype at all." A blood pressure cuff squeezed my upper arm, then released. "Besides, they've got their hands full with the blackouts and the solar field being throttled."

Solar field. Deadeye and Bandit's conversations about the possibility of summer blackouts stirred somewhere in my consciousness. We'd been concerned about winter—heating took more energy than cooling, especially with the shorter days—but production had already been trending downward as we approached the deadly summer heat. *No wonder they haven't come for me. They're trying to save everyone else.*

Abuela pulled a fleece blanket up to my shoulders. "Bundle up, mijo, *and stay close to me." We'd lost power, and the house was so, so cold. I could tell from overhearing her conversations with the neighbors that things were bad. Her voice, though, was warmer than hot chocolate as she reassured me, "It's okay,* angelito. *This won't last forever."*

She'd been right. But this time, there wasn't anyone looking out for me.

This won't last forever. Right?

STAGE TWENTY

COLD. *Cold, cold, cold.*

My limbs stirred fitfully under the thin blankets, dingy walls wavering in my vision as I clawed my way into consciousness. The aching from yesterday hadn't subsided, and this time I knew it had nothing to do with sedatives. Anger stirred at the sight of the line snaking from my arm to the IV pump, and I wrapped my fingers around it. *No more.*

A fine-boned hand landed on mine. "Don't."

Wheels squeaked against the floor as Sierra slid around on an office chair to face me. I hadn't even felt her in the room.

You've gotten so used to your power, you forgot you had ears.

As soon as I saw her face, I could tell something had changed from the last time we'd spoken. Dark shadows had grown around her eyes, her hair was unbrushed, and her face was thin like she'd lost weight. The torn jeans and tank top she'd been wearing had been replaced by a shapeless top and trousers in a desaturated blue color—hospital clothes if I'd ever seen them.

As difficult as the last week had been for me, it was apparent they hadn't gone easily for her, either. *Captive? Collaborator? What have they been doing to her?*

She repeated herself, looking me seriously in the eye. "Don't bother. You won't like what happens if they have to put that back in."

I let my hand drop from the IV.

"Better." She settled one knee over the other, fixing her gaze on the opposite wall. I wasn't entirely sure why she'd been allowed near me, but the change in her demeanor suggested she'd been wrestling with more than one of her own demons. My muscles had finally relaxed when she softly asked, "Why'd you do it?"

"Do what?"

"You had the chance to bring that building down on all of us. You could've killed *everyone*—finished us off once and for all—and you didn't." She turned her face back to me, eyes haunted as she demanded, "You surrendered—why?"

It took a long moment for me to remember what she was talking about. Finally, I shook my head, even that small motion making the room spin. "Because even with everything you've done, you still deserved another chance."

Her cyan eyes widened, and she shrank in her chair. "*That's* your reason?"

"That's why my shield dropped, yeah."

"So you..."

"I told you," I insisted. "I don't want to hurt you. I never did." Sierra gave a long, slow exhalation as I added, "I had no idea they'd all get killed. I'm sorry. I know some of them meant something to you."

One of Sierra's shoulders hitched in a half shrug, her forehead furrowing. "They took care of me when I had no one else."

"But they were still afraid of you," I said. "Why'd you go back to them after they joined Vanguard?"

She took a deep breath—in and out—a whisper of despair I almost recognized. "Vanguard told me they were working on a way to make our power less likely to kill us. I don't know about you, but I want to live longer than fifteen years after Shattering."

I drew in a pained breath. Hadn't I felt the same way? Hadn't I almost agreed to something horrible, just for that reason?

She gave me a pained glance, and her elbows drew tighter to her ribs. "We made a deal—weapons and security, and I could be the first recipient of whatever cure was discovered, if I helped them capture you."

"That's—that's why you ambushed me?" Between exhaustion and pity, my voice came out softer than I'd antici-pated. "Don't you realize they're not going to follow through?"

Sierra bit her lip and looked away.

"I mean it, Sierra." I'd been lying down this whole time, but now I levered myself to an elbow, my arms shaky after the miserable night. "They don't care about you any more than they care about me. They just want our power; to use us however they like. The only reason they aren't using you for this project is that the field's already calibrated to me."

"You can't know that for sure." Sierra's shoulders hunched, like she could shield herself from the lie lurking behind her words. "They gave us a place to hide after Santana took over. Besides, I've spent too long surviving to stop now." She shook her head and got up, her voice dropping as she reached for the door. "I doubt they'd let me leave, anyway."

"You could if we worked together." The words left my lips without my stopping to consider. A heartbeat later, I decided I didn't regret them. "We could overcome the guards long enough to get out from under this field. And once we did, there's not much they could do to stop us." I pushed myself up against the head of the bed, a wave of dizziness making my eyes water. "We could be free—*you* could be free."

For a moment, I thought Sierra might agree. She ran a hand through her tangled blonde hair, cyan eyes fixed on the ground. Finally, her shoulders straightened. "I—I'm sorry," she whispered. "I'm too tied up in this to stop now."

She opened the door, and my heart sank as she took a half-step out...then stopped. Her head lifted, and she turned decisively back to my bedside.

I flinched involuntarily, setting my jaw in anticipation of a jolt of electricity.

"Calm down."

There was no flash of lightning, no burst of pain as Sierra wrapped her fingers around my wrist. Instead, warmth spread up my arm. The pain I'd been doing my best to ignore faded, leaving only a faint tingling under my skin. I took a tentative breath, then a deeper one, the relief bringing tears to my eyes.

"What—how—"

"The field's tailored to block *your* secondary, not mine," she said, fingers still warm against my skin. "I can't shield, or throw a whirlwind, or anything like that, but I can still weave electricity. It's not just lightning, you know," she said without meeting my eyes. "Pain is carried by it too."

A voice sounded nearby in the hallway, causing both of us to stiffen. Sierra pulled her hand away. "I—" She ducked her head. "I should go."

The door clicked shut behind her, and I heard her in conversation with someone outside. Their voices retreated down the hall, leaving me alone and—for the moment—free of pain.

With my mind clear, I let our conversation replay in my head until I came to a disheartening conclusion. *She's convinced they'll still help her, and I can't say I blame her. If I thought there was even a small chance to reach old age, I'd take it.* On instinct, I reached for my power, but the tiny specks clinging to the edges of my mind refused to cooperate. *I can't believe it's possible, though. Even if they did have some solution, they'd only use it to make sure we stayed in fighting condition as long as possible—like a program to make your computer run longer. I shuddered. And Shattereds would stop being people. We'd be tools. Weapons.*

I can't let them win. I can't. I have to stop them. The pain was already returning, forcing my eyes closed as the room spun. *Even if it takes everything I have left.*

IT TOOK several hours of foggy thinking, but finally I came up with a plan. That afternoon, I realized that the tubing going into my arm had a small plastic clip attached. It took some fiddling, but eventually I was able to wriggle it loose and replace it just above where the line entered my arm. Once there, a tiny adjustment was enough to clamp the tubing shut. With that safeguard in place, I waited and rested, closing my eyes against the constant dizziness and conserving my energy as much as possible.

Just like the previous night, nine o'clock arrived with another dose of sedative administered by the same green-uniformed technician. Evidently, Vanguard no longer trusted me to sleep through the night without causing trouble. As in pain and exhausted as I was, I had to hide a satisfied smile as she finished her rounds and left my room. She hadn't bothered checking to make sure the IV line was unobstructed before pushing more drugs into it.

They've gotten lazy. I put an even tighter crimp on the plastic line to keep the sedatives contained in the tubing and out of my bloodstream. I didn't *think* anyone was going to be back in my room before morning, but it wasn't worth the risk of pulling out the IV before I was ready to make my move. With eight hours of alertness ensured, I curled into a ball and waited.

Time ticked slowly by, marked by shivers crawling across my skin and the weight of the Unbreaking Field pressing into my body. I'd wondered in passing what Caleb's experience had been like in xeno custody, and now I didn't have to guess. If I succeeded in getting out of this, I promised myself, he and I would have a lot to talk about.

Finally, a chair scraped outside my door, and footsteps walked away. I sat up with an effort and squinted at the clock. Two in the morning. I'd been banking on the assumption that there weren't guards outside my room 24/7, and it seemed I'd been right. I waited another hour, just to be safe, but the footsteps never returned.

Time to go.

The adhesive cover over my IV site pulled at my skin as I

worked it loose. The catheter slid free, followed by a bubble of blood, which I staunched with a corner of the blanket. Once the bleeding stopped, I slid my feet over the side of the bed. The room spun around me as I got to my feet. Blinking away the worst of the dizziness, I steadied myself and opened the door.

The hallway was dark, lit only by the glow of exit signs and lines of brightness emitting from beneath a few doors. I caught my breath—just getting out of the room had made my muscles quiver like I'd been sprinting—and set off with one hand on the wall toward where I'd felt the generator's presence the other day. My hurried mapping of the facility had placed it in a room adjacent to the lab where I'd first spoken with Dr. Kartchner, but the corridors proved an almost impossible mess to traverse. It wasn't until my headache spiked when I turned a corner that I realized I could navigate via discomfort alone. After that, my mental map proved accurate, and soon I stood in front of a door.

A locked door.

I sagged against the wall, despair circling my heart. *I can't break through metal. Not while the field's up—and I can't even reach it to turn it off.*

My knees gave out, and I slid to the floor with my hands against the unyielding metal. *What was I thinking? They'll find me, and—and—*

This time, I didn't have the strength to push away the fragments of Caleb's nightmares as they assailed my mind. Crimson and cold, searing pain, and unending helplessness blended into the darkness of the hallway until I couldn't tell what was real or imagined. *No matter what I do, I can't win. Sierra was right. Fighting back never ended well for anyone.*

I couldn't hold my head upright any longer. It smacked

into the doorframe, the impact sending stars of white light through my vision. Shaken from memory and despair, I swore at the pain—then a realization cracked through the darkness.

People never change, Deadeye had said. *Somebody wrote the code on the doorframe.*

"The code!" My muscles cramped as I hauled myself up, fingertips straining over every surface of the doorframe that I could reach. Just as I thought my luck had run out, my fingertips scraped over something—digits, etched into the metal—and I couldn't contain a gasp of relief.

"Hold it right there!"

Blinding light flooded my eyes, and terror jolted through my system. Footsteps pounded toward me. A flash of red light illuminated the hall, a cry bursting out of my mouth at the sudden, shocking pain.

From there, everything blurred. There were shouts, footsteps, the overhead lights turning on, and more flashes of red as I yelled and fought back as well as I could. No matter what I did, nothing worked. My blows felt like they took forever to land, the world tipped each time someone hit me, and my headache became blinding. Finally, I dropped under the weight of both assailants and Unbreaking Field.

"Knock it off, Mendoza," one of the troopers gasped behind me. "You're only going to make this worse."

The statement, so like everything I'd been thinking only a moment before, ignited something furious inside my soul. *You don't get to tell me when I'm done fighting. And there's nothing left for me to make worse.*

I squirmed around until I had a hand free. Slapping it onto the linoleum, I closed my eyes and concentrated on light tracing each of the hallways and breaking into the open air. In an agonizing moment that made my heart feel like it was about to stop, the imagined map became reality as cyan swirled through my vision. The pressure of the Unbreaking Field lessened, and for a split second I could feel the threads of emotion that marked each of the men restraining me.

They'll knock me out any second. I have to—

My power didn't let me decide what to do. Another stunning shot hit my leg from one of the troopers who realized what I'd just been able to accomplish. A single image popped into my head—his stray memory, crystallized by power.

A man in an EDF uniform stood at the front of a room, staring down each person with intensity. "Shattereds and their abilities are the super weapons of our generation. They're too dangerous to leave free, but their value in the right hands is incalculable."

The image vanished as fast as it had come, and my power went with it. I let my head drop to the floor, exhausted, in pain, and on the verge of tears. *Someone high in the EDF is in on this, and I can't do anything about it. I can't even call for help.*

The thought had barely percolated through my head when Dr. Kartchner's voice came from the end of the hall.

"Gabriel, I have to say I'm impressed." He approached and knelt to look me in the face. "I didn't think you were able to stand, let alone pull something like this. Good thing we did an extra round tonight; you might've gotten away with it." He turned his attention to the troopers holding me to the floor. "Get him up. I think tonight's incident proves we're ready for Phase Two."

"Sorry if I don't cheer," I muttered as the pressure on my limbs decreased and I was hauled to my feet. "You're insane, you know."

I hadn't expected the jab to have any kind of effect, and it didn't. Dr. Kartchner only snorted and turned away, calling over his shoulder, "Sleep well."

I didn't bother resisting as the troopers hauled me away, didn't fight as my hands were bound and a guard remained in my room. Sleep claimed me soon after, the last thought in my head regret that I hadn't been able to reach the others.

At least I tried.

PHASE TWO STARTED the following day. The technicians sounded concerned, their voices tense with uncertainty as they carried out their usual routine of taking vitals, checking sensors, and replacing the IV I'd pulled out. This time, however, there was a new addition to their protocol.

"Hold still, please," one of them murmured, his hands gentle but firm as he swabbed behind my right ear with alcohol, a few centimeters below where my bio implant sat. "This might hurt."

"What a surprise." I'd been lying flat on my back with my eyes shut, the better to conserve energy and manage dizziness. I cracked an eye open to glare at the tech. "Nothing you people do is ever painless."

His brow furrowed, a flash of regret passing through his eyes before he set the alcohol to the side. "This time, it'll be just a pinch."

I bit the inside of my cheek as dull pressure swelled, then subsided. When the man released my shoulder, I reached up to discover a new adhesive cover over yet another foreign piece of plastic. "What's this for?"

The technician turned to adjust settings on the medication pump. "A frequency disruptor." He tapped behind his own ear. "To cancel out whatever latent signals that implant might be sending."

The other technician glared at him from across the bed. "Shut up."

"What?" He rolled his eyes. "He's not going to be able to *do* anything with that knowledge." They'd lowered the side railings on the bed to be able to work. Now, the railings clicked into place and the frame juddered as brakes were released.

The bed began moving with an accompanying surge of vertigo, and I stuffed down a burst of panic. *I can't do anything.* I tried, frantically, to collect enough power to call out or break free or *something*, but nothing happened. I was so dizzy I couldn't even move. *Helpless.*

The cold air of the lab hit my face, stark lighting illuminating my vision even from behind closed eyelids. The new device on my neck began humming, a whining tone that set my teeth on edge. Another high-pitched sound reached my ears as a girl's voice rang out in frustration. "—could think this is a good idea!"

My eyes snapped open, and I realized in a glance that things were different than when I'd first met Dr. Kartchner here. Several pumps and monitors stood by the procedural table, and the control room was crowded with people. I recognized Sierra's blonde hair as she stood mid-argument with someone in scrubs. The man shook his head, his posture utterly confident and patronizing as he turned Sierra away, both disappearing beyond the edge of the window.

"All right, here we go."

The technicians' words jarred me from eavesdropping as they slid me from bed to tabletop. Before I could squirm away, several sets of hands landed on my wrists, chest, and ankles, holding me still as restraints snaked to bind my limbs fast.

"Hang on, what are you—mmph!"

One of the technicians' gloved hands clamped over my mouth. For once, there was sympathy in his voice. "Don't. Don't make it worse." He reached into a pocket of his scrubs, and I felt my rosary being stuffed into my restrained hand. His voice dipped to a whisper, almost an apology. "This'll be over soon."

I closed my fingers tightly over the rosary, the ends of the cross digging into my palm. The technician stepped back as Dr. Kartchner's voice came from the edge of the room. "Is this working?"

I peered through wavy lines of vertigo to see him standing outside the control room, holding a recording device very similar to mine. There was movement from inside the control room, and someone gave him a thumbs-up.

"Yeah? Okay." He cleared his throat and addressed the control room like it was a camera. For that matter, there may have been one. "Phase One of the Vanguard Project was to perfect a field to contain Shattered abilities for future testing. With Phase Two, we're approaching the answer to the questions of what exactly happens when Shattered Power is unlocked within an individual."

He shifted from foot to foot, then began pacing in front of the window. "Now that we've completely blocked Subject 7's abilities, we'll be able to measure and quantify the electromagnetic changes that occur as his power attempts to break the barriers placed on it. This process will give us an understanding of exactly what conditions need to be replicated for repeatable results in those who haven't Shattered previously."

This is it. The words swelled at the edges of my foggy mind. *This is the data they've been chasing.* I felt for the tiny dregs of power that coated my veins and throbbed in the knots of my muscles. *Whatever happens, I have to contain it. I can't let them get their answers from me.*

Dr. Kartchner had kept talking while I'd been distracted. "...in many previous instances, the initial Shattering event typically occurs in a moment of extreme stress. To replicate that in Subject 7, we'll utilize a short-acting agent to temporarily induce high heart rate and nervous system response."

A pair of the researchers had been busy somewhere behind me while he'd been talking. Now, one of them twisted a chunky plastic syringe into a space on the medication pump over my head, the other giving emphatic tugs to each restraint on my limbs. The sciencey jargon had taken its time processing through my mind, but the beeping of the pump and muttering from the scientists as they scurried away made things sink in.

I glared up at Dr. Kartchner as he reached for the pump's controls. "You're a monster."

"Me?" He input a command before looking straight into my eyes. "I'll be the man who brought Shattered Powers under control. History will remember me as a hero."

I yanked fruitlessly on the binding holding my upper arm, adrenaline clearing my head enough to let me spit, "Not if I have anything to say about it."

"You? A ghetto kid from a dying region?" He smiled thinly. "Nobody would believe you."

With that, he stepped away. The control room door closed on his heels, and the lights inside the room dimmed.

I struggled against the restraints, expecting a shock, the

cold of a sedative, or for the Unbreaking Field to tighten its hold enough to make me black out. Instead, my heartbeat sped up—a little at first, then more, as a burning sensation spread through my arm.

I'd made the mistake exactly once in my childhood of annoying a spider-killing wasp. Its sting had been a streaking, hot thing that set every nerve alight and made my muscles tense in silent agony. I'd fallen to my knees and cried, unable to move while the wasp flew away unscathed.

That pain had lasted only for a minute.

The fire spread faster and faster with my increasing heart rate—across my chest, down my torso, into my bones. A moan escaped from between clenched jaws.

Then, a voice through the intercom. "Don't give up!"

I opened my eyes as the voice cut off. Sierra struggled against the arms of a burly trooper as he hauled her away from the control window.

For a single moment, the pain calmed on the heels of her words, and I could breathe. *She's fighting back. Finally.*

Then, Dr. Kartchner yanked a technician away from their station, and his hand slammed a button.

In the Unbreaking

I SCREAMED. I know I screamed.

No power rose in answer to the sound as it ripped through my vocal cords, no cyan tendrils or blue glow or earthshaking rumble. Light exploded through my vision, pain speeding through mind and body as moments shared with the squad blurred with nightmares. I struggled to keep their faces in my mind, but they shredded into nothingness as the edges of my vision went dark.

No. No!

My body was giving up. The screaming had become nothing but background noise as my mind collapsed, Shattered edges imploding into a bright, swirling core of cyan. All my being focused into a single thought.

I'm going to die here.

STAGE TWENTY-TWO

SUDDENLY, I wasn't there.

I lay on the kitchen floor in Station Somewhere, broken glass scattered across the cracked tiles. I struggled to my elbows, blood welling from a handful of cuts on the outside of my arm—one whose inside was laced with dully gleaming circuitry. Overwhelming pain and panic surged through my head, and as someone slammed open the bay door, I realized where—in whose mind—I was.

Gabriel!

The pain from outside faded in a burst of relief, and I felt my physical body slump into unconsciousness even as my mind calmed. *Caleb?*

In answer, a wash of strength swept across the edges of my mind. *I'm here.* His voice was strained; pain tempered by urgent determination. *What's going on? Where are you?*

What—his mental voice faltered, and I flinched at the memories fighting their way through our bond. *What are they doing to you?*

I don't know how, and I don't have much time, I said, struggling to put the words together instead of dumping the information at him. *I think I'm unconscious, but they won't let that last for long.*

Okay. I could feel him take a deep breath. Tara had pulled him upright, her voice high with worry and face panicked as he asked, *Where are you?*

I answered with as much of the mental image of the complex and its location as I could conjure. *It's Vanguard. EDF leadership are in on this—they've been playing us this whole time and they're trying to replicate Shattered powers. Caleb, I—*

If I'd been conscious, I wouldn't have been able to keep the tears at bay. *It hurts. I don't know how long I can hold on. I just want it to end.*

I was certain he was crying as well. *I know, buddy. I know.* His own memories battered at our connected minds in a swirl of freezing crimson, and this time *he* was the one to shield *me* from the horrible images. *Hold on as long as you can.* Fierce protectiveness surged past the pain. *We're coming for you.*

Something jostled my body, and a jolt of electricity sped through my limbs. In the distance, I could hear angry voices. I know Caleb felt my alarm as I said, *They're waking me up. Be careful. There's a field—it blocks Shattered powers. Tell the others to—*

Light flared through my eyelids, and someone rubbed my chest roughly. My throat grated on a gasped breath, cold air flowing through a mask over my nose and mouth. My whole body throbbed, and as I slipped into consciousness, I heard Caleb's voice once more in my head.

Hold on, Gabriel. You're not alone.

"MENDOZA, WAKE UP. MENDOZA! GABRIEL!"

A girl's voice.

A girl's voice?

Sierra?

My limbs were free, and darkness covered my eyes. An oxygen mask rubbed against my mouth and nose, freezing puffs of air dissipating around my face with each breath as I blinked at the ceiling. Wherever this was, it was not the lab.

"Where am I?" The words scraped out of my throat.

There was a gasp. "You're awake!" A hand landed on my chest. "They panicked when you went under. Once I got you back, they stuffed us both in here until they could decide what to do next." Sierra's cyan eyes glowed in the dusk of the room as she turned to squint at something out of sight. "You're still attached to the medication pump. I'm going to see what I can do about that, so *don't move.*"

Sierra disappeared, leaving a faint smell of citrus to compete with the freezing air coming through the mask. The pain from earlier ebbed in different areas of my body, my heartbeat sluggish after having sped to such a high rate. Some part of my mind informed me that the jolt I'd felt had been Sierra's power, pacing a rhythm for my body to follow into life, but the greater part of my awareness was too occupied in breathing to fixate on that fact for long.

Gabriel?

I gasped, my eyes snapping fully open despite pain and

dizziness. *Caleb? You're still here—how are you still here? I don't have... They blocked my... How?*

I don't know, and I don't want to know. The barriers that normally surrounded his mind were barely enough to contain the lethal danger flooding from him. I had the sense of armor weighing his shoulders, the bouncing of the truck, and the crackle of comms in his ears. *We're on our way. Are you able to take any action?*

No. I didn't try to formulate a coherent sentence in return, instead allowing a fraction of the pain, dizziness, exhaustion, and helplessness to slip through our bond.

Caleb shuddered as everything hit him, and for an instant Tara's voice sounded in the distance, concerned and angry. *Okay,* he said. *I wonder if—*

I couldn't tell what he was trying to do, but my breathing calmed and some of the shaking in my limbs subsided. I reached up to pull the oxygen mask away, the stickiness of drying blood from my nose meeting my fingers as they brushed against my face.

Anything? he asked.

If that was you trying to boost my power, no. Another breath rasped through my throat, still raw from screaming. *I felt something, but only barely.*

I think I have to be touching you for it to work. If we'd been face-to-face, I was certain I'd have heard him sigh. *We'll work with what we have. Oh*—distraction flicked somewhere in the distance. *Hang on.*

With that, my sense of him dimmed, as if layers of blast padding lay between us. If I concentrated, I could feel his emotions churning behind his mental walls, but the effort left me gasping for breath.

"Hold still."

Fingers circled my wrist, and panic jolted painfully through my veins before I realized it was Sierra. Her hands were surprisingly warm as she removed the IV catheter from my arm, the itch of a paper towel immediately coming to press into the spot afterward. "I figured taking this out is better than trying to disconnect the tubing. I got the disruptor off your neck while you were still out, so at least now they can't—" Her voice faltered in the darkness. "Ugh, why am I doing this?! I'm so stupid!"

"No." My arm moved with agonizing slowness as I reached up to brush her fingertips. "If I'm not mistaken, you saved my life."

"Yeah," she replied bitterly. "I save yours and you spared mine. Now we're even." Her fingers whisked away from mine. "Not that it'll do either of us any good. Lightning alone can't get us out of here, and we have a snowball's chance in hell of them letting us leave alive."

My hand closed weakly into a fist. "We have to try. I don't know if they got the data they wanted, but—"

"I think they must've. When you went under, that string bean with glasses was staring at the screens like he'd just rediscovered DNA." Sierra's voice had filled with more sarcasm than Deadeye's on a migraine day. "He didn't even care that you were about to flatline, after they'd made your heart beat fast enough to go into orbit. It was one of the *other* doctors who let me help you." Her voice softened, and I could've sworn I heard tears choking it. "I can't believe them. They didn't even care that you—that it—" She cleared her throat. "You were right."

My breathing was steadier now. I groaned as I shifted my limbs, still too weak to even consider trying to sit. "I know." My breath caught on that truth. "If they find a way to make

Shattering a repeatable event, they'll inflict that pain on so many more people. I have to stop them, no matter what it takes." I sought out Sierra's eyes in the gloom, her blonde hair tangled and obscuring their light. "And I know we've spent the last six months fighting each other, but I can't do anything without your help."

The silence in the room stretched, broken only by footsteps and raised voices outside. Whatever had happened in the lab when I'd passed out—*when you died,* my cynical side reminded me—it'd sent the staff into pandemonium.

At last, Sierra cleared her throat again. "I'll never understand why you lot are so stubborn. If it were me, I'd be content with getting out alive, and forget doing the noble thing. But you're right; we can't let them do this to more people." She tapped the back of my hand in the darkness, a weak fist bump that carried more weight than any handshake. "Let's see what we can do to stop them."

I took a shaky breath. "Okay." *Caleb? Did you hear that?*

Nothing came from him, but as I focused a little harder, the cadence of an intense conversation in Spanish filtered through our bond. The effort it would take to get his attention was beyond me for the moment, so I let my focus return to Sierra. "Don't ask me how I know, but the others are on their way. Something—" I stopped. *I have no idea how to explain this, and I don't know if I want to try.* "You'll just have to trust me. There's backup coming, but it does us no good if I can't reach them. I can't even stand right now, but can we at least get these sensors off?"

"Yes—wait. Are you sure?" Her fingertips rested on the monitors embedded in my chest. "It'll be obvious that something's up when you disappear from the screens."

I groaned. "Good point..." *I'm going to have to find out how far the others are from us.* "Give me a minute to think."

Her hand withdrew, and she retreated to where the crack under the door made a tiny pool of light. "Better make it fast. They won't ignore us forever."

I didn't bother answering, closing my eyes instead and reaching out to Caleb. *Are you there? Can you hear me?* My limbs still throbbed with the memory of the pain from before, and I bundled up a knot of it before pushing it into him.

Caleb jumped, the surprise reverberating between both of our minds. His attention returned, sharp and clear as he asked, *You okay?*

I'm fine. Sorry. Needed to get your attention. What's going on?

I'd expected him to tell me, but instead the walls around his emotions retreated and I dropped further into the bond. The darkened room fell away, and for the moment, I was in Caleb's mind.

"...down across the entire area, but at least now we know what area it is." Deadeye's sharp features were visible through the open visor of her helmet as she sat in my usual seat in the truck, her fingers busy over the keyboard of the surveillance station. The angle of her screen showed a map, a homing beacon blinking off the edge of a massive blob of buildings. "They'll be using standard sensor arrays, but luckily your guys are experts at dropping those in their tracks."

A familiar laugh crackled through comms, whether in-ear or through the truck's speakers I wasn't certain. "Yeah, but there's no need. Your pilot says he can jam the frequency from the air, but the Thunderbird isn't built to hover for that long. The moment the sensors go down, we'll need to move."

"Thanks, man," Caleb said. "Stand by for our mark. We have a fairly good idea of which building, but we'll know for certain when Banshee starts throwing up inside her helmet."

His shoulder was jostled by someone, and he turned as Tara glared up at him. "Shut up. I'll be fine; it's not the first field I've been under."

No! Tara can't go! I grabbed as much of Caleb's emotions as I could, dragging his attention toward me. *Her power won't react well and she's still hurt—Caleb, don't let her near here!*

He lost his balance as the weight of my determination struck, a hand going up to steady himself against the roof.

"What's wrong?" Tara asked, grabbing his armored forearm.

Caleb caught his breath with a gasp, and my own chest heaved in response. "It's Gabriel. He—" His breath hitched again, and I realized my pain was ebbing over to him. "He's worried about you being close to that field. He doesn't want you to risk yourself."

Tara's brow furrowed. "The two of you are connected, yeah? He can hear us?"

At his nod, Tara released Caleb's arm and grabbed the edge of his helmet to pull his face down to the level of her own. Something like acceptance flickered in her gaze as she and Caleb locked eyes, before Tara looked past her husband's soul to stare into my own.

"Okay then, Gabriel. You listen to me, and you listen good. You're worth enough to all of us that we don't care what we risk by coming after you." Her eyes shifted focus, and I had the distinct idea that she was talking to both me *and* Caleb as she said, "Whatever happened in there earlier, whatever happens now, I'm not leaving you in there to die."

And that makes two of us, Caleb added silently. *No matter what.* His head rocked backward as Tara released his helmet, and he asked aloud, "Did you hear that, Gabe?"

I heard. I couldn't tell if the tears I was feeling were mine or his, but at this point it didn't matter. *I heard, but—*

"Good." He steadied himself against the ceiling. "Pipe down and save your strength."

"Focus on getting to the point where you can move," Deadeye admonished without looking up. "It'll be easier to get you out if we don't have to drag you. And keep your head down when the bullets start flying."

I'll try.

I jumped as Sierra touched my arm again. It took some effort to return my consciousness into my own body, but soon the darkened room resolved around me once more. Sierra had turned on a light under a cupboard, the glow enough for us to see each other clearly.

"What happened?" she whispered. "You blacked out again."

I shook my head. "It's the others. They're closing in. And"—I blinked hard as I recognized the voice I'd heard through Caleb's comms as Santana's—"I think the Blood Angels are joining them."

Sierra's voice went hushed. "Really?"

"Yeah." I tried to sit, spasms catching my muscles and my breath going ragged before she came to support my back. "They're as pissed as we are at Vanguard—oh, hang on. That hurts." I remained still for a moment, taking a few deep breaths before continuing, "Some of them might also be worried about you. Tía Gloria certainly is."

"I had friends on both sides of the split," she confessed distractedly as she pulled me upright. The room swam, then stabilized as she added, "I probably hurt them when I did what I had to do—well, what I *thought* I had to do."

"I know. They're waiting outside the campus, outside of sensor range. Once they move, we won't have much time to react." I eased the cramps in my shoulders, the prickling of sensors less bothersome after the horrific pain I'd endured in the last hour. "If these monitors are still stuck in me, Vanguard will be able to shock me enough that I won't be able to do anything but scream." My stomach churned at the thought. "I know it's a risk, but we need to get them off."

"Okay, if you say so."

Gabe, are you ready?

I jumped at Caleb's voice in my head. I was used to the mind bridge's constant two-way flow of information, but it seemed like he was able to control more of this connection than usual.

I guess. We're getting the sensors off, so you'd better move fast. They're going to know something's wrong when I drop off their radar.

Who's 'we'? Caleb asked. *Gabe, wait, who's—*

I stifled a yelp and slammed a barrier between our minds as Sierra ripped a sensor free. "Ow," I hissed from between clenched teeth. "Geez, that hurts."

"I shocked you to life a few minutes ago, and you're worried about *these* hurting?" Even with the tartness in her voice, Sierra was gentler with the next sensor, its teeth sliding from my skin with hardly a whisper of pain. "Just hold still. I'll get them."

It was quiet for a bit, as Sierra painstakingly peeled adhesive covers away and pulled the sensors off. While she worked, I let the barrier between Caleb and I drop enough to catch a glimpse of a parking lot lined with light poles and the sharp rooflines of concrete buildings. The bouncing of the truck had stopped, and he stood with one foot on pavement and the other in the dirt at the edge of the lot. His own heartbeat was mounting, if the flickers of tension running through his mind were any indication.

"Okay, Banshee. Signal 'em."

Beside him, Shattered power flared. A bolt of blue light streaked into the sky, reminiscent of the beam I'd used to get Sierra's attention so many months ago.

"Okay, they're moving," Bandit announced. He jumped down from the truck to land next to Caleb, slinging his rifle over his shoulder. "Let's go."

Brace yourself, Gabriel, Caleb warned, lethality running through his voice. *It's about to get loud.*

STAGE TWENTY-THREE

"THERE!" Sierra said from somewhere far away. "That's the last one." I shook off the images from Caleb's mind as she dropped the last sensor to the floor. "Now let's see what we can do to get you on your feet again."

I caught a cyan glow before she was touching my back, a tingle sliding through my skin. Like the last time she'd demonstrated the ability, the pain wracking my limbs subsided, and I took a full breath for the first time in what felt like hours.

"That might do it," I whispered. "Can you keep this up without burning yourself out?"

"Not long," Sierra said. "The field might be tailored to you, but it's still giving me a heck of a fight."

I took another breath, counting the seconds in and out as her hand left my back. "Better save your power, then. I think we're going to need it."

Sierra crossed to the door, opening it a crack. "No one's outside. I think we—"

Both of us tensed at the sounds of gunfire, muffled through several layers of architecture. "We need to go," I finished quickly. "Now."

Somehow, I was able to get to my feet and stay upright. The other symptoms of the Unbreaking Field assailed me as I got into the corridor, nausea and dizziness threatening to send me right back to the floor. Sierra caught sight of me wobbling and immediately came to steady me. She was several inches shorter than me, but unexpectedly strong as her arm tightened around my chest.

"They're coming for *you*, right?" she said, her hair whisking against my bare shoulder as we hurried down the hall. "Not supplies or tech or anything else?"

"Yeah, they're here for me." I took a sharp breath as a misstep sent a jolt of pain up my leg. Even with the lingering effects of Sierra's power, my body was barely responding to my mind's commands. "Caleb knows there's a loading dock; I told him as soon as I could. We need to get there—duck!"

I slid free of Sierra's arm and let myself drop, ducking my head as a pair of troopers darted into the hallway in front of us. An electrical hum built in the air before lightning arced between their guns and armor, leaving both of them in quivering heaps on the floor. Sierra lowered her hand, a glow fading from her eyes as she bent to get my arm over her shoulder.

"Loading dock, right."

We made it through the first corridor, then another, my consciousness splitting between my location and Caleb's as the squad faced off against the Vanguard resistance. Elsewhere, I could hear more gunfire, and once, a rumble that could only be Tara's destructive subtype at work.

Gabe? Caleb's voice broke through the rumbling. *Can you hear me?*

You're clear, I responded. We'd made it around another corner, leaving behind several huddled troopers who'd hesitated firing their weapons long enough for Sierra to send lightning through their bodies.

We're outside the loading dock. Caleb's vision overwhelmed mine, jumping between targets faster than I could process. Another rumble shivered through the soles of his feet, and Tara swore nearby. *The opposition is a lot worse than we expected. We're doing what we can, but Tara's having a hard time with her power.*

I felt it just now, I said, catching my breath as a twist of nausea from the field skewered my stomach. *She figured out her subtype is working?*

Yeah, Caleb replied, his chest spasming in response to the pain stifling my breathing. *Her subtype works, but nothing else does. And she can't use it too much. I'm afraid that—*He clenched his jaw and his muscles tensed. An unprompted image slid through both of our minds; the building crumbling in an avalanche of concrete and rebar. *We need her help, but her power's getting harder to control near this field. Is there any way to shut the field down from the inside?*

I took a deep breath, the action less painful with how deep in our bond was. *I think so. It's controlled from inside this building, and I know where it is. But I don't know...* I paused, uncertain if I should even say what I was afraid of. *I can't do much. Sierra can fight, but I can't help her. I don't know if I can shut it down on my own.*

Just get to the generator, then, Caleb ordered. *I'll have the others cover me so I can get inside. I'll find you, and we'll end this together.*

My stomach settled, despite the ongoing nausea from the Unbreaking Field. Taking out the field generator could set back the Vanguard project by months, possibly even halt its progress completely. And with him to help, Sierra wouldn't have to keep me upright *and* fight. *Okay,* I told him. *I'll find it. You're sure you can*—I paused, mind spinning with worry—*Will you be able to find me?*

Assurance skittered through my head, along with a crackle of voices from Caleb's in-ear comms. *Don't worry,* he said, then added aloud, "Whatever linked us seems to be working both ways. I'll find you."

I snapped out of the bridge and grabbed the edge of Sierra's sleeve. "We need to get to the field generator."

"Why? The loading dock is *that way*." She pointed toward the gunfire, which hadn't let up in the time my attention had been diverted.

"I know, but look." I pushed myself up from the floor, muscles quaking as I did. "The others are outside, but there's a bunch of troopers between us and them. We can't get out that way, and the others can't break through without Tara using her subtype—which could bring the building down with us inside."

Comprehension lit Sierra's eyes. "Got it." She pulled me to my feet and steadied me as I wobbled under the Unbreaking Field's influence. "They didn't bother moving it after you tried taking it out last night. This way."

We had to backtrack, sidestepping fallen equipment and Sierra's previously downed opponents as we went. Finally, we approached a door marked with red warning signs. "Here!" Sierra exclaimed. "We'd better hurry. Do you know the code?"

"It's..." I scanned the doorframe. In the daylight, the scratched letters were easy to pick out. "There. Try those."

"Nice." Sierra released my arm and let me stand on my own, punching in the code and testing the handle. The whir of an electric lock sounded, and the handle turned in her grasp. "We got it!" Without another word, she threw her weight against the door and took a step inside.

I flung out a hand. "Hold on—"

Before I could say anything else, a single shot rang out. Sierra screamed, and there was a sound of something falling to the floor.

No! Terror streaked into my heart as I staggered through the door—and froze.

"Well, that's twice now that I've underestimated you." Dr. Kartchner stepped away from Sierra's downed figure, holstering a gun and picking up a tablet. A bizarre but familiar machine sat atop a heavy work table behind him, Deadeye's and my work butchered and patched together with new components to create an alien device that exuded corrupting energy. "You keep surprising me, Gabriel."

I dropped to my knees alongside Sierra and reached out to shake her shoulder. I couldn't see any blood, but her cyan eyes were unfocused with pupils jittering back and forth. *A stunning frequency in the handgun?* "Sierra? Sierra!" I looked up with growing anger. "What'd you do to her?"

"The xenos had some useful tools for keeping prisoners contained," Dr. Kartchner commented. "Hit the right frequency, and the mind itself shuts down. I understand it feels a little like a nightmare, but it does the trick to stop attackers in their tracks. And as for you..." Dr. Kartchner skimmed a finger across the tablet's surface, and I crumpled to the floor under the amplified weight of the Unbreaking Field's effects.

"Let her go," I managed between surges of nausea. "She's not part of this."

"Oh no, she's coming with me." Dr. Kartchner turned to stuff a pile of printouts into a bag on the table, speaking over his shoulder. "You both are. I'm not going to let anyone with so much potential go to waste."

I took a deep breath, then another, my body working to master itself against the waves of vertigo and exhaustion. A sharp jolt of pain went through my hip, and I gasped before the sensation subsided. *Caleb?*

It took a moment for the sense of him to filter in, distraction and focus overriding pain from multiple sources as weapons' fire sounded nearer than ever. *Almost there. There's a lot of guys in here. I took a hit, but it's not too bad.* Another burst of pain caught the attention of both of us before he insisted, *Don't worry about me. Are you all right?*

I was about to reply, but caught sight of Sierra's fingers twitching and a hand closing on a flash of lightning. Letting the connection to Caleb sink to the back of my mind, I lurched forward and bore her wrist to the ground. Praying that she'd understand what I was trying to communicate, I gestured at the field generator. She jerked her head in the briefest of nods and I removed my hands.

I need to get his attention for Sierra to make her move.

The dizziness was getting easier to stand. I didn't stop to wonder why as I pulled myself up, using the table to balance.

"I don't know what you think this is going to accomplish, but I can't let you continue."

"Courage again." Dr. Kartchner turned to face me, shoving his glasses higher up his nose. "We talked about that at our first meeting, if I recall." He rested a hand on one of the machine's components with a sigh. "It doesn't have to be like this, you know. Even now, you could go down in history as someone who changed the world. Courage never gets anyone anywhere without power, Gabriel, and you could have both if you just cooperated." Dr. Kartchner's gaze flicked to the door. Clarity flickered through my mind as gunfire sounded outside it.

He's stalling. I caught my breath on another stab of pain. *Caleb?*

Hostiles outside. The words cut through the mental bond with grim certainty. *I'll hold the door. End this, or they'll—*

Cold. Silver. Red.

I took a deep breath. Banished the memories.

Then I raised my eyes to the scientist, words coming out hushed but gaining strength as I spoke. "You're all the same. You, the gangs, even the xenos. You think power solves everything, and controlling others with it will ensure your own importance." Something Bandit had told me finally made sense. I'd asked him why. Why, when the option was there to protect others, would some choose to exert their own authority instead? "You're afraid that without power, you'll be nothing."

Determination shot through from Caleb. *You tell him, Gabriel.*

Dr. Kartchner's face tightened, blue eyes freezing cold. "Those are bold words, when you know what I'm capable of." He pulled the gun from its holster and aimed right between my eyes. "There's still so much I could do with you."

Fury surged through my veins. "I *don't care* what you do to me." I pushed myself free of the table and stood straight. "You can steal my power, break my mind until there's nothing left of my will *or* my courage, but there's one thing that will never change." New strength stirred as I became aware of a figure in bloodied armor standing just beyond the door. Threads of emotion tangled, and I felt both Caleb's fierce pride and the doctor's cold desperation as I spat, "I will *never* stop fighting to make sure no one else has to suffer like I have."

The air hummed, vibrations building faster than thought. Electricity cracked through the metal table, the force throwing me to the floor. Sierra was on her feet with her hand wrapped around a power cable, her eyes illuminated with terrible light.

"He's right. Shattereds aren't a weapon to be wielded."

Dr. Kartchner's face contorted with rage as he turned on Sierra. "No!" His finger tightened on the trigger and the gun went off. A control panel threw sparks as the shot went wide. She ducked another shot, raised a glowing hand, and a stream of electricity poured into the field generator.

In the blink of an eye, my dizziness lifted, the nausea evaporated, and the world snapped into full sixth sense. Dr. Kartchner swore and reeled back from the crackling energy surging into the device, firing several times in my direction as he ran for the door.

Fiery pain streaked through my right shoulder and chest even as a shield exploded around me, the wind driven from my lungs and brilliant crimson light flashing across my vision at the force of the gunshot. I fell back, unable to do anything more than gasp raggedly while my hands went to staunch the blood flowing from my chest.

Only, there was no blood.

A shout came from the hall, followed by several gunshots as my vision resolved into the sparkling blue of a full-strength shield. The device on the table threw off gouts of acrid black smoke, its sharp smell a vibrant contrast to the input pouring through the restored edges in my mind. Sierra stood under a shield of her own a few feet away. The cable she'd been holding fell to the floor as she gasped, "You okay?"

I gulped in another breath. "I'm fine. I think." I looked down at my chest, checking my shoulder, my collarbone, my arm. "He shot me, he—" I frowned. "He...*didn't* shoot me." The relief at being alive morphed into confusion at the confirmation of unbroken skin. "But I definitely felt—OH NO." I didn't wait to see if Sierra would follow as I scrambled to my feet. "CALEB!"

I skidded out the door. Dr. Kartchner's presence was fading down the hallway, and a shout rang through the air as two troopers pounded toward us. Before either of them could fire their weapons, I launched a pair of energy balls. They staggered a few steps before toppling with gurgles, the shocks of their deaths muffled in contrast to the pain spreading through my chest and shoulder.

I dropped to my knees beside Caleb, lying on the floor where he'd fallen just outside the door. Bullet marks ripped through the front of his armor, the underlayer was shredded beneath his right arm where the vest didn't cover, and a pool of crimson was beginning to spread across the tile. More blood marked the outside of his thigh and higher on his left side, soaking the fabric of his cargo pants and what remained of the underlayer.

And circling his mind, closer than ever before...darkness.

"Caleb! No!" A brilliant shield burst to life around us, and I looked toward where—several corridors away—a loading dock door opened onto sunlight. *Tara!* My power surged in response to the thought, and I screamed her name through the ground.

TARA!

I wasn't sure she'd heard me, but then something shifted in the air. A tremor shook the building.

"Sierra! I need you!" I shouted over my shoulder before returning my attention to the mess of blood and armor that was my best friend. A scream cracked through my mind as I pulled off his helmet, and my chest hitched in time with Caleb's bloodstained one as a spasm shook him.

And in that scream, I thought I heard my name.

Caleb! Stay with me. My hands shook as I planted them on his chest, letting power flood into him with a memory of sunlight. *You can't give in.*

Caleb spasmed again, uncontrolled tremors shaking his body. The world shook, spun around me, and *I stood surrounded by darkness.* "Hey, stay with me!" I yelled. "Caleb, stay with me!"

The echoes of my voice yelled back at me. Mocking.

"Fight it! Don't let it win!"

Nothing answered. Even the blue glow of my power had faded, and all I could see or hear was blackness.

"Caleb, come back." Tears stung my face as I sobbed, "We still need you, and your story's not over yet."

Silence.

Then, a bright spark flared in the darkness, growing until my eyes stung and the darkness fled. Suddenly, I knew how he'd survived the past. Hidden behind the pain was something that burned fiercer than any Shattered power or xeno technology.

There was fire in Caleb's soul that nothing could dim.

"Okay, Gabriel," he said, voice growing steadier as my eyes opened on the bloodstained hallway. *I hear you. Just don't let go.*

I steadied my hands against his chest. *I won't.*

Footsteps sounded nearby, citrus and ozone melding to identify Sierra. She didn't stop to ask questions, but fell to her knees beside me with energy pulsing through her hands. Before I could say anything, the ground began trembling. Near the end of the hall, a wall cracked, crumbled, fell, allowing daylight and dust to spill into the corridor. Sierra looked to me as several armored forms blocked the light, her surprise changing to panic as the figures resolved into Tara, Deadeye, and Bandit.

"Get away from him!" Tara screamed, raising a blue-glowing hand.

The plasma bolt rebounded against my shield with a sputter of light, the shock through my stomach a sharp reminder of everything my body had been through in the last few hours.

"Tara, **STOP!**" I threw an arm between her and Sierra. "She saved my life and she's trying to help!"

"Banshee." Bandit's voice was commanding, even muffled by his helmet. "He's still alive." He grabbed her elbow, arresting her forward momentum as he ordered, "Focus."

Rage and protectiveness played across every line of Tara's posture before resolving into desperation. She yanked her arm from Bandit's grasp and pushed past him, shoving Sierra to the side and planting power-wreathed hands beside mine on Caleb's chest. Blue light suffused every torn spot in his armor, every scratch, every bloodied spot, until the light winked out and she sagged against Deadeye. "I can't—I don't have any more." She looked up at me frantically. "Gabe, is it enough?"

Before I could answer, Caleb stirred under our hands, coughing and groaning as his eyes fluttered open. The relieved words I'd been about to say died in my throat.

The irises of Caleb's silver-grey eyes had become shot through with cyan, like cracks of blue light appearing through a broken mirror.

Shattered.

"What—what did I do?" I whispered. "Why did you—"

His hand circled my wrist, the grip from his augmented arm frighteningly weak despite the power that Tara had just poured into him. "It's not your fault."

My voice cracked, tears breaking through and coursing down my face. "If I hadn't—If you hadn't—"

"Hey." Caleb's grip tightened, and strength flowed into me; subtle blue light that eased the aches from the last few horrific hours and settled my heart all at the same time. "It's going to be okay." His breathing was still labored, but growing less so as he glanced up at Sierra. "It doesn't hurt anymore...are *you* doing something?"

Sierra's eyes widened, and she yanked her hand away from where it'd been resting on his shin. "Sorry! I—" Her shoulders slumped. "Yes. My secondary, it—" She shot a panicky glance at me.

"She's able to dull pain with her subtype," I said, acutely aware as I did that everything in my own body hurt. Twice over, now that I was face-to-face with Caleb and feeling the spots where he'd been injured. "Sir." I looked up at Bandit with urgency. "We have to get him to a hospital. He's stable, but there are things that *really* need to be fixed."

"For more than one of you," he said, kneeling to help me to my feet. Behind him, sunlight streamed through the holes broken in the wall as he ordered, "Let's get you *all* out of here."

STAGE TWENTY-FOUR

THE SQUAD HADN'T PULLED their punches with their response. The Thunderbird came to land outside, and within a few minutes had taken off again with Caleb, Tara, Sierra, and Deadeye inside. I'd paused for a moment when Bandit insisted on Deadeye's inclusion in the aircraft, but the sharp glances Tara was shooting at Sierra quickly proved his point. Bandit and I rode in the back of the truck, driven by a Blood Angel and careening toward St. Augustine's at a pace that would have been deemed unwise by anyone with an interest in vehicular maintenance.

I leaned against the side of the truck, consciousness splitting between my own mind and Caleb's every time a stab of pain hit one of the phantom injuries. He was talking to Tara, explaining the last half hour to both her and Deadeye, but his focus and mine kept wandering as waves of pain and exhaustion struck both of us.

Eventually, a blur of sleepiness passed over my senses, and when I woke it was to Josephine's voice and a rocking motion as Bandit carried me through the emergency room doors. The bright lights and antiseptic smells immediately hit my senses, and I tensed against his shoulder. "What—where—"

"*Mijo*, it's okay," Bandit's voice rumbled. "I've got you."

"No, let me go." I twisted my shoulder from his grasp as he set me on a gurney. "Caleb—where's—" *Caleb! Where are you!* I looked up at Bandit with panic. "Where is he? I can't hear him!"

"Gabriel, he's okay." The gurney padding shifted under Josephine's weight as she sat beside me, putting a gentle hand on my knee. "They landed here fifteen minutes ago. The OR team was already standing by, and he's in surgery right now."

"You're sure? He's not—" My breathing was growing ragged as I sent power racing through the hospital halls until I found him, a silver and cyan figure asleep on a table and surrounded by the humming of machines. My hand went to my shoulder, where I could still feel the pain of something tearing through tissue, blood vessels, and bones. "He's...going to be okay?"

"We'll know for sure soon enough," Josephine said gently. "Right now I'm concerned about *you*." Her face pinched with concern as her gaze skimmed my torso. "You're hurt too, and it'll get worse if I don't take care of it."

Suddenly the lights in the emergency department were too bright, the air too cold, the stares too perceptive as fear flooded my system. I closed my fists tightly, blue light beginning to shine from between my fingers.

"*Mijo?*" Bandit asked, rounding the gurney to kneel in front of me. "You okay?"

The innocent question, the answer so achingly clear, sent tears burning down my face. In an instant, his arms were around me as I sobbed into his shoulder like a little kid. Everything from the moment I'd been captured to now flooded out, shaking through my limbs, choking off my voice. Minutes stretched into what felt like hours, until finally, I'd cried it all out.

When I looked up, a curtain had been drawn around the bed and Josephine was gone. Bandit was still holding me, running his hand gently through my hair.

"Sir, I—"

"Shh." He scooted to sit beside me, moving his arm to settle around my shoulders and pull me closer to him. "I've got you, *mijo*. Whatever's going on, we'll figure it out. One thing at a time."

IT WAS hours before I was able to let the medical staff do their jobs. When they did, it was clear from any angle that I'd been lucky to survive. Between the broken ribs, stitches, cuts where the monitors had been embedded, burn marks from when Sierra's power had saved my life, and more bruises than anyone could count, there was hardly a spot on my torso that didn't hurt. Bandit didn't leave my side, talking me through everything and keeping the curious—and their stares—far away. Finally, I was showered and wearing my own clothes, and the injuries were out of sight beneath my red hoodie.

Almost six hours after our arrival at St. Augustine's, Santana stepped through the door with Sierra beside him. She was still wearing the same shapeless scrubs she'd been wearing that morning, and kept shifting from foot to foot as he addressed Bandit. "We cleaned out the rest of the facility. Looks like they were already shutting things down when we hit. The cops showed up, and they're getting things locked down until you're ready to take a closer look at all of it." His narrow shoulders raised in a halfhearted shrug. "Figured there's no rush, with all of them running."

Running.

My voice was as worn out as the rest of me. "They got away?"

Santana winced, though I wasn't sure if it was at the question or at how beat up I looked. "I knew some of my guys had issues with working together, but I didn't realize how bad it was. I guess there was a back door, and someone looked the other way. Whoever was running that place is gone."

I was too tired to curse, but Bandit wasn't.

Leaden exhaustion weighed my heart as I said, "They got the data they were looking for. If we can't stop them, they'll keep developing this technology. Everyone who's suffered will have done it for nothing." I balled up a fist against my knee, too tired for anything beyond grim resignation. "I have to warn Central Command—I'm not convinced they know what's happened here—and I have to do it in person. I'm not trusting information like this to a transmission."

Sierra crossed her arms, uncertainty behind her mental walls. After a moment, her expression hardened. "I'm coming with you. The EDF might not believe one eyewitness, but they'll have trouble ignoring two of us." Her gaze dropped to the floor, and her voice hushed. "And it'll give me a chance to repay what I've taken from you."

I shook my head, grateful that I could finally do so without dizziness marking my every movement. "If it weren't for you, I'd be dead. I know you don't believe me, but I trust you." I glanced at Bandit. "And I can't continue this fight without you, sir. I know you and Josephine just started life together, but will you—"

Bandit pulled me into a hug. "I'm not letting you out of my sight, *mijo*." He released me and added, "And I've told you about the 'sir' thing. You know you're more of a son to me than anything else." He gave me a lopsided smile, his expression that of a man who'd lost more than I could imagine but had chosen to love anyway. "Josie'll understand if I'm gone for a while."

He looked up to continue his conversation with Santana, but his arm stayed around me. After a few minutes, the talk blurred until I could no longer hold exhaustion at bay. From there things moved to waking and sleeping, nightmares blending with comfort as familiar voices soothed the panic each time I startled awake. Eventually, my surroundings changed from an ER bay to a glass-walled room lined with curtains, and when I woke next, it was—once again—with someone calling my name.

Gabe?

I blinked away fogginess and looked around the room. No one was there, but I'd *definitely* heard something. Which meant...

Caleb? You're awake?

A soft laugh came through the mental link. Now that I

was properly alert, I could tell he was in the room next door to mine.

Hang tight; I'm coming.

You don't have to— I couldn't know for certain, but I thought he was rolling his eyes. *Okay, do whatever you're going to do. Just don't hurt yourself.*

I pushed myself up from the bed, undoing the blood pressure cuff and peeling away the adhesive holding an IV site in place. They must've set the new line while I'd been sleeping. I took a deep breath and slipped out of bed, relieved when the world stayed steady after a few moments upright.

What happened? Caleb asked as I stepped around the curtain covering the door to my room. *The last thing I remember is someone running out of the generator room.*

The stupid scientist, I said, padding the few steps to his doorway. The sliding glass door was open, but the curtain had been drawn across the aperture. *He got away, too. And the weapon he had—I think that's what sent you under.*

I pulled the curtain aside and breathed a sigh of relief at the sight of Caleb lying with a blanket tucked around his chest, a single set of tubes and wires snaking from beneath the sleeve of a greenish hospital gown. He opened his eyes at my approach, and my breath caught at the sight of mixed cyan and silver in his irises. Of all the nightmares to have come true...

"Oh no." I dropped into a chair near the head of the bed, explanation forgotten. "I'm so sorry."

Caleb's quiet laugh came again, raspy at the edges like he'd forgotten how to talk out loud. "Kind of a shock, huh? It was to me too." He turned his head to examine the monitor panel affixed to the wall. All the usual readings were there:

heart rate, oxygen saturation, blood pressure...Shattered power. "Even weirder when they confirmed it."

"I'm so sorry," I repeated. "I can't believe it. When... how...what *happened?*"

Caleb winced. "I think it was yesterday—no, wait." He frowned at a whiteboard beside the monitor screen, where smudged writing proclaimed the date. "Okay, I guess it was three days ago. Damn, they kept us asleep for that long?"

"Kept *you* asleep," I said. "They didn't need to do anything to me."

He snorted tiredly. "I know the feeling. Once you're safe, it's like you lose all ability to keep going." The eyes hadn't gotten any less unsettling as he winced again. "It happened at the same moment that I started hearing your voice in my head. That's what Tara said, anyway. Whatever it is, it's only partial. At least, I've never seen anyone keep some of their original eye color when they Shatter."

"Yeah..." I let my head drop into my hands. "I'm so—"

"If you say 'sorry' again, I'm going to hit you," Caleb warned with a ghost of a laugh following the words. "And then the nurse will kick you out."

I had to laugh as well, my chest aching as I did. "Well, what else am I supposed to say? 'Welcome to hell, hope you brought your sunblock'?"

"It's a start."

"What...what did happen?" I asked, nodding to his bandaged right shoulder. I'd felt the pain from it, the intensity rising and falling according to what I assumed were doses of painkillers. For that matter, it *still* ached, though not nearly as badly as earlier. "I thought *I'd* been shot, then I realized it was you."

The memory flashed through my mind in an instant,

even without physical contact between us. He'd heard a gunshot from inside the generator room after clearing the hall of oncoming troopers, had wheeled around to look for the source, and was hit by a lucky shot from one of the opponents he'd thought dead. The impact had thrown him to the ground, and he hadn't had time to return fire before something else sent him into the darkness.

"It was stupid of me, but I thought—" Caleb rubbed his eyes. "I thought he was aiming for you, and I panicked."

"He was shooting at Sierra." I tipped my head and conceded, "Then at me. I think he was trying to down both of us so he could get away."

"Which he did?" Caleb asked, then swore as I nodded. "He has to be stopped."

I nodded. "He said he still had plans for me and Sierra." A chill spread through my limbs, and I tucked my arms to my torso with a shiver. *I never want to be cold like that again.* "I don't know what those plans were, but I don't think they'll end now that the Unbreaking Field's been destroyed. Santana said he's long gone... I didn't even think to go after him once I saw what'd happened to you." Silence fell as I thought back to the hopeless moments in the darkness of Caleb's mind.

Without a word said, I knew he was remembering it too. After a moment, he asked, "Was it you who got me out?"

I looked away. Nodded. "Yeah." My voice choked at the word, and I didn't bother saying the rest out loud. *Even if it was your time to go, I couldn't leave you there.*

Caleb reached to rest his fingers against my arm. *Thanks, bud. I owe you one.*

No you don't. I raised my eyes to his. Bandit's earlier

words came back, and I repeated them with a warm glow of relief. *Whatever's going on, we'll figure it out. Together.*

Caleb cracked a smile. *Glad you're okay, Gabe.*

Yeah. You too.

———

THE CAMERA EYE stared at me unblinking, as the red light of my recorder pulsed on the table below it. Anger tugged at my heart, wrapping the sharp edges in my mind and lending lethality to my voice.

It's time to end this.

"You made a serious mistake when you decided that this region was the key to gaining power." New scars shifted against the inside of my T-shirt as I uncrossed my arms, still sore after more than a week of rest. "The desert is *dangerous*, and you made yourselves the enemy when you decided the lives here were disposable. We chose this place." I glanced at Sierra, standing behind the camera next to Deadeye. "We chose *each other*. We're resilient, determined, and willing to set aside our differences if it means protecting the things we love most. You tried to break us, but we've come out stronger, and we're not going to let you go after what you've done."

A fist closed on the paracord loop dangling from my pocket—the rosary that Sierra had retrieved from the lab after she'd saved my life. I'd tried to find Diego at St. Augustine's, but no one there seemed to know of any chaplain by that name. Whoever he'd been, I doubted he'd ever know how close to despair I'd come until his intervention that had seen my faith restored.

Deep breath, Gabriel, Caleb said in my head. *You can do this.*

I looked up to see him get to his feet with Tara and Bandit's help. His right arm was in a sling and he'd barely been able to get out of bed a few days ago, but he'd insisted on being here nonetheless.

Yeah. Yeah, I can. I glared into the camera. "We're done playing your games, Vanguard. We know what you're planning to unleash on the world, and we're not going to let you get away with it." I closed my fists as power began thrumming through my veins, flickering and strengthening until I stood surrounded by blue light. "Brace yourselves," I told the enemy. "You angered the protectors of the desert. Now we're coming for you."

GLOSSARY

ADOBE: A material made from hardened clay, commonly mixed with straw to construct houses and other buildings. Adobe homes have thick walls, which insulate well against both cold and hot weather.

BARRIO: The term for a neighborhood within a Spanish-speaking city. These neighborhoods often hold their own cultural distinctions, and function as micro-communities within a larger metropolis.

BOUGAINVILLEA: A large shrub, with sharp thorns and large clusters of brilliant magenta blossoms.

CATALINAS: The mountain range directly north of Tucson, reaching over 8,000 feet in elevation at the tallest point (Mt. Lemmon). Officially named the "Santa Catalinas," but universally abbreviated to just the second word.

CHOLLA: A large cactus with segmented limbs and heavily barbed spines. When brushed up against, segments will break off and embed their spines in skin, clothing, and flesh. Spines can additionally pierce some shoe materials and work gloves. Not for hugging.

COCHITO: A large, soft gingerbread cookie flavored with molasses and cinnamon and cut into the shape of a pig.

CREOSOTE: A short, shrubby bush common to the Sonoran Desert. Blooms in spring with small yellow flowers, and has a distinct smell when it encounters moisture.

DUST SPINNER: Also known as a "dust devil." A towering column of spinning air and dust, created when warm updrafts collide with each other to pick dirt up from the ground. While related to tornadoes, they're not typically dangerous.

FOLKLÓRICO: Mexican folk dance, characterized by elaborate costumes with regionally based variations. Dresses worn by folklórico dancers have extremely full skirts, which are used as part of the dance to create mesmerizing patterns of movement.

LUMINARIA: A candlelight lantern, made by placing a votive candle in a paper bag weighted with sand. Typically used to line driveways as a decorative feature, these lights are traditionally associated with Christmas Eve in the desert Southwest.

MESQUITE: A native desert tree with twisted trunk and branches, craggy bark, and small, feathery leaves. Some varieties produce edible, protein-rich pods, and wood is widely used in smokers to impart a distinct flavor to meat dishes.

MONSOON: A brief July-August phenomenon in which moist air from the Gulf of Mexico combines with hot desert updrafts to create massive thunderstorms. Provides most of the annual rainfall for the desert.

NOPAL: Prickly pear cactus pads, eaten sauteed or grilled as a vegetable in Sonoran cuisine. Blooms in late spring with large yellow flowers, which develop into clusters of bright magenta fruit in the fall. Fruits are often used to make jellies, syrup, and juice.

OCOTILLO: A tall cactus that grows as a cluster of 12-foot-tall stick-like stems. Leafless and mostly lifeless in appearance for most of the year, they grow bright green leaves along the length of the stems after a period of rain. Ocotillo stems can be broken off and planted to make living fences.

PALETAS: Mexican popsicles or ice cream bars, usually fruit-based. Mango, strawberry, and coconut are all popular flavors.

PALO VERDE: A native desert tree with green bark, large spreading branches, and tiny leaves. In late spring, they bloom with a riot of bright yellow flowers, covering the entire tree.

PAN DULCE: The umbrella term for Mexican pastries, whether yeasted, puff pastry, or deep-fried. Each region has its own specialty, often incor-porating sugar paste which is applied to the dough before baking and scored or shaped to form decorative designs.

SKY ISLAND: A term used to describe the mountains in the Sonoran Desert. Often soaring abruptly from sea level to heights of 5,000 feet or greater, they are integral in helping form the life-giving monsoon storms.

TAMALES: A main dish consisting of a shredded meat filling (usually beef or pork braised with red chile) encased in corn flour "masa" dough and steamed in a cornhusk wrapper. Labor-intensive and time-consuming to make, tamales are usually reserved for holidays or special occasions.

TORTILLERÍA: A bakery whose specialty is tortillas, literally "tortilla factory." In Sonoran cuisine, tortillas are thin and pliable, and primarily made of flour and lard. They go stale very quickly, and are best eaten within a day of being made.

WASH: A dry riverbed, which floods during monsoon storms. Sometimes called an "arroyo."

CAST OF CHARACTERS

GABRIEL MENDOZA

The youngest of Squad 36 at age nineteen, Gabriel was born and raised in the city he's now sworn to protect. A kindhearted chronicler of others' stories, he's keenly observant and determined to stand up for the undefended. With recently developed Shattered abilities, growing confidence, and a newfound adoptive family, he now has the power to make a difference in the region no one cares about.

TARA "BANSHEE" FLETCHER

Once considered a wild card even by her allies, Tara's unpredictable nature and devastating power come second to her kind, caring nature. After training Gabriel and helping him destroy an enemy facility several months ago, she now wields her destructive Shattered subtype on behalf of Squad 36. A long way from her birthplace in Appalachia, she considers "home" to be wherever her family—especially her husband Caleb—is.

CALEB "PHANTOM" FLETCHER

Appalachian rebel leader, Defense Force veteran, and survivor of xeno captivity, Caleb runs point for Squad 36 with his wife Tara, dealing out damage and bolstering her Shattered abilities as needed. Steady in the midst of chaos with lightning-fast reflexes and cool-headed lethality, he fights on more than one battlefront to protect others from the pain once visited on him.

JOSEPHINE FLORES

EDF-trained doctor, Bandit's girlfriend, and the maternal heart of Squad 36. After returning to Tucson with the rest of the squad, she joined the Medical Corps to staff the newly recommissioned St. Augustine's Hospital. Has known Bandit for over twenty-five years, but only confessed her affection for him in recent times.

CARLOS "BANDIT" ESPINOZA

In his late forties, Bandit holds command of his squad with loyalty, steadfast leadership, and sharp intuition. In the wake of the Defense Force's departure from Region 520, he's stepped up as a community leader and is determined to protect his squad—especially the doctor he's in love with, and the young Shattered who looks up to him.

RENEÉ "DEADEYE" ZIEGLER

Communications Specialist, engineer, artist, and not a half bad cook, Deadeye has settled into urban life with only a few loud complaints. As the mistress of all things technology for Squad 36, she carries secrets behind her eyes—well, eye, and don't ask how she lost the other one—and pushes the boundaries of known science in order to make life better for those she cares about.

ALEXI "JUDGE" MOROZOV

A cocky Shattered who never hesitated to use his mental control subtype (or his collection of silly T-shirts) to humorous effect. After becoming fatally wounded during a rescue mission, Judge summoned a vortex powerful enough to level the entire area—losing his own life, but saving his squadmates.

MICHAEL "CYBER" LEROUX

Founder of the Earth Defense Force, now deceased. A powerful Shattered with a telepathic subtype, who led humanity's resistance against xeno occupation. Although his legacy has become urban legend and propaganda, those who knew Michael well describe a man who fought tire-lessly to defend humanity at the cost of his own life.

COOK FROM THE BOOK

TACO TOPPINGS

What's this? Don't we all know how to make tacos? Well, yes. In fact, I'm not even giving suggestions on what meat to put inside these ones. Do carne asada, shredded beef, ground beef...heck, you can even get a rotisserie chicken and hack it into pieces. The point is the stuff you put ON your taco. Get some family together and have fun!

Pico de Gallo:

- 6 Roma tomatoes
- 1-2 jalapeño peppers
- 1 sweet onion
- ½ bunch cilantro
- Juice of 3-4 limes
- Salt

Halve tomatoes and scoop out the seeds and membranes with a spoon, then dice. Do the same with jalapeños (be careful not to touch your eyes!). Dice the onion and roughly chop the cilantro. Combine all ingredients in bowl and add salt to taste (about a teaspoon).

Cabbage Slaw:

- ½ head green cabbage, sliced very thinly
- ½ red onion, sliced very thinly
- ½ bunch cilantro
- Juice of 2-3 limes, plus more if needed
- 2 tbsp. vegetable oil

- Salt

Combine onion, lime juice, and a pinch of salt in a small bowl. Let sit for ten minutes while you prepare the other ingredients. Slice the cabbage very thinly, chop the cilantro, then add the onion/lime/salt mixture. Pour in the oil and toss to coat. Taste, adding lime juice and salt as needed.

Avocado Salsa:

- 6 fresh tomatillos, husked and roughly chopped
- 1 ripe avocado, seeded, peeled, and roughly chopped
- Juice of 1 lime
- ⅓ C. cilantro, roughly chopped
- 1 jalapeño pepper, seeded and minced
- ¼ C. white onion, roughly chopped
- ¼ C. water
- Salt

Combine all ingredients in blender and process until smooth.

Pickled Red Onions:

- 1 red onion, very thinly sliced
- ½ C. apple cider vinegar (or white vinegar)
- 1 tbsp. granulated sugar
- 1 ½ tsp. salt
- 1 C. hot water (not boiling)

Combine vinegar, sugar, salt, and water and stir until sugar and salt are dissolved. Pack onion slices in a jar and pour brine over, making sure they're immersed in the liquid. Let stand for at least an hour before serving. Keeps in fridge for up to three weeks.

Black Beans:
For Soaking:

- 1 lb. dry black beans
- 1 tsp. baking soda

- 3 tsp. salt

To Cook:

- ½ lb. ham, diced
- 1 yellow or white onion, diced
- 1 tsp. cumin
- 1 tsp. minced garlic
- 2 tsp. chili powder
- 1 bay leaf
- 1 tsp. salt

The night before you want to eat, combine beans, baking soda, and salt in a large pot and cover with water. Cover and let soak overnight. The next day, drain the soaking liquid and add more water to cover beans. Add remaining ingredients and bring to a boil, then reduce to a simmer and cover. Simmer over low heat for at least two hours and up to three hours, stirring occasionally, until beans are soft enough to mash with a fork. Remove lid and simmer a bit longer, until liquid is somewhat thickened.

To Serve:

- Small tortillas
- Cooked rice (add lime juice and cilantro if you want)
- Guacamole
- Shredded cheese
- Meat of your choice (In most Southwest states, you can buy marinated meat at grocery stores to grill at home, but any protein will work!)
- Sodas in glass bottles (Jarritos brand is fun!) or lemonade

ACKNOWLEDGMENTS

The Homely House
Tucson AZ
Spring, 2025

You know that feeling when you reach the finish line of a race, realizing that you're here, it's done, you conquered the thing you set out to do?

Yeah, me neither.

I don't run unless I'm being chased.

Finishing this story (and being proud of it) felt as impossible as running a marathon. Second books of trilogies are tricksy, after all, and this one almost gave me a run for my money. But suddenly, inexplicably, here we are. And it's time to thank the people, places, and non-corporeal entities that made it possible.

Let's start with the obvious one. Many thanks to Le Buzz (where I typed the first draft), and to the Bear Canyon Library (where I *edited* the first draft). Honorable mentions include Tucson Coffee Roasters and The Scented Leaf—especially since I'm writing this section far in advance, and will be camped out in one of those two places to finish proofreading.

Very special thanks to Paradox Interactive and Jon

Everist for the *Battletech* soundtrack. You provided the background to my editing through all seven (count 'em, SEVEN!) drafts, and your service is greatly appreciated.

A tip of the hat to Matthew Parker, Owl City, and Apollo LTD, for writing music that captures the heart of Squad 36's story—in particular the tracks "Breathe", "Bird With a Broken Wing", and "Soul Worth Saving". There's fierceness and light in your lyrics, and I so appreciate your work.

Ordinarily, I'd have a few more non-corporeal entities to thank for their support, but *In the Unbreaking* was a community effort in more ways than one. So without further ado, the producers would like to thank...

Emmy, for being with me every step of the way and reminding me to look to the third rail—the *why* of every story. Brittany, for being the voice of reason when I needed it, and for always—*always*—reminding me to dream bigger. Laurel, for the enthusiasm (you still can't date Judge). Robin, for letting my characters take up residence in a new universe (you're doing marvelously with them, too). Elisabeth, for tolerating my ups and downs and only laughing at me *a little* when I try new things. Jenni, for putting me on the "favorite person" shelf and always shining a light to remind me of the way home. Deborah, for the edits and endless support (you now hold all the spoilers. Take care of them, okay?).

To the beta team—Amanda, Amber K., Amber D., Caitlyn, and Melissa—who read the earlier versions and yelled at me in varying degrees of "How could you!", I'm sorry? Thank you? I hope the current canon makes up for the pain I've caused.

To the Menace (yes, you get your own paragraph, deal with it) who talked me out of a certain decision, thanks for being brave enough to tell me that I was making a mistake, and for being understanding when I admitted that I was scared to walk it back. You'll never know (or maybe you do) what type of story—what type of *series*—this would have been if you hadn't dumped me on my behind and helped me back up again.

To the readers who picked up book one of this series and continued to book two, thank you. When I say that every message, every tag, every reaction made my day, I mean it from the bottom of my frosty heart. I can't count the number of times I cackled at someone's reactions, and I can only hope that this continuation of the series lived up to your expectations. Readers are what keep stories going, and I hope you know that I value each and every one of you.

To the place that I live, my beautiful desert, thank you. Thank you for the monsoon storms, the cracked streets, the mango *paletas*, the murals on the sides of abandoned buildings. Thank you for the jagged edges of the Catalinas and the bougainvillea scraping my gate when it's windy. Thank you for the memories. I may have Shattered here, but it's also here that the cracks were mended.

Now then, onward and upward. Let's finish this story together.

The Homely House
Tucson, AZ

Brigitte Cromey didn't plan on falling in love with the desert. After ten years, it's safe to say that it's grown on her. In addition to admiring the glorious Arizona sunsets, praying for rain, and reminding her children not to touch the cactus, she enjoys playing video games with her friends and family, reading entire fantasy books in one sitting, and listening to Christian Reggaeton with the bass turned up. She may forget to drink enough water, but the tea kettle will always be on, and her Homely House in the desert is always open to those seeking refuge from the cares of life.